"W[...]
Al[...]

Robin was leaning forward on the table, gazing intently at him as she spoke.

He went all cold inside. What had happened to their innocent conversation? "I don't deal in fantasies," he replied.

"But you should. Come on, think about it," she coaxed with a smile. "How do you *see* yourself?"

He turned away and stared out into the darkness. A sudden urge to tell her everything washed over him. He could unburden himself, be rid of hiding, of pretending. It was as if Robin had seen into his heart and knew his secret war name, Changing Man. Yes, this woman who dealt in fantasies would accept and understand.

He turned to her, noting the eyes filled with hope. Expectant. *No.* No woman would *ever* understand what was wrong with him....

ABOUT THE AUTHOR

"Romance," asserts Lynn Erickson, the writing team of Carla Peltonen and Molly Swanton, "is a genre that, first and foremost, has to be thoroughly fulfilling to the reader." With nine Superromances as well as many historical novels to their credit, these two women know whereof they speak. Molly is the idea person in the partnership, while Carla does the research—they tackle the writing together. Fans should watch for a new Lynn Erickson story set in sizzling Cozumel!

Books by Lynn Erickson

HARLEQUIN SUPERROMANCE

132–SNOWBIRD
157–THE FACES OF DAWN
184–A CHANCE WORTH TAKING
199–STORMSWEPT
231–A DANGEROUS SENTIMENT
255–TANGLED DREAMS
276–A PERFECT GEM
298–FOOL'S GOLD

HARLEQUIN INTRIGUE

42–ARENA OF FEAR

Don't miss any of our special offers. Write to us at the following address for information on our newest releases.

Harlequin Reader Service
901 Fuhrmann Blvd., P.O. Box 1397, Buffalo, NY 14240
Canadian address: P.O. Box 603,
Fort Erie, Ont. L2A 5X3

Lynn Erickson
FIRECLOUD

Harlequin Books

TORONTO • NEW YORK • LONDON
AMSTERDAM • PARIS • SYDNEY • HAMBURG
STOCKHOLM • ATHENS • TOKYO • MILAN

Published August 1988

First printing June 1988

ISBN 0-373-70320-1

CHAPTER ONE

IN TWENTY MINUTES it would be too late, Robin Hayle thought as she unlocked the door to her shop. It was already 6:05 a.m. and shortly the sky would turn from pearl to pink then gold, and the shadows in the plaza would be all wrong. She switched on the lights in the back of her photography studio and hurriedly loaded her camera, snatching up a long telephoto lens just in case.

"Good morning!" came a voice from the front. "Miss Hayle? You here?"

"In the back," Robin called. "I'm heading out in a minute, though." Picking up an extra roll of film, she went to greet her salesgirl, Ericka. "What on earth are you doing up at this uncivilized hour?"

Ericka was already behind the counter, her round pretty face as cheerful as usual. "It's Indian Market, isn't it?" She began to wipe down the display cases. "I knew you'd be busy, so I figured I'd get here early."

"Early is right. Listen, I'm going to try to get some shots of the plaza before the hordes arrive."

"Go ahead, I'll get everything set up."

Nineteen, Robin reflected, and already the girl was efficient. Her own teenage years were receding into a comfortable haze, but she was darn sure she hadn't been as responsible as Ericka Dalton. She'd certainly never gotten up before six in the morning and gone off to a real day's work.

Robin's photography shop was located in the Sena Plaza right in the heart of Old Santa Fe. A short half block from her store was the nearly four-hundred-year-old core of the city, the Santa Fe Plaza, a tree-lined square that was bordered on one side by the Governor's Palace, the *Palacio Real*.

The *Palacio* had been built in 1610, Robin thought as she walked beneath the cottonwoods toward the plaza. Even by European standards, that was an old building. The Pueblo Indians still sold their rugs and pottery, their jewelry and trinkets beneath its shaded portal.

Robin stood on the corner of the plaza and checked the light meter on her camera. In the mother-of-pearl dawn she was a study in casual elegance, tall and graceful, dressed in a full calf-length blue chambray skirt and an oversize white silk blouse tied in a knot at her waist. A string of bright turquoise beads hung around her neck and swayed as she moved.

Usually at 6:15 a.m., the plaza was silent; only the occasional fluttering sound of a pigeon rising from a church belfry broke the morning calm. But not today. It was the last weekend of August, the weekend of the Santa Fe Indian Market, an affair that brought buyers from all over the world into town; already there were dusty pickup trucks and vans unloading their wares, and Indians in brightly colored shawls moving around, setting up their booths.

Robin walked in her usual long-legged stride toward the far end of the plaza. The Sangre de Cristo Mountains that rose to the east of town could be seen in the quickening dawn, their tall peaks turning rose in the champagne-clear morning light. With the low portal of the palace giving depth to her pictures, Robin shot half a roll of film of the mountains. A pigeon lifted from the palace's flat roof; she caught the peaceful portrait on film.

She moved around the plaza, snapping pictures of the women at work, trying to capture the shy yet proud demeanor singular to the Pueblo Indians.

"There you are." Shelly Dalton, Ericka's mother, crossed the brick street and walked toward Robin. She was carrying a white bakery bag. "Want a squishy, low-cal doughnut?"

"I ate already, but...." Robin shrugged and took one. "Can you believe these crowds?" she asked rhetorically. "I know I've only lived here a year, but still, I've never seen so many people in the plaza all at once."

Both women glanced around. Even though it was barely light enough to see, early-bird tourists were milling, handling intricately patterned Navaho rugs, eyeing the turquoise and silver jewelry, exclaiming over the pottery and stylized ceramic animals.

"Maybe I should wear a sign on my back," said Shelly. "Shop at the Dalton Fine Arts Gallery."

"You've had a good summer, haven't you?" Robin asked as she licked sugar from her fingers.

"A record season. And yesterday, with the annual market going on, we sold more than we did the whole month of June. I'm going to *make* Chuck buy me that Volvo I want."

"Must be nice," Robin said flippantly to her friend.

"Some got it, some don't," Shelly quipped good-naturedly. "Ericka's at your shop already, isn't she?"

"Bright and early. In fact," said Robin, "I better get on back. I've got a nine o'clock."

"What is it this time?"

"It's a lady from Los Angeles who wants a picture of herself selling jewelry with the Indian women under the portal."

"I *love* your stories," replied Shelly. "You meet the neatest people."

"Isn't that the truth? Sometimes I feel like a psychiatrist. Dealing in people's fantasies." She shook her head mock-seriously. "You know, I should probably sign an oath, like a doctor, never to divulge my clients' secrets."

"Don't do that. I'd miss your tall tales." Shelly laughed.

Robin specialized in portraits in which any fantasy of her clients was met. A client might want to be photographed as an Indian warrior, a Hell's Angel, Aphrodite rising from the sea or a local Spanish noblewoman from the 1600s. To Robin, anything went, so long as her client's fantasy was indulged. She saw to every detail: costume— even if it had to come all the way from Denver—makeup, hairstyling, props. It was exhausting work at times, but since Robin had moved to New Mexico from Illinois a year ago and opened her own shop, she'd been a great success. She was thirty-two years old; things could be a lot worse.

"Guess I better get these doughnuts on over to Chuck," Shelly said. "We left the house so early he didn't get a chance to eat."

"Can I have just one more?"

"Honest to God, Robin Hayle, I don't give a hoot *how* tall you are—how can you eat so much and stay so skinny?"

"One hundred and forty pounds is *not* skinny." She snapped a picture of Shelly, catching her friend with no makeup on and her shoulder-length, permed brown hair still in damp coils.

"Thanks. Now please destroy that film."

"Sure."

The plaza was bathed in gold, the sun just peeping over the rim of the Sangre de Cristo Mountains, and the old dun-colored adobe buildings glowed in the warm rays of light. Robin shot another roll of film, trying to capture that lucent sense of peace, that contemplative mood peculiar to the City of Holy Faith, Santa Fe. There was no place else where man and landscape came together with such mutual advantage, where the landscape was brought to human measure.

Robin had first fallen in love with New Mexico three years ago when she'd come for a visit. Like the hundreds of various artists who'd preceded her, she'd been mesmerized by the unique light found only in the Southwest, a clear, precise light that made every pine needle stand out with purity and far-distant objects appear with clarity against the sky. She'd known then that Santa Fe would become her home.

And she'd made her move at the right time; this particular corner of the Southwest was a cultural center, but unlike Paris or New York, New Mexico had space—lots and lots of open space. She had traveled all over the state and taken thousands of pictures, yet she felt that she could explore the land for the next fifty years and still only see half of it. The Land of Enchantment, read New Mexico's license plates. And that was exactly what it was, Robin thought.

Shelly had once said, "I can tell how much you love it here from the photographs you take."

Robin was glad it showed. Although she mostly did portraits of clients, she also sold lots of landscapes. Every square inch of the walls in her shop was covered with studies of the land: the tortured red buttes and great mesas, the gentle, rolling grasslands, the blinding sand dunes and the sun-bronzed cliffs that had been inhabited long before the time of Christ by the Mysterious Ancient Ones, the Anasazi Indians.

Many peoples had come to New Mexico over the centuries. And each new group that had settled there had become assimilated, had found its niche, its style. The Anasazi Indians had left their mark, the Navaho and Apache raiders theirs, the Spanish, the Mexicans and finally the Anglos.

As each successive wave of newcomers had found their home in the Rio Grande Valley, so Robin hoped she would. Having lost her parents in an airplane accident when she was nine, she had always craved that feeling of belonging, of being secure, of being loved. True, she had been raised properly by her aunt and uncle in Waukegan, Illinois, and they had loved her, but it just wasn't the same as having a mother and a father.

In Santa Fe, Robin felt she was on an equal footing with everyone else, as all were new to this ancient, evocative land.

Robin snapped one more picture before returning to her shop. It was the face of that particular child that drew her camera like a magnet. An Indian child, a dignified, secretive face, a quiet moment in which the child sat beneath a booth twisting a string of silver jewelry in his fingers slowly, his mother close by. What thoughts, Robin wondered as she threaded her way through the gathering crowds, were behind those silent black eyes?

When Robin arrived at the shop, playfully named Robin's Nest, there were already a dozen customers in line waiting to buy film. "Oh, Miss Hayle," Ericka called, "can you give me a hand?"

Ericka was a delightful young college student. Her parents, Chuck and Shelly Dalton, had moved to Santa Fe from Ohio fifteen years before. They'd opened an art gal-

lery in the Sena Plaza and scraped by for years until Santa
Fe had become a mecca for art collectors.

Robin had been luckier in a way. Her parents, even
though they'd died early, had left her financially secure,
although not with enough to buy that adorable adobe
house on Canyon Road that Robin craved. She had modeled part-time while in college, not because she was forced
to, but because photography fascinated her. And she did,
of course, have that five-foot-ten-inch frame, not to mention a great head of shoulder-length, thick, curling ash-
blond hair that she helped along with a yearly frosting job.
Her eyes, a dark blue, were striking with makeup. She
could have modeled for years, but the other side of the
camera had begun to lure her and before Robin knew it,
she was taking pictures of everything and everyone, eventually studying the art in school.

True, the Daltons had struggled to make it, but at least
they'd always had one another. They'd had family holi-
days, family squabbles, warmth and loving and belonging. Robin often felt cheated of those things and admitted
to herself that she harbored a stockpile of insecurity because of it. Oh, she hid it well, always seeming to be in
control of her life, always ready with a joke, a witticism,
a funny story. She tended to talk too much, but deep down
inside there was that sense of being an outsider, of wanting to belong.

She hated to leave Ericka on one of the busiest days of
the tourist season, but Robin's client from Los Angeles
walked in shortly after nine.

"Ericka, honey, I've got to go for about a half hour.
Can you manage?" Robin asked apologetically.

"No problem, Miss Hayle." The young woman went
back to selling film without a word of complaint. Tomorrow morning, even though it was still Indian Market,

Robin thought, she'd let Ericka sleep in and come into work at noon.

And in a couple of weeks, when Ericka was off to college again, Robin planned on writing her a large bonus check.

Robin's client, a Mrs. Hartmann, was a very short, stout woman of about sixty. She was well dressed, her rust-colored purse and her high-heeled sandals matching, her jewelry strictly from Tiffany's.

In the back of Robin's Nest, Mrs. Hartmann changed into the traditional Pueblo outfit Robin had provided: a sleeveless green striped dress caught at one shoulder over a blouse, a blue shawl patterned with roses, long necklaces of red and jet beads, silver earrings and bracelets. Robin helped her into a black wig that had thick bangs and a blunt pageboy cut.

When Mrs. Hartmann was dressed, she looked in the mirror and practically jumped up and down with satisfaction. "Oh, this is wonderful!" she exclaimed.

"Mrs. Hartmann," Robin said, standing back and viewing her handiwork, "you look positively gorgeous."

Mrs. Hartmann's life story came out as the two women walked up Palace Avenue. "I *always* wanted to be an Indian. You know, dear, for a day. Like *Queen for a Day*, the old TV show. You see—" Mrs. Hartmann nudged aside some shoppers "—my grandfather was a full-blooded Navaho Indian. He got into oil."

Robin didn't question that one.

"And you, Miss Hayle? Surely you have a fantasy."

"About a trillion of them," replied Robin. "My biggest, if you can keep a secret, is to find a *really* tall man."

Mrs. Hartmann tipped her head back and looked up at Robin. "I see what you mean."

The sun was already hot in the eastern sky by the time they crossed the street to the Governor's Palace and sought the shade beneath the portal. It was crowded. Hundreds of tourists pushed and shoved, fingered the Indian wares, exclaimed over the high prices.

Mrs. Hartmann chatted away with two Indian women, then Robin asked if her client could sit by their jewelry-laden blankets, her back against the old *Palacio* wall. The Indians giggled shyly behind their hands and nodded.

Robin shot a full roll of film. She had to admit that Mrs. Hartmann looked the part and was having a grand time.

"When do I get to see the pictures?" she asked excitedly when they were done.

"The proofs will be ready Monday morning. About eleven. I'll go over them with you and we can pick out the best. Okay?"

"That will be fine, Miss Hayle." She led the way back to Robin's shop, turning and saying, "Now, about that tall young man of yours . . ." By the time Mrs. Hartmann had changed and was gone, Robin had an earful of information on the advantages of short men. But Robin could just see herself at five foot ten on the arm of a short man—like back at those junior high school dances.

Before lunch, Robin had one more client coming; he was a young student from a seminary in New York State who was vacationing with his brother. He wanted to be photographed in front of the Cathedral of St. Francis dressed in priests' robes of the sixteenth century. Robin had had a devil of a time finding the robes but finally had managed to talk one of the fathers at the church into lending the boy the antique clothing and only because he was of the faith. She arrived at Robin's Nest starving and hot, her feet tired from hours of standing on the hard bricks of the streets. But Ericka obviously needed help.

The young woman's big blue eyes, with those heavenly dark fringes of lashes, implored Robin. "Just an hour? I really promised Shane I'd have lunch with him and—"

"Say no more." Robin took over for Ericka behind the counter. "When true love calls, one must follow. Or something like that."

"Geez, thanks, Miss Hayle." She was off and running, the energy of youth propelling her out the door. Ah, wondered Robin, when was the last time she had run to meet a beau?

The customers kept coming until Robin was, for the first time in a year, sold out of thirty-five mm film. And she wasn't about to go into her private stock in the back, not with yet another portrait to do that day. She sold two silver-framed color landscapes she had taken herself. Both were quite expensive, too. And she sold her favorite print of autumn wildflowers with the Taos Pueblo in the background. She'd won an award for that one, first prize in the New Mexico State Art Fair last spring. Of course, she could print as many as she liked. Signed and numbered, she might end up selling dozens of them. Oh, that adobe house on Canyon Road—what she wouldn't do to get out of her downtown apartment.

Finally, when the local restaurants filled up for lunch, the shop quieted down. Robin walked to the open door and took a deep breath, stretching her arms over her head. Then she leaned against the doorframe and sighed. Her shop was situated on a picturesque street. Like all the old streets in Santa Fe, its twisting, narrow path was lined with adobe walls and tall cottonwoods that formed a lush, cooling canopy overhead. On both sides of Robin's shop were art galleries and shops that sold Indian jewelry and rugs in a profusion of color, baskets, pottery, oil and watercolor paintings, posters.

Shelly popped her head out of her shop, as well. "Hi!" she called from two doors down and gave Robin a wave. "Busy?"

"It's slow right now," Robin called back.

"It'll pick up." Shelly made a tired face.

Santa Fe was experiencing a renaissance. Indian art was in demand in collectors' circles, and the city was the center of one of the largest concentrations of Indians in the country. There were the Pueblo Indians, heirs of the Anasazi cliff dwellers of a thousand years ago, a placid, community-centered people who lived in tiered adobe dwellings.

And there were the Navahos and Apaches, totally different tribes, relative latecomers to New Mexico, nomads, then herders, but above all fierce warriors.

The art of the Indians stirred Robin's senses. Their pottery, their silver and turquoise jewelry, their rugs and blankets—all came from Mother Earth herself: the clay, the wool, the metal and stones, the dyes, even their paintbrushes of yucca fiber.

What had the Indians thought when the first conquistadores had made their hot and dusty way into New Mexico? It had been exactly four hundred years ago, and they'd come from Mexico, looking for the fabled Seven Cities of Cibola, which supposedly had streets paved with gold.

Robin opened a bag of potato chips and munched, watching the tide of people in the street. There, bent over an Indian's handicraft, was a classically Spanish face, a woman with dark hair, huge dark eyes and a high-bridged nose. Perhaps one of her ancestors had been given a land grant from the Spanish king back in the 1600s.

And next to her was a blond man, sweat stains under his arms, arguing ferociously with the Spanish lady over a piece of silver jewelry that they both wanted. The Indian artisan watched them both with timeless patience, waiting for their quarrel to subside.

History repeats itself, Robin thought with a smile, popping another chip into her mouth.

The Anglos had been the last to arrive in New Mexico, forging the Santa Fe Trail through the wilderness, only to find the city, already centuries old and quite pleased with itself.

But the Anglos stayed. And the Indians, Spanish and Anglos warred, finally tiring, until an uneasy peace came to New Mexico and the trinity was complete, ungainly but enduring.

Robin stood in the door and drank a can of Coke, polishing off the chips. The restaurants began to empty and the streets became crowded again. She decided to get out her stock of film, after all, and was in the back sorting through cartons of thirty-five mm film when the bell over her door tinkled. She turned automatically to see if the customer was in need of assistance. Suddenly she stopped still. A thought winged through her mind: *Oh, Mrs. Hartmann, he's definitely not for you.*

For an indecently long time, Robin stood undetected in the back of her store observing the man. He was tall, very tall, maybe six three or four. He was big and broad and well-muscled, strong-looking from his neck down to his well-shod feet.

He didn't appear to need any help at the moment. He was probably browsing, most likely waiting for his wife, who must surely be window-shopping nearby. Still, the stranger seemed quite interested in a window display Robin had recently arranged. Maybe he had a fantasy and was thinking about having a portrait done. What would this man's wish be? Her mind was filled with vivid images just thinking about the possibilities.

As if setting up a shot, Robin studied him with a professional eye. He was about forty years old, she guessed, and obviously Indian in descent. His skin was copper colored, smooth as satin. He had the most perfectly shaped head, and his cheekbones were high, powerful, framing his strong, slightly hooked nose as if sculpted by expert hands. From Robin's angle of view his shadowed, deep-set eyes looked as black as a moonless night.

He has to be married. A strange, disturbing jealousy shot through her. Why couldn't she have a man like that? Of course, maybe he was all looks and dull as dishwater.

There was a vitality to him, though, emanating from that well-set body, an unquestionable force. There appeared, from his carriage, to be pride as well, but not necessarily arrogance; rather, this man exuded competence and self-esteem.

He was an Indian, yes, but his attire told her a different story. He was wearing a forest-green polo shirt and khaki trousers, and on his wrist was an expensive-looking European watch.

Robin had him completely framed for a portrait when suddenly he turned and caught her studying him. Embarrassed, she dropped her gaze to her hands.

But he fixed his attention just as quickly on her display, and then she wasn't sure if she was relieved or insulted. Moving out to stand behind the counter, Robin saw him not only studying the display in her window but fingering it as well. Before she could object, he was pulling a framed photograph from the arrangement. Darn it all, she'd just finished setting that up!

"Excuse me," she said.

He turned abruptly and faced her full on, his black gaze falling directly on her for an unsettling moment before he looked again at the picture. "Where," he asked finally, "did you get this photo?" His tone was polite, but demanding a response in some indefinable way.

Robin's hands felt curiously empty; she placed them on her hips. "I shot that photo myself. Is there something—"

"And do you recall exactly *where* you shot it?" He sounded businesslike, but now she sensed a note of urgency in his voice.

"I took it at San Lucas Pueblo. I think it was two weeks ago. Why?"

The stranger strode over to her and tapped the print with his finger, indicating a lovely clay pot she'd used as a part of the background. "This pot is a counterfeit," he began, "a blatant forgery. The real one is in the Peabody Museum at Harvard University. You see that?" He pointed to a blemish on the pot. "I recognized the piece by that dark marking. It's what we call a firecloud, a smudge made when the piece was originally fired. That pot is unmistakable."

"Oh," replied Robin, at a loss. Of course, she distinctly remembered taking that portrait. She'd taken a client up to the pueblo for background and, as they arrived, a potter had been firing his work outside in the open, in the traditional way, so they'd stopped to watch. She'd asked the man if she could use one of his pieces in her picture; she'd tipped him and he'd been very proud and cooperative.

What was this stranger getting at? "Listen," she said, her head cocked to one side, "I don't quite understand..."

He regarded her for a long time with those Indian-black eyes then finally said, "I should introduce myself, Miss…"

"Hayle, Robin Hayle."

"Robin's Nest," he mused aloud. "Then you're the owner."

"That's right."

"I'm Adam Farwalker," he said, "from the University of New Mexico in Albuquerque, the archeology department." He tapped the picture once again, and Robin noticed his long-fingered brown hands. "I saw this photograph as I was walking by. I couldn't believe it at first, this copy being displayed right out in the open."

Robin was still puzzled. What was he trying to tell her, this man from the university, this archeologist?

He leaned against her counter, his strong arms folded across his chest, a knee bent so that their eyes were on a level. "Antique pieces, *true* ones, are bringing outrageous prices these days, Miss Hayle. The original of this piece—" he indicated the photograph "—is priceless. And, I might add, against the law to sell."

"The one in the picture is a fake then?" Robin asked.

"A very good one."

"And my kindly potter in San Lucas is really a crook?" Robin shook her head; it was hard to swallow.

"He could be. Or he could be innocent." Adam Farwalker's jaw tightened almost imperceptibly, but Robin saw the tension beneath his smooth skin. "The Indians are often exploited. They're given some cock-and-bull story about making a reproduction for a museum. It's been done with oil paintings for years, and now that Indian artifacts are in such high demand, we're starting to see these kinds of forgeries springing up like mushrooms. It's big money for unscrupulous art dealers. You see, it's harder nowadays to get hold of prehistoric pots. You can only sell pottery found on private land since the Archeological Resource Protection Act was passed."

"I see," said Robin thoughtfully. She glanced up at Adam Farwalker's chiseled face and wondered if he was a Pueblo Indian. He didn't really *look* like the Pueblo Indians she'd seen... Curious, hoping he didn't take offense at her ignorance, Robin asked, "You seem to know an awful lot about this pottery. Are you, uh, a Pueblo Indian?"

A corner of his mouth lifted; he was obviously amused. "I'm an Apache," he said with quiet dignity. "Prehistoric pottery is my field. In fact, I'm on a dig right now in Chaco Canyon." He paused then went on. "Would you recognize the potter again?"

"Well, sure. He was middle-aged, kind of thin..."

Ericka returned from lunch then, interrupting them. Robin introduced the young woman and assumed that the subject of the forged pot was closed. She was very wrong.

"If Miss Dalton can watch the shop now," Adam Farwalker said, "we could get going."

"Excuse me?" said Robin.

"Get going to San Lucas Pueblo."

"I..."

"To find this pottery maker of yours." Robin was so stunned, so taken aback by his suggestion, that for a minute she merely stood there.

"You've got an appointment, Miss Hayle," came Ericka's voice. "It's at three, I think."

"Oh," said Robin, snapping back to reality, "I *did* almost forget. I'm awfully sorry, Mr. Farwalker, but I can't really be of any help."

"Of course you can," he replied easily, as if asking her to drop everything was the most natural thing in the world. Oh, he was the perfect gentleman, and obviously very professional, but there was something else, too, something hidden in that calm expression. "After your appointment," he continued, "we can drive up to San Lucas. I assure you, Miss Hayle, this matter is vital."

"Well, I . . ."

"I'll wait for you in the plaza."

"But I don't know how long this shoot will take," Robin protested, amazed at how easily this man had taken control.

"No matter. I'll wait." And then he was gone.

Robin stood unmoving, watching the vacated space, staring into nothingness until Ericka's voice tugged her reluctantly back to reality.

CHAPTER TWO

ROBIN HAD A DEVIL OF A TIME keeping her mind on Mr. Norgard's photography session. He was a large, blond, muscular man who posed as a Viking. It was for his girlfriend's birthday, he explained somewhat sheepishly. Luckily the shoot didn't take long, and Robin was soon telling him when to stop by for the proofs, glancing at her watch and wondering if Adam Farwalker was actually still waiting for her. Should she go meet him? He was, after all, a complete stranger. Maybe he wasn't who he said he was...

It was Ericka, however, who set Robin's mind at rest. "Aren't you supposed to meet Mr. Farwalker?" she asked. And then it came out. "Oh, sure, I know him. Well, I know who his family is, anyway. They have a big ranch south of here."

"A ranch?"

"Yes, they're a real old family in these parts." Ericka shrugged. "I don't know them personally, but everybody says they're really nice people."

"I guess it's okay if I go meet him then," reflected Robin.

"Oh, sure," said Ericka.

"You'll lock up at six?"

"No problem. I'll see you tomorrow, Miss Hayle."

"At noon. You sleep in."

"Okay, you're the boss," Ericka said eagerly.

Robin grabbed her shoulder bag and camera, ran a hand through her mass of hair, pulled her skirt straight and stepped out into the hot yellow sunshine of midafternoon. Although the plaza was half a block away, she could hear the noise from the crowds at Indian Market, and the sidewalk in front of her shop was jammed with people who jostled her as she walked along.

What if she couldn't find Adam Farwalker in the mass of humanity? It struck Robin suddenly: she wanted to see him again. There was something about that man, Adam—she even liked his name—something very special, but hard as she tried, Robin could not put a finger on what it was. He was certainly the cerebral type, but there was nothing dull behind that implacable expression and those courtly mannerisms. What excited him, what pushed his buttons? She crossed the street, threading her way through the stalled traffic, and craned her neck to see. What if he had grown tired of waiting and had left already?

But she saw him instantly, just as she reached the shaded portal in front of the *Palacio Real*. He towered above everyone else in the crowd, yet it was his aura of stillness, of imperturbable calm that caught her eye. She started toward him then stopped, unable to resist studying this stranger who had just barged into her life.

She stood beneath the cool, shaded portal and observed Adam while a sea of people ebbed and flowed around her. His head was bent; he was talking to someone. He shifted his position and she saw who it was—Julien Cordova. He knew Julien, then. Well, of course he did. Julien had been born and raised in Santa Fe and was the curator of the *Palacio Real* Museum. It would be odd if Adam *didn't* know him.

A lady burdened with parcels bumped into Robin. "Excuse me," she mumbled, shouldering her way past.

When Robin looked back, Adam was smiling at something Julien had said. How handsome he appeared, his teeth flashing white against his copper skin! She would dearly love to do a series of portraits of Adam Farwalker, to see if she was skilled enough to capture on film that poise, that self-containment. His was a face that belonged on the cover of a magazine. In black and white, she decided, so that color did not interfere with the line and shadow of his features. It was a face that was seasoned but without blemish, full of strength and energy, proud, the face of a warrior, containing a harsh beauty and a store of secrets—like the land from which he came.

Robin shook herself; he was only a man, after all, and he was waiting for her. She started toward the pair of men, comparing them in her mind. They were so different— Adam big and dark and quiescent and Julien small, elegant, animated, with the pale skin and sad eyes of his ancestors, the Spanish noblemen who had settled Santa Fe nearly four hundred years ago.

She knew Julien well. He was the president of the newly formed Santa Fe Business Association, of which Robin was a charter member. He'd been elected unanimously, because his knowledge and leadership abilities and political acumen made him the only logical choice.

"Hello, Julien," she said, a little more breathlessly than she would have liked. "I see you know Mr. Farwalker." Glancing at Adam, she said, "Sorry I took so long."

Julien was lifting Robin's hand to his lips, kissing it in his intimately continental manner, but all the while Robin was aware of Adam, sensing his gaze on her.

"My dear Robin," Julien was saying, smiling with charm and a total disregard for the four inches she rose above him. "I do hope you're getting some additional business this weekend to tide you over the quiet times."

"Oh, yes, Julien, the studio's doing fine, thanks."

"Good, good." He glanced humorously around at the hordes of buyers who were grabbing at Navaho rugs and silver jewelry and pottery and paintings from the booths, or even snatching at things before they were unloaded from the vans that had been driven into Santa Fe for Indian Market from hundreds of miles away. "I must leave you. Today is one of the most loco of the whole year. No doubt there are dozens of crises I must attend to, and I've been shirking my duties." He laughed and shook Adam's hand. "So good to see you again, Adam. And I'm looking forward to your mother's fiesta tonight."

"She couldn't put it on without you," replied Adam genuinely.

"Oh," Julien added, turning to go, "good luck finding the man who made that counterfeit pot."

"You told him about it," Robin said when Julien had left.

Adam Farwalker shrugged. "It's bound to get out. And Julien's in a position to warn people about this sort of thing."

"So you really think it's that important?"

"Look, Miss..." He hesitated.

"Hayle. *Robin*," she said firmly.

"Miss Hayle. The economy of this area depends to a great extent on the art collector's dollar, especially the collector of Indian art. Aside from being against the law, counterfeiting pottery—or any kind of art—could ruin the reputation of every honest gallery owner in the state."

"I see what you mean," she said ruefully.

He took her elbow then, and she could feel the strength of his hand as it enclosed her arm. "Let's get out of this mob scene," he said impatiently. "Did you bring the picture along?"

She patted her fringed leather bag. "It's in here, don't worry."

It was amazing how easily Adam made his way through the throng. It was like the Red Sea parting for Moses. Was it his size or merely the determined look in his eye? Whatever, she was content to be swept along next to him for three blocks, to where his mud-caked Land Rover was parked.

"San Lucas, you said?" he asked as he unlocked the passenger door for her.

"Yes, that's where I took the picture." She couldn't help but notice that, as she climbed in, he stood by her door, ever the gentleman, until it was closed.

When he was seated, he asked, "And you don't know the name of the man, the potter?"

"No, I never asked. It just sort of happened, you know. I saw some people firing pots and we started talking."

Adam pulled the vehicle out into the busy street, winding his way through the traffic until they were headed out of the city on the main highway to the north. They passed DeVargas Mall, a modern shopping center named for the Spaniard who succeeded in the reconquest of Santa Fe after the Pueblo Revolt in 1692. It always tickled Robin to consider what Don Diego DeVargas would say about this monument to his name.

She would have liked to share this pleasantry with Adam Farwalker, but his drawn brows and silence stopped her. She shivered deep down inside somewhere, drawn by this man but a little wary of him, too. This wasn't like her at all. Robin could usually laugh and joke and talk a blue streak. She had a tendency, she knew, to talk too much, to overpower people—men, anyway. But not this man.

"That pot is extremely valuable. Priceless, actually. It's held up as the archetype of Anasazi black-on-white ware," he finally said. "There's only one like it in the world. There are collectors who would pay in the six figures for it."

"For a pot?" Robin asked in astonishment.

"It's nearly a thousand years old. If a collector really thought he'd found an original, sure, he'd pay that."

"But he wouldn't be able to show it to anyone, would he? I mean, he'd know he got it illegally."

"Well, possibly. Some collectors are content to just own a piece and never show it to anyone. And there *are* some valuable pieces for sale. You see, it's only illegal to sell the artifacts found on federal land. If a piece is found on private land, it's fair game."

Robin pulled the photograph out of her bag and looked at it once again. Her client was dressed as a conquistador in armor, helmet and tall leather boots. He stood in front of the pueblo, the stepped adobe cubicles making lovely checkerboard squares behind him. On the ground was an artful display of pumpkins and cornstalks, red chili peppers and the graceful round pot with its narrow neck and black geometric shapes on a white background.

"It's a beautiful piece," she said. "It even looks old. I could swear I see a crack in it. And some chips."

"It was very well done," Adam admitted.

"You're sure there couldn't be another one like the original? Maybe somebody found one...."

"I'm sure," he said and then turned his attention back to the road.

The harsh dry land sped by the window of the car as Robin stared ahead. It was parched by the August sun, but there was still a subtle array of color: ocher, vermilion, orange, sand, yellow. And a sky so blindingly blue that she always wore sunglasses. There were mountain peaks to the east of them, a dark, beckoning green mass that shimmered distantly in the heat haze. It was disquieting, untamed country, full of enigmas—hidden spots of startling beauty and dangerous barren stretches like the one named the *jornada del muerte*, the journey of death. It was a land that could bear men such as Adam Farwalker, professor of archeology, all man, all Indian. Something primitive stirred in Robin.

"So you teach?" she ventured.

He nodded, his eyes on the road. His profile was vigorous and blunt, the swell of his lips perfectly carved. He was a powerfully attractive man.

She tried again, determined to get him to talk. "Are you on sabbatical? I mean, if you're on a dig in Chaco Canyon..."

"Yes," was all he said.

"Is your university funding the dig?" she pressed, not one to give up easily.

"Partly. The university and *National Geographic* both. It's a follow-up to the Chaco Project of the seventies."

Well, at least she'd gotten something out of him. "Are you there year-round?"

"No. Usually just summers, but this year I'll be there until the second semester begins."

"Beautiful country up there," Robin found herself saying.

He finally had a reaction. "Have you ever been to Chaco Canyon, Miss Hayle?"

"No, but..."

He was smiling skeptically. So she'd finally pushed one of his buttons. "The canyon is in brutal country. It's a dry spot in the driest state in this nation. The sun drains the water from a man's body faster than he can drink it in. Beauty, Miss Hayle, as they say, is in the eye of the beholder."

She smiled to herself. Ignoring his tone, she said, "Please, call me Robin."

He turned to flash her a glance. "Robin it is, then."

Fifteen miles north of Santa Fe in the mesquite-covered red hills was an enclave of several pueblos. Following the sign, Adam pulled off the highway to drive the twisting mile to San Lucas. A sunlit plaza shaded by dusty cottonwood trees was the stage; the backdrop was the adobe dwellings piled one upon the other, built of the earth itself as the Anasazi had learned to build in this arid region devoid of forests. Indian children played under low trees; dogs barked; women in bright shawls and colorful skirts went about their daily business. The scene was timeless— except for the several pickup trucks parked nearby.

Adam pulled up alongside the trucks and switched off the Land Rover. He turned to her, his dark head inclined slightly in her direction. "Where to?" he asked.

"I told you," Robin began, "I met the man purely by accident, behind the pueblo where they were firing pots."

"Then we start there."

But the area behind the buildings was deserted, and the fires were out that afternoon. Only a skinny dog lay panting nearby in the shade.

"Now what?" inquired Robin.

"We ask around, show the picture. This is a small community." He stopped in the middle of his long stride. "I *am* sorry about dragging you away from your work, Miss—Robin. But this is very important."

"That's okay," she said, grateful for his sudden concern, realizing that this man did have other sides to him.

Adam approached an elderly Indian whose chair was tipped back against the wall of an adobe house. He asked the man in English, "Do you know who made this pot?" He motioned for Robin to show her photograph.

The man stared at him. Adam tried the same question in Spanish, but the man continued to gaze unblinkingly at him as he inhaled deeply on his cigarette. Finally his head moved from side to side; he blew smoke out of his nose in a stream.

Adam asked him in Spanish if there was a headman of the pueblo that he could talk to. Robin caught the impatient tone of Adam's question and wondered if he were making their job harder. They were, after all, practically in a foreign country, as Indian pueblos, like reservations, were autonomous bodies governed by their own tribal councils.

The man said something; Robin caught a few words of Spanish. She wished she could talk to him. She'd try smiles and charm and persuasion, but he seemed not to understand English.

"We'll try the headman. He speaks English," Adam told her. "This fellow knows nothing."

But Robin wondered.

She followed Adam's broad back up stairs and around corners to a door painted bright blue. Adam knocked. A heavyset woman answered, then called her husband.

"I am Reynaldo Sanchez. How can I help you?" the headman asked, and Robin heaved a sigh of relief that he spoke English. Maybe *she* could talk to him.

Adam explained their problem, showing Robin's photo to the Indian. "I'd like to locate the artisan who made this pot."

The man looked wary. "Do you wish to buy the pot?"

"No, not exactly, I'd just like to talk to the man who made it."

Oh, no, Robin thought. *Now we'll never find out.*

She was right. Reynaldo went stony-faced and called something in Tewa to his wife. He turned back to them and smiled deliberately. "I am sorry. I have never seen this pot, nor do I know who it belongs to. Perhaps this picture was taken in some other pueblo, *señorita*?"

"Oh, no," Robin was quick to say. "It was right in the plaza under that big tree. I'm sure—"

A little boy, probably the headman's son, scurried out the door, brushing Robin's skirt. He was in a hurry, intent on some errand. Robin didn't give the incident a thought—until later.

"I can't help you," Reynaldo said, closing his blue door in their faces.

They went back to the square, and Adam showed the photograph to a couple of women. They stared at him blankly and shrugged their shoulders.

"Let's ask in that store," suggested Robin, pointing to a small grocery on one side of the square. "I bought a Coke from the man. He'll remember me, I'm sure."

But he didn't. And Robin was sure it was the same man: she remembered his concho belt with its turquoise sunburst design. "No, I have never seen that pot. No one in San Lucas makes pots like that. Maybe you should try Cochiti or Acoma."

"The lady says she took the picture right over there," said Adam irritably. "Look, we just want to talk to the man who made it."

"Nobody here made that pot," the store owner said patiently, unmovably, enveloped in the obdurate privacy of the Pueblo Indian.

Leaving the store, Robin glanced sideways at Adam. He was angry, his dark brows drawn together in a bar. "Why won't they talk to us?" she asked.

He muttered something, a swear word, she suspected, in a strange language. Apache? "Because they're afraid and stubborn and secretive. They don't trust anyone outside their community," he finally said.

"But you're—" She stopped short.

"Yes, I'm an Indian." Adam halted and turned to her. "But I'm the wrong kind. Apache and Pueblo have been hereditary enemies since before the Spanish came here." He shrugged, his broad shoulders stretching the fabric of his polo shirt. "Unfortunately, they don't trust me any more than they trust you."

"Oh, dear."

"Yes. I'm afraid we won't find out a thing here. They've closed ranks."

"But how did they all know so fast? Oh, the little boy..."

"Probably." He grimaced and made a fist, hitting it into the other hand. "I should have known. If we'd come up here asking to *buy* the pot maybe we'd have gotten somewhere."

"Well, now what?" Robin asked, wondering if she should return to San Lucas without Adam and make some more inquiries. But no, they knew who she was now.

"I'll take you back to Santa Fe. It's getting late."

The sun was low, its rays long and bronzed, reaching across the plaza, lighting the adobe cubicles. The pueblo appeared to be a golden pyramid set against purple mountains. A boy drove goats home through clouds of gilded dust.

"Do you mind?" Robin said, pulling out her camera. "The light is irresistible."

"No, go ahead."

Flashing him a bright smile, Robin shot some pictures of the goats, of the pueblo itself, of some women dressed in traditional Indian garb, of a tree with the sun slanting through its branches. Several children, brown and round-faced, gathered to watch her curiously. She captured the array of childlike expressions, too: open, friendly, shy, impatient.

Adam waited for her, his shoulder against a rough adobe wall, his hands in the pockets of his well-cut trousers. She wanted to ask if she could photograph him, but she lacked the nerve. Maybe some other time—if she ever saw him again.

It was funny, but in her shop, when she'd first seen him, she had only noticed his sporty clothing and his self-confident demeanor. But now, as he stood there against the old pueblo wall, he looked Indian to her. She could see him mounted on a pinto war horse, the arid, unforgiving mesa lands behind him, his ebony hair in thick braids, his painted, sun-coppered skin gleaming in the harsh sun. An unaccountable chill crept down her spine and tingled in her scalp.

She had to shake herself, realizing that he'd been watching her. Finally something flashed in Adam's eyes—anger, amusement, disdain?—and he moved away from the wall and squatted to talk to two of the children. What did he tell them? They giggled and he smiled in return, his face relaxed and open, as he'd been with Julien. Why was he so guarded with her? Why couldn't he laugh and joke with her that way? What was there about the man that made him seem so . . . so mysterious, so closed to her?

Secretly, while his attention was on the children, Robin snapped a picture of him. She couldn't resist. It wasn't even an artistic shot, nor was she sure she'd focused properly. She just wanted his image; it was as if she possessed something once she'd photographed it. It was an odd concept but one Robin had always felt was the reason she became a photographer. Once she captured something on film she owned it forever.

Dusk dimmed the stark hills around them, softening their harshness, as Adam drove toward Santa Fe.

"Thanks for waiting for me," Robin said, still trying to break the ice. "I just can't bear to let a single scene go to waste."

"Will you use all those shots?" Adam asked.

"Oh, no, some will turn out lousy. Others I'll file away. A few I may enlarge and frame and put in the shop. The tourists buy photographs of the Southwest like mad."

"Interesting," he commented.

"Well, it's a living. No, I shouldn't say that. I love photographing things. I used to model in college, but I was always much more interested in the other end of the camera," she said, realizing that she was talking too much. "Photographs can capture something, a mood, a place, a personality. And I love fulfilling people's fantasies."

"Their fantasies?"

Robin had to explain about her studio and the costumes and props. She was half tempted to tell Adam how she saw *him*, but thought better of it.

He smiled as he listened to her stories. "You must have fulfilled some very bizarre fantasies," he remarked.

"Well, sure, but those are the fun ones. Once I had to arrange for a man to dress as a gorilla, but he wanted to be photographed in the zoo, with the gorillas."

"Did you do it?"

"Of course." She laughed. "It took all kinds of arranging and I was scared half out of my wits, but it's my job."

"Mine seems pretty dull compared to yours."

"Oh, no! I think it's fascinating. Ancient artifacts and ruins and figuring out how people lived thousands of years ago have always fascinated me."

"Have they?"

"Oh, yes. I'd love to see your dig. I mean, is it possible…well, for me to see what you're doing out there some time?" Oh, dear, there she was, being forward again, inviting herself.

"You'd like to see Chaco Canyon?"

"Oh, yes. And I could get some great shots, I bet."

"I'm sure it could be arranged," Adam said noncommittally, but Robin couldn't tell whether he meant it or not.

She changed the subject, not sure she really wanted to know. "Gosh, I'm starved. I'm always starved, it seems. Do you think we could stop?" She noticed that Adam glanced at his watch. Darn it! She was pushing again. His wife—or girlfriend—was probably waiting for him at that party Julien had mentioned. "Listen, I'm sorry. Maybe you have to be home for dinner or whatever."

He looked at her for a moment, as if considering something. "There is no one at home, Miss Hayle—Robin— waiting for me. I'd be glad to stop somewhere," he finally said.

Relief flooded her. So he wasn't married. Wonderful. Although why it was wonderful, Robin didn't even begin to explore. "Well, I eat like a horse so I insist we go Dutch treat."

"Sorry, Robin, I really do have to draw the line somewhere. I dragged you up here. It's the least I can do to buy you dinner."

"All right. I give up pretty easily, don't I? How about Maria's? She makes the best burritos."

"Maria's it is," he said.

Maria's was situated on a hillside just on the outskirts of Santa Fe. Adam and Robin were seated outside, facing the west, where the last pink glow of the sunset still stained the sky. Strings of lights surrounded the patio, twinkling spots of brightness that complemented the candles on their table.

Over her menu Robin studied Adam's face in the gathering darkness. Inadvertently, unable to escape habit, her mind conjured up yet another image of him: Adam on his haunches by a camp fire, dressed in leather leggings, his thick coal-black hair held back by a strip of cloth, his eyes searching the darkening land, his visage reddened in the fire glow.

Yes, he belonged to this land. She decided what it was about his people that held her fascination. It was their uncompromising yet utterly secure sense of belonging to the natural world, a unique gift granted to the Indian. Or, perhaps, a gift that had been given to all of humankind once but lost by Robin's own race.

She'd very much like to know Adam better. She'd like to break through his impenetrable constraint and see him laugh. She screwed up her courage, took a deep breath and said, "Maybe tomorrow, after work, I could drive to the pueblo with you and look for the pottery maker again."

His eyes lifted to hers, so still, so dark, reflecting twin points of light from the candle. Once again he seemed to be weighing up her words. "All right," he finally replied with equanimity, and Robin realized that he'd missed the invitation in her voice completely.

CHAPTER THREE

ADAM HAD NOT MISSED the invitation at all. On the contrary, it tempted him with exquisite irony. From the first moment he'd seen Robin Hayle standing in her shop, he'd been much too aware of her, uncomfortably aware. She had a way of looking at a man with frankness, her emotions surfacing vivaciously like rushing water flashing with sunlit jewels. And she met his eyes nearly on a level when they stood together, a singular experience for Adam, but he found himself liking it.

Robin Hayle.

He tried to withhold judgment, to suppress the attraction he felt. The Middle Way of the Apache was to avoid all excesses, even of happiness, and he had found the Way useful in his life.

"So," she was saying, "tell me some more about your dig."

Oddly enough, he wanted to tell her. "I'm doing follow-up research on Pueblo Bonito.... Are you familiar with any of the ruins there?"

She tilted her head and regarded him with her dark blue eyes. "Well, just the usual stuff."

"Pueblo Bonito is the best known community in the canyon, but there are a dozen others. What I'm trying to do is date the pottery periods more specifically, tie them to the few facts we know. Uh, Robin, I must be boring you."

"No, not at all." She was resting her chin on her fist, elbow on the tabletop, watching him closely, studying him as if she wanted to take a photograph of him.

He leaned back in his chair, as if to distance himself from her, aware of the disquieting interest he felt. "Well, that's all, really. I teach at the University of New Mexico in Albuquerque in the archeology department. Southwestern Indians and their pottery are my area of specialty."

The waitress arrived, and they ordered. Robin *did* eat a lot; she asked for the "grande" platter, and she wasn't a bit self-conscious about it.

He eyed her across the table surreptitiously. What attracted him to her so much? Was it her lighthearted manner? Her beauty, her long, lean body? Was it her quirky way of making a living?

"Tell me about how you happened to end up in Santa Fe," he said, a little surprised at his curiosity.

"Ah, so you can tell I'm not a native." She hesitated then flushed. "I'm sorry, I seem to be full of thoughtless remarks."

"Don't apologize. I'm a native, yes, but not so far back as you might think. It's the Pueblo tribes that were here a thousand years ago. We Apaches are newcomers; as nomads, we only arrived in the fifteenth century, just ahead of the Spanish. Almost everybody is an immigrant here."

"Thanks," she said wryly.

The dry hills around them were dark, their own oasis of light standing out like a beacon. Warm air caressed Adam's face and arms. He watched Robin eat while he picked at his own food; his mother was expecting him for the annual barbecue. He was late already, but just now that didn't matter. He folded his arms on the table. "And how did you come to live here?"

"Oh. Well, I visited once with a friend from my home-town, Waukegan, Illinois. That was three years ago. I fell in love with the place. The possibilities—" she waved her hand, gesturing around her "—for my craft are endless. And the people. You know how it strikes someone from the Midwest? Like a foreign country. Exotic."

"So I've been told." He liked her enthusiasm, the way she smiled with fun and humor. Yet when she was quiet she seemed almost like a vulnerable child, a woman who should be treated gently. The parody struck Adam; here was a person full of life, a tall, confident woman, and yet she was definitely hiding something. He could discern it in her eyes, behind the humor, could sense it from a stolen glance when he'd caught her off guard. Instinct and experience told him that there was pain somewhere in Robin Hayle, and if there was one thing Adam could recognize in another human being, it was pain. He wondered what had happened in her past.

Adam caught himself and smiled sardonically. This curiosity of his about a woman he'd probably never see again was futile. Nothing was going to happen between them; he wouldn't allow anything to come of this meeting. They were as far apart in their separate worlds as the sun and the moon.

She pushed her empty plate away and sighed. "That's better, I feel human again." Then she folded her hands in front of her on the table and said, "Do you mind if I ask you about yourself? I'm terribly curious. You see, I've never really met an Indian before." She stopped and pressed her lips together. "I sound so dumb, but I don't know how else to ask."

He smiled at her candidness. "Sure, what do you want to know?"

"Everything," she said then laughed at herself.

"That's a tall order."

"Well, how about the Apaches then? What are they like?"

Adam was finding that he wanted to talk to Robin, to explain things to her. He felt as if he hadn't conversed with an interesting woman for ages. What harm could come of a simple conversation?

"Everyone always thinks of the Apaches as warriors, you know," she was saying, drawing him out. "But I suspect they're a lot more."

Adam nodded. "They fought because they had to. Although," he admitted, "my tribe, the Mescalero Apache, did have a terrible reputation. The Eastern newspapers loved to play it up, of course. But the truth is, to us, the family and the clan are everything. We even introduce ourselves by who we're related to."

"So a hundred years ago," said Robin, "the Apache got a bum rap from the press?" She smiled faintly, challenging him.

"Well," said Adam, "I will admit that the name Apache comes from a Zuni Indian word, *ápachu*, meaning enemy."

"Aha."

"But believe me, the welfare of the clan was, no, *is* the focal point of our existence. We call ourselves the Diné, which means the People. It makes us sound very self-centered, and perhaps we are. And we call this land Dinetah."

"Dinetah," Robin said, savoring the word, "I like that."

"The U.S. Army fought us for fifty years. But before the Spanish or the Americans came we were peaceful farmers and herders."

"Farmers," she said, "I never would have guessed."

"Well, we're good with horses, too. And we never lie."

"Never?"

He shook his head. "You might find this interesting," he explained, "but the Apaches are what you could call the original women's libbers." Adam had to smile at her look of curiosity. "We're a matrilineal society, meaning that the mother is the hereditary head of the family. When the daughter marries, she brings her husband home."

"Amazing," said Robin, "and all along I thought the Apaches were warlike, you know, an all-male society, machoism at its height."

"Apache warriors *were* fierce in their day, but contrary to popular belief, they never took scalps. Apaches have a horror of mutilation, even of their enemies."

"Are you fierce?" Robin asked.

He looked at her blankly for a minute then cleared his throat. "Me? I'm one of your civilized Indians. College degree and all. I've made a compromise of my life. My subject allows me to stay in touch with the past of my people."

"You look like you could be fierce," she mused.

"Isn't that a strange thing to say to someone you hardly know?" he stated flatly.

"I suppose it is, but, you know, I can't help imagining people in photographs with costumes on, and backgrounds. Silly, isn't it? I see you in buckskin with long braids, on a horse, a fierce warrior."

"You've seen too many movies," he said dryly.

She disregarded his statement and leaned forward. "What is your fantasy, Adam Farwalker?" she asked, staring at him intently.

He went all cold inside. What had happened to their innocent conversation? "I don't deal in fantasies," he replied.

"But you should. Come on, think about it. How do you *see* yourself?"

He turned his face away from her and stared out into the darkness. The muted voices of the other diners, the tinkle of silverware, the sound of a cork popping from a wine bottle reached his ears. He was aware of her, still scrutinizing him, expectant, curious, attentive. A sudden urge to tell her everything washed over him. He could unburden himself, be rid of hiding, of pretending. It was as if this strange woman had seen into his heart and knew his war name, Changing Man, the name given him when he was a child, a secret inside his family. Changing Man, an apt description, he'd always thought. And this woman, this Robin Hayle, who dealt in fantasies, would accept and understand.

No. No woman would understand what was wrong with him. *Fierce.* He wanted to laugh at her assessment of him.

"Come on, you must have imagined yourself in some kind of scene. Everyone does," she urged.

"I hate to put a damper on everything," he said, "but I think we better go." He glanced at his watch. "I'm expected someplace."

"Oh." Her face fell, and he hated himself for being the cause of it. "I'm sorry. You should have told me. Really. Maybe I should call a taxi," she said.

"I dragged you out to San Lucas, Robin, and I'll get you back to Santa Fe. It's still early."

"Okay, if you're sure. I mean, sometimes I go on and on. My friends've learned to tell me to shut up when they've had enough." She was gathering her bag and pushing her hair off her shoulders as she rose, flashing him a too-bright smile.

The night wind flowed in the open window of the car as Adam drove toward the city. He could smell the pungent odors of sage and creosote bush and piñon, all mixed with dust, a familiar aroma.

He wondered again if Robin saw through his coolness. She couldn't, she hardly knew him. He'd learned to control himself, to consider every gesture, every expression, every word when he was with a woman. He'd had years to school himself in the hard lesson of keeping his distance from women. He'd had to.

"It's really too bad we couldn't find the man who made that pot," Robin said. "What are you going to do now?"

"I could try asking around at San Lucas again," he answered.

"Is there anything else you can do? Can the police help?"

"Not really. I have no proof, nothing but your photograph. That's not enough to convince them to do anything."

He sensed her hesitance, as if she wanted to say something but was not sure if she should. He wished he could joke and laugh with her, lay a hand on her arm, feel the thick silkiness of her ash-blond hair. He wished he had the freedom to still do that.

Adam stared at the road, at the lights of cars coming toward him. He wondered how he would act with this woman if he were a whole man.

Ridiculous. The entire situation was laughable, senseless. Ten years ago he'd caught the mumps from a young cousin. The mumps! A grown man with a ludicrous childhood disease. But in adult males the mumps could be devastating, causing clinical sterility. The doctor had shaken his head gravely and informed him he could never father any children.

He had the normal urges and his performance was not affected; in all outward respects he was perfectly normal.

He'd made a conscious decision to avoid serious commitment, though. Oh, he'd had a few superficial relationships, but the women to whom he was attracted seriously were all looking for something he couldn't give them. So he spared them the decision, threw himself into his work with a fervor and masked his shortcoming with aloofness. He was aware that he appeared to be arrogant at times, and prideful. But hidden, like a worm in an apple, was the bitter ever-present knowledge. What woman would accept that knowledge without derision or, worse, pity?

Robin's voice intruded into his thoughts. "Are you, um, from Santa Fe originally?"

"Yes, born and raised. My parents live here, just outside of town."

She sighed, and he wondered what it meant, then she drew her knees up under her full skirt and turned sideways toward him, one arm resting on the back of the seat. He was acutely aware of her, of her scent, of her hair catching the flashes of outside light like ribbons of silver, of her tilted head and questioning eyes. "You're so lucky," she was saying in a soft voice. "You belong to this place, you know. You have roots, your family lives here. Sometimes I feel so unattached that it's scary. My parents died years ago. I hope you appreciate what you've got."

There was the trace of pain he'd noted. She was lonely, that was all. Where were all the men that surely must be interested in her? Why wasn't she married? Against his will he glanced over at her; she was staring out the front window of the car, her neck long and lovely, her profile classic. Regret seized him like a fist.

Adam pulled up in front of Robin's Nest. "Thanks for dropping everything and going up to San Lucas with me," he said.

"Even if we didn't find anything. Oh, well, we could try again, couldn't we? Thanks for dinner, anyway," she said, smiling. "And I got some great shots."

He went around to her door and opened it while she gathered up her shoulder bag and camera from the back seat. Her breast pressed against the white fabric of her blouse as she reached behind her, and Adam flushed and looked away.

She slid out of the car and turned to him. "Thanks again," she said genuinely. "I enjoyed this afternoon.... That is, it was good to get away for a while, from Indian Market. You will let me know if there's anything I can do to help?"

"I will," he replied, making an instantaneous promise to himself never to see Robin Hayle again. She was too disturbing to his hard-earned peace of mind.

"Well, bye," she said, turning away. Then she stopped, cocked her head and looked at her shop front. "I wonder why Ericka pulled the blinds?" she mused.

"Excuse me?"

She kept staring at the shop. "We never close the blinds, it messes up the displays. Why would she...?"

He looked. The blinds were all the way down. "You mean, you never close them like that when you lock up?"

"No." Robin turned to him, a frown creasing her forehead. "Did Ericka forget? But why on earth...?"

Then she rummaged through her big bag for her keys, pulled them out and started toward the door.

The sixth sense is only the other five senses working to their limits, noting anything out of harmony. Adam's brain tested his impressions, listened to his five senses, the way his father had taught him when they went hunting, listened to his instincts. "Wait," he said, putting a hand on her arm.

She stopped abruptly and peered at him through the dimness. "Yes?"

"Is there a back door, a window, something like that?"

She frowned more deeply. "Sure, there's a door to the studio on the alley, and my office window. Do you—"

"I'm going to take a look," he said. "Stay here."

"But what do you think happened?"

"I don't know," he said tightly, "I'm just going to take a look."

When he got to the back of her shop he saw it immediately. Someone had broken the window, knocked the glass out and entered the building. The back door was open, too. Could whoever had done it still be inside? He stuck his head in and listened. Utter silence greeted him.

"Adam?" he heard from the alley behind him. "Oh, there you are. What . . . ?"

"I told you to stay—"

"What happened? Oh, my window!"

"Someone's broken into your store."

"Oh, no!" She brushed past him and flicked the lights on inside the back door. He heard her gasp.

Stepping inside, Adam understood why. Her shop was in a shambles. Every drawer and cupboard had been opened and the contents dumped out on the floor, every picture pulled off the wall, every camera and roll of film tossed helter-skelter, many unrolled, exposed, ruined.

"Oh," she said in a distraught voice. He could see her sag, her hand going out for support. He took her arm quickly and led her to the nearest chair he could find. She held onto his hand tightly and stared around at the mess.

"Are you all right?"

She looked at him, tears welling in her eyes, then she seemed to shake herself. "Yes, sure, I'm just . . . Oh, boy, I don't know."

"Have you ever been burglarized before?"

"No."

"Any of the other stores around here been robbed?"

"Not since I opened the shop." Her head rose. "Did they steal the cash? It's in a drawer..."

He left her there and checked beneath her cash register. The day's cash, checks and credit-card receipts had been neatly stored by Ericka in a bank deposit bag, with the register tape. He handed her the bag silently, watched as she checked the contents then looked up at him, bewildered. "It's all here," she said, "just as Ericka left it. I don't understand."

But Adam was beginning to. There was evidently nothing missing in her shop—even the cash had not been disturbed. It was as if this ransacking were a message of sorts.

"I just don't get it," Robin was saying.

"I do," stated Adam, his mind working logically and clearly now.

Robin looked at him anxiously. "What's going on here?" she asked. "Why didn't they take the money?"

Adam folded his arms and looked at her upturned face. "I'm beginning to think this was not a simple burglary, Robin. It's too coincidental. It's a warning."

"What *are* you talking about?"

"Somebody found out you were at San Lucas today, asking about a forged pot—the lady photographer who was there two weeks ago. Word must have spread like wildfire. Did anyone at San Lucas know your name?"

She thought for a minute. "I gave the man, the potter, my card, in case he wanted a copy of the picture." Then she stared at him openmouthed for a second. "What are you saying?"

Adam felt a sudden burst of anger at himself for getting an innocent person involved in what was already a messy situation. "Damn it," he muttered. "Look, your potter at the pueblo, or someone working with him, probably did this to warn you off."

"Oh, come on," she said skeptically.

"Robin, I'm not sure you realize what we're dealing with here. Some of these art counterfeiters run huge rings. There are hundreds of thousands, maybe millions of dollars at stake. Apparently they don't take kindly to investigations."

Adam stalked out to the front of the shop, regarded the clutter once again and cursed himself. He'd marched through that pueblo like a blundering white eyes, and in his wake had left an entire community suspicious and doubting. Why hadn't he been more subtle; why hadn't he used his head? It couldn't have been because he was with Robin, uncertain, ill-at-ease, not thinking quite straight. He couldn't be that careless.

"Adam," came her voice behind him, "I think I should call the police and report this."

"I suppose so. Can I do it for you?"

"Oh, no, that's all right. I'll do it. But I would like to ask a favor of you. I know you have a…a date, but maybe you could stay and face the police with me. I…I have this awful feeling they won't believe me. Can you call and say you'll be late?"

She was so shaken, so apologetic, so terribly vulnerable that all Adam could do was stand there, helpless. "Sure," he replied softly, "my appointment doesn't matter."

"You can use the phone…"

He wanted to hold her tight, stroke her thick silver-blond hair, tell her everything was going to be fine. He trembled with his need, steeled himself against it and kept his distance from her.

He watched while she phoned the police, saw her gather herself together and look around at the chaos in her little shop. A gleam of anger shot from her eyes when she hung up.

"Those *slobs*," she said. "No wonder they closed the blinds!"

"I'll help you clean up," he offered.

"The police said not to touch anything."

"Perhaps later then. Tomorrow."

"I won't say no," she answered wryly.

She heated the day's coffee on a hot plate, and they sipped while they waited. It wasn't more than five minutes before an official car drove up. Robin unlocked the front door for the policeman, who introduced himself, flashed his badge and grimaced at the mess.

"Detective Cordova," Robin said, "are you any relation to Julien?"

Adam's head snapped up. "Rod!" he called. "Well, I'll be damned!"

"Adam, that you?" The two men shook hands. "It's been a few years," said Rod. "Now, what's this burglary all about? You say no money's been taken?"

"I'm sorry, Robin," said Adam. "Rod's an old schoolmate of mine. Julien's younger brother—well, one of his *many* younger brothers."

"You know Julien?" Rod asked. "Sure, everybody does." He laughed, answering his own question. He was a trim man, small like Julien, but not so elegant. He gave the impression of sharpness, of being in control, of seeing to the bottom of things. He pulled out a pad, fixed his eyes on Robin and said, "Okay, what's the story here?"

Robin told him about the pot, about their trip to San Lucas that afternoon, about Adam's theory. Adam added a few of his own comments but mostly let Robin vent her anger and confusion on the patient Detective Cordova. Rodriguez wrote quickly, nodded, listened, asked a few pertinent questions.

"I'll send my fingerprint man over on Monday," he said when he was through writing. "Maybe they left some prints."

But Adam could tell he was doubtful. "You don't sound like you're convinced, Rod," he remarked.

"Well, it's like this, Adam. I have to go on facts. So far the facts are clear: nothing's been stolen. The window was broken, yes. Probably some teenagers getting into trouble. You know." He shook his dark head. "There are a few nasty gangs around."

"But why *my* shop?" asked Robin.

"You've got a teenager working for you, don't you?"

"Ericka?"

"I'll question her. Maybe she has some friends, they heard her talking. You know how it is, Miss Hayle. Happens all the time."

"Ericka Dalton had nothing to do with this," Robin said defensively.

Adam put a hand on her arm. "Rod's only doing his job. I'm sure Ericka had nothing to do with it; it's only that Rod's got to check."

She said nothing more, but Adam could see that she was still hot under the collar. Rod was not taking this as seriously as Adam would have liked. Of course, if you looked at the break-in from an outsider's point of view, it was merely a petty crime.

"Look, Rod, keep the pottery angle open, okay? There could be a connection," Adam suggested.

"Until I find otherwise, I'm open to any and all possibilities," Rod answered. "Stranger things have happened. Good night, Miss Hayle. Sorry about the mess."

He grinned at Adam and said, *"Buenas noches, amigo.*
See you around."

"Well," said Robin when her door was closed behind the
detective.

"He's just doing his job."

"Of all the nerve! Accusing Ericka." She turned
around, made an angry gesture with her hands. "I wish *he*
had to clean this up!"

"I was afraid the police would react like that."

"He wasn't much help, was he? But it does sound crazy.
I hardly believe the story myself." She looked imploringly
at him. "Maybe it's just a coincidence, a group of teenagers, like he said. Maybe somebody broke into the wrong
shop. It could be that, couldn't it?"

"Robin . . ." He didn't want to upset her any more than
she already was; neither did he want to give her false hope.
"I don't know for sure who did this. I don't want to scare
you, but if we disturbed a ring of forgers, this may not be
the end of it."

She stared at him with those wide, dark-blue eyes, then
she strode across the littered floor, her sky-blue skirt
swirling around her long legs. "Oh, I don't know," she
said, "it just seems like someone should do *something*
about crime these days. It's as if no one cares. Even the
police."

She was brave, he'd give her that. Too brave, maybe, for
her own good.

"You know," she stated emphatically, "if I could do
something myself—like find out who did this—I'd con-
front them. I swear I would."

She was angry, and she sure had a right to be. But there
was something Adam had kept from her, something he'd
remembered when Rod Cordova had been here. It had
happened in Albuquerque two, maybe three years ago. A

local policeman had gotten a lead on one of the counter-feiting rings. The papers had been full of stories of art counterfeiting back then. But it had all ended abruptly—the police officer's body had been found in the desert alongside his car. Some had called it an accident; others were not so certain. Needless to say, the follow-up investigation had led nowhere.

Good God, what had he gotten Robin involved in?

CHAPTER FOUR

SUDDENLY ADAM LONGED to take off for Chaco Canyon and bury himself in his work, to turn back the clock to that morning before he'd passed by Robin's window and spotted the photograph. But firmly imbedded in his genes was the Apache sense of honor, of duty and fairness. He had gotten Robin into this ugly situation, and he could not conceivably walk away from his responsibility.

"You better stay at the ranch tonight," he said.

"Oh?" she replied and, by the tone in her voice, he decided he'd better rephrase his suggestion.

"I want you to be my guest at my parents' place, Robin. Of course, I can't force you to stay there, but for safety's sake, I'd feel much better. I'm sure, if you think about it," he added carefully, "you'll agree."

"I couldn't. I don't even know your parents."

"They won't mind. There's plenty of room. I'm sure they'd want you to stay with them under the circumstances."

"I feel so foolish. My goodness, you make it seem as if we're involved in some cloak-and-dagger plot."

"Perhaps we are," he replied gravely.

She put a finger on her chin and tapped her foot for a minute, thinking. "Can I be back early in the morning?"

"As early as you like." He glanced around the shop. "And I *am* going to help clean up in here."

"Oh, I didn't really mean that. You don't have to."

"I insist."

He drove Robin to her apartment on Bishop's Lodge Road, which was only four short blocks from her shop.

"I believe," she said tentatively, "that there's an affair going on tonight at your folks' place. I'm afraid this is a really bad time for me to intrude..."

"The annual fund-raiser, yes. But you won't be intruding in the least."

"Are you sure? I feel awfully silly about this. I mean, it isn't a formal sit-down dinner, I hope."

"Not at all."

"What is the fund-raiser for?" she asked.

"The proceeds go to the Native American Art Museum here in Santa Fe. My mother likes to stay active in local affairs."

"Is it dressy?"

Adam parked his car and glanced at Robin for an instant. "You look fine," he said. "It's not formal, like I said. A mesquite barbecue, an auction." He shrugged, climbed out of the Land Rover and went to open her door. "May I have your key?"

Robin looked at him askance. "You're not thinking someone might have broken into my apartment, too?"

"It's a possibility." He took the key ring and walked up the narrow flight of stairs ahead of her. He could sense her reluctance to believe him, to comprehend the danger she might be in. There was a stiffness to her now, a hesitance. He only hoped she was not making more of his invitation to the ranch than was meant.

Cautiously Adam tried her doorknob. It was locked. He inserted the key and let the door swing open noiselessly, listening, trusting his senses.

"Well?" she asked from behind him.

He found the light switches inside her door and flicked them on. Good. No one had made a mess in her apartment.

"Oh, thank heavens!" she breathed, starting to go in.

"Wait a minute," he warned.

He poked his head into the kitchen and the bedroom then, satisfied, he told her to come in.

"I'll just change and throw some things into an overnight bag," she said. "I should only be a couple of minutes."

As Adam stood in the middle of her living room alone with his impressions, an acute sensitivity, a peculiarly Indian sense of environment, of place and time, surfaced in him. There was, of course, the scent of the place, of Robin in particular: a female scent, neither sweet nor flowery but simply natural. Then there were her surroundings and, to Adam, surroundings revealed a person's inner self. The white man called it taste—so and so's taste was good or bad—but to the Indian the things a person gathered were either for utility or reminders of their heritage. Robin's possessions told nothing of her upbringing in Illinois. They were new, all of them, and traditionally Southwestern in style.

So, Adam thought, she'd left her past behind, the past that he surmised was clouded by some sort of pain. There was a feel to these possessions, however, that was not lost on him. Robin had collected Navaho rugs and lovely baskets and intricately woven coverings for the cushions on her couch. On the clean white walls were prints of Hopi Indians and pueblos, of striated tabletop mesas gilded in afternoon light. There were framed, limited-edition posters advertising the Santa Fe Opera. Pots of lush plants and bunches of chilies and ropes of rosy garlic hung from the beamed ceiling. Beige, moss green and muted pastels caught the eye. A pleasant place. Oddly, though, there seemed to be none of her own fine photographs on display. Adam wondered why. It was as if she'd grasped a feel for his land and his heritage, but somehow she had not yet fit her own self into the scenario.

"I'll be out in a sec," she called. "Fix yourself a drink if you like."

"No, thank you," he replied, his hands in his trousers pockets as he stood, rigid, uneasy with his thoughts. She was just behind that door, only steps away. He tried not to let himself dwell on Robin in there, changing her clothes, brushing her hair...

Despite the fact that his back was to her, Adam sensed her presence in the living room the moment she entered. It was as if she had suddenly brought life to an inanimate place. He turned to face her. She was lovely, like sunlight sparkling; she brought with her a freshness and vitality that filled his being with a unique longing.

"Well," she said, "how do I look?"

"You look fine," he remarked noncommittally, taking her overnight bag from her hand, but his eyes stubbornly refused to leave her. She had put her hair up with combs, the effect of which was informal yet elegant, feminine and sensual all at once. Adam experienced a stirring in his groin and suddenly he felt closed in, as if he needed to run for miles in the cool night air.

"Hold on a second," Robin said, then she strode purposefully into the kitchen where she began to write something on a notepad. Adam watched as she leaned over the spotless countertop. She certainly looked better than *fine*. She wore a salmon-pink, calf-length skirt with a matching blazer whose sleeves were pushed up to the elbows. Underneath was an off-white top with a low scoop neck. And he couldn't help but notice as she finally straightened and the fold of her jacket parted, Robin wore no bra beneath the shimmering material.

He was seized by sudden regret.

"What do you think?" Robin asked, handing him the note.

Adam looked at it. "Don't bother wrecking this place," he read, "I got the message loud and clear." He glanced at Robin's amused expression and found himself smiling.

"You're putting this on your door?" he asked.

"I sure am. I've no intentions of cleaning up in here, too, *if* your theory about the counterfeiters is right." She brushed past him and tacked up the note, and he was gripped by her scent as it floated in the air. It was her perfume, of course, a light, unfamiliar aroma that filled his head. It was as if she were tormenting him on purpose.

"Let's go," Adam said, turning away.

The drive to the ranch didn't take long. His family's old Spanish hacienda sat at the end of Canyon Road only a few miles from the center of the city, enfolded in hills above the Santa Fe River.

"I never realized there was this much open land so near Santa Fe," remarked Robin from her seat in the darkened car. "I mean, it's really *big* up here."

"The ranch," said Adam, glad to slip into his role as professor, "has been in the family for over three centuries." He heard her mild gasp of surprise.

"But . . . but you're an Apache," she said. "I mean, Apaches didn't have ranches here three hundred years ago. Or . . . did they?"

"Well, no, they didn't. The ranch was originally a Spanish land grant to an ancestor of mine—and this is purely family legend—but my mother says the Spanish king gave it to one of his bastard sons."

"Then you're not entirely Apache."

He shook his head. "I'm about ninety percent Indian, though. My great-great-grandmother, Cassandra, married a wealthy American after her father died. By doing so, she saved this ranch when the United Sates won the war against Mexico. Most all the other Mexicans lost everything. But not her."

"So," said Robin, "that's all fine, but how did the Apache get into the family?"

"Cassandra's husband died of wounds from the Civil War and she married again, a half-breed Apache."

"I see," answered Robin.

"Yes. His name was Adam."

"So you're named after this illustrious ancestor. How wonderful."

"My mother liked the story. Of course, there's a question as to how illustrious he was. He was a wild sort, off in the mountains half the time, but his children inherited the hacienda. And from then on they kept the land, but they all married Apaches."

"Wow, what a story," said Robin.

"I often wonder how much of it's true, although the original land grant is on file in the historical library. This is one of the few haciendas that survived American taxes and surveying laws."

"Cassandra," mused Robin, "a strong woman. I would have liked her."

"She probably would have liked you," he found himself saying.

"What a remarkable inheritance," Robin said softly.

And Adam felt like adding: *But it's all going to end with me.*

Before them spread the rolling hills of the ranch. Cattle, mere shadows in the moonlight, dotted the countryside above the Santa Fe River, which in the late summer was a mere trickle. And beyond several camel-like humps of land stood the sprawling hacienda, Las Jaritas—the Willows—lit like a strand of diamonds on the hillside.

"If you listen," Adam said, "you can hear the music." Indeed, when the night wind shifted, they could hear faint guitar music as if it were being played in a distant time and carried on the breeze through the decades.

"Oh, that's beautiful," Robin whispered. "It gives me goose bumps."

Carrying her bag in one hand, Adam took Robin's arm with the other and led her across the crowded, lantern-lit courtyard to where his mother stood talking. Christina Farwalker looked charming; she was a small, plump woman who wore a calf-length, full skirt, a conch belt and peasant blouse and lots of turquoise jewelry. Her lustrous black hair was cut in a modern style, feathered and swept back—the perfect combination of ethnic and chic.

Adam was aware the moment his mother saw him. Her black eyebrows raised, she excused herself from the man to whom she was talking and made her way through the crowd toward him. He'd have to explain to his mother; she'd think he'd brought a date and be thrilled to death. Abruptly he released his hold on Robin's arm.

"Hello, Adam," Christina said, stepping forward to greet him. "You're awfully late."

"Hello, Mother," he replied. "This is Robin Hayle. She owns a photography studio in town and due to some rather peculiar happenings today, I've asked her to stay in the guest house. That's why I'm so late."

"Nothing's wrong, I hope," said his mother. "But, my dear—Robin, is it?—you're most welcome here." She was looking back and forth from Robin to Adam, obviously puzzled.

"Robin got involved with a crazy idea I had..." Adam offered. "I'll explain later."

"I *am* glad to be here, Mrs. Farwalker," Robin was saying brightly, shaking the shorter woman's hand and taking control of the conversation.

"Call me Christina, please. And Adam, take Robin to her room and then get her something to eat."

Robin laughed lightly. "I know I look like I'm starving," she said. "I always do. But Adam already bought me dinner."

"I won't tell a soul." Christina laughed, and they were friends already. Somehow the notion disturbed Adam.

The low, one-story hacienda spread along the hillside behind an aged adobe wall. Built onto and expanded countless times over the centuries, it was an intricate jumble of adobe walls and small, square windows covered with the ubiquitous wrought-iron grills of the Southwest. A century-old chapel still stood apart from the main structure. Nearby was a building that had once been the servants' quarters, but now, newly renovated, served as private guest housing.

"I'll get lost coming back to the party," joked Robin as Adam swung open her door.

"Just follow the noise. The louder it gets, the closer you are." He placed her bag on an armchair and turned to leave.

"I'll be ready in a second."

"I'll see you there," he said quickly. "There's someone I have to talk to for a minute. Do you mind?"

"Oh, no. Of course not." But she sounded disappointed. A pity, he thought, as he closed the door and fled into the shadows, but he was doing her a favor.

There actually was someone Adam had to see. He threaded his way though the throng and found his mother again. He had every intention of warning her off before she said or did anything embarrassing to either himself or Robin.

"Got a minute?" he asked his mother, tactfully steering her away from the group. Quickly he explained Robin's situation and how he had gotten her involved.

"And you're convinced that there really is a counterfeiting ring and someone deliberately broke into Robin's shop to warn her?" asked Christina.

"I'm going to act on that theory," said Adam. "I want to make sure Robin is safe."

"Of course. She can stay as long as she wants."

"Mother, you do understand that's why I brought her out here? For her own protection?"

"Such a lovely girl," Christina observed with a sigh. "Don't you think so?"

"Yes," Adam said impatiently. "But if she'd been a hag I still would have done the same thing."

"Well, son, I see you finally got here. A little late. You've missed the auction," came his father's voice.

"Adam's had a little problem," offered Christina, and then she repeated the story to her husband. "So that's why he's so late. But you must meet Adam's friend, Robin. She's absolutely delightful. She's a photographer, Ray, and that's how this whole thing got started."

Ray Farwalker was an exceptionally tall, rawboned man who wore a studded, Western-style shirt, boots and dress pants and kept his long, graying hair tied back in the old way, in a ponytail. He was a quiet man who worked hard every day of his life, and he had an aura of peace to him, a peace Adam had come to envy. Soberly he asked his son, "You reported this to the police?"

"Rod Cordova's taking care of it."

"Good," said Ray. "Now where's this lady of yours?"

"She is *not* a lady of mine," replied Adam tightly. "I just felt responsible after what happened to her shop."

"And well you should," said Christina. "Poor girl. Why don't you go get her, Adam? Your father would like to meet her."

"Mother..." Adam warned.

"She's a *guest* in my house," Christina pointed out. "I do think we owe her certain courtesies, Adam."

"I'm sure I'll get a chance to meet her later," Ray said.

"Well, I better get back to the party," Christina exchanged a meaningful glance with her husband, a glance Adam caught. Anger coiled within him. She was doing it again—assuming, pushing, *hoping*.

"Mother, don't read anything into this," he warned again.

"Son," Ray said, "your mother—"

But Christina laid a hand on her husband's arm to silence him. "Adam," she said quietly, "you have been taught to adjust yourself to remain in harmony with life. If nature withholds children from you, it is up to you to seek the pattern behind it, to find its beauty and accept it. Not to fight nature, as the white man does." Then she stood on tiptoe and kissed Adam's cheek. "You and Robin enjoy the party." She took Ray's arm and the two of them disappeared into the noisy, laughing crowd while Adam watched, his face devoid of expression.

ROBIN SAT, SLUMPED, her hands on her cheeks, contemplating the situation. She wished Adam had never paused at her shop window. She wished she'd never seen him or talked to him. He was someone she could like, a lot, but it seemed he had no interest in her.

She looked around the guest house. It was typical of the charm of old Santa Fe she'd come to love. The furniture was simple and spare, with cleanliness and a Spanish flavor. On the four-poster bed was a black and red Indian blanket, on the floor a Navaho rug. The bathroom was utterly modern. The room itself, she decided, was a trinity of cultures. Like Adam Farwalker.

She really didn't feel like joining the party. Sighing, she stood and walked to the open window, drawing aside the curtain. Guitar music lifted from the courtyard and floated along the paths to her room. Everywhere she gazed there were potted flowers, dark in the night shadows. Over near an old chapel was a lonely little bench resting against the high adobe wall, a wall, Robin guessed, meant to keep out intruders. She felt suddenly lost, out of place, out of her time.

Leaving the guest house, Robin strolled aimlessly toward the chapel. She couldn't help thinking about the story of Adam's ancestor, Cassandra. The woman had walked these same paths, smelled this exotic profusion of late summer flowers. Of course, the walls had probably been new then, and the chapel in better repair.

A soft footfall behind Robin made her turn. It was Adam, tall and broad-shouldered in the dark. She put a hand to her throat in an unconscious gesture. "Oh, you startled me."

"Sorry. I was worried you'd actually gotten lost."

"I was poking my nose into corners. This place is so fascinating, so old. I think it's marvelous your family still lives here." She wondered who would inherit all this. "Are you the eldest son?" Robin asked casually.

"Yes," he replied. "I have two younger sisters."

"Then your children will be the ones to carry on your name and live here."

Adam stood leaning against the adobe wall of the old chapel. He folded his arms. "Apache society is matrilineal, as I told you. My sisters should be the ones to bring their husbands home to this place. Unfortunately, they've become so thoroughly modernized they both moved away with their husbands. My mother isn't happy about it.''

For a long moment Robin stared at him pensively. Why had he sidestepped the issue of his children inheriting? Didn't he plan on *ever* marrying? "You know your heritage is worth preserving," she said softly, trying to draw him out. When he said nothing, she couldn't help but add, "It's beautiful here, Adam. I'm very jealous. I wonder if you know how valuable your inheritance is."

"Oh, I do know, Robin, I do," he said simply, almost bitterly, she thought.

They stood in mutual silence, history embracing them. Yet Robin felt that distance Adam was purposefully cultivating.

"You must be hungry," he stated after a time. "Shall we join the party?"

She would have preferred to say there in the darkness with Adam, but how could she possibly tell him that? "I suppose we should," she said, chiding herself for being a fool.

As they passed by the solitary wooden bench against the wall, Robin slowed her pace. Had Cassandra once sat on that very seat and secretly kissed her wild Apache lover? she wondered.

"Are you coming?" asked Adam and she nodded quickly, tearing her mind from the past and following him toward the gathering.

On the lamp-lit central patio the party was in full swing. A wonderful mélange of faces greeted Robin: elegant Spanish grandees whose families had lived in New Mexico for centuries; heirs to East Coast fortunes in town for Indian Market; collectors in their own right; Westerners with sun-faded eyes, snakeskin boots, string ties and Stetsons; stoic Indians who were local artists or friends of the Far-walkers.

Dutifully Adam left Robin's side for a minute to get her a plate of ribs and chicken from the mesquite grill, cole-slaw and salad from a long trestle table. She looked around, wishing she could take some photographs in the flickering light.

It was then that Christina took the opportunity to speak to her. "Are you enjoying the party, Robin?"

"Very much so, Mrs. Farwalker."

"Christina," she said easily. "This is my favorite event of the year. It's my way of bringing the Indian and the white communities together."

"It's very generous of you."

"My husband writes it off our taxes," replied Christina with good humor, and Robin laughed along with her. How different the Farwalkers were from most Indians, she thought. They chose to bridge two worlds, and obviously they did it very successfully.

"My son told me about the photograph," Christina was saying, "and about your shop. It's terrible."

"It makes me furious," Robin answered.

"You know, these rings of counterfeiters can be very dangerous. You have to be careful. I don't know what my son was thinking when he dragged you out to that pueblo. Usually he's very levelheaded—"

"I realize I should have consulted you first, Mother," Adam said lightly as he returned with a plate for Robin and one for himself.

At that point a couple from New York who owned a gallery joined in the conversation. Robin couldn't help but notice how easily Adam talked with them, how alive he became while discussing his role as one who treasured and

preserved history, who protected the marketplace as well
as the museum. He even laughed once, his black eyes
dancing in the soft light. How could he be so at ease with
others, barely acquaintances, and so stilted with her?

Nonetheless he was a perfect host, escorting Robin from
group to group; taking her arm occasionally, introducing
her to so many people she knew she'd never remember all
their names.

Julien Cordova was there, talking animatedly to a group
of collectors. "How nice to see you again, Robin," he said.
"I must say, Adam, this meeting you so often is becoming a pleasant habit. Delightful party."

And then they drifted on, pushed here and there by the
eddying throng. The music grew lively, and a young man
sang in Spanish, a lilting song about *amor* and *la vida*, love
and life.

Two effeminate men who owned a Western art gallery
in Scottsdale, Arizona, were talking to Adam, but Robin
wasn't listening. Instead, she was staring at Adam's face
unashamedly, at the strength of his bone and muscle, at the
strong set of his chin and those finely molded lips.

He caught her staring at him and turned away slightly,
his animated expression closing as if the door to his soul
had shut. Maybe, Robin told herself, it was the Indian in
him, the innate privacy he used to protect himself from
outsiders. In time she might come to know him, to understand.

She was probably kidding herself about that, though.
He was so distant with her, he was obviously just not interested.

By midnight guests were starting to leave. The music
quieted; unobtrusively servants cleared tables; the flames
in the gas torches were lowered. A few night owls still hung

around, however, sitting and chatting over wine spills on the tablecloths.

Robin was tired. She'd been sitting talking to Ray Far-walker about a portrait she'd shot on the Apache Reservation near Santa Fe, but he'd had to leave her and say his farewells to some visitors. She felt suddenly alone, an alien in Adam's world, a place she had no business being.

Self-consciously she sought out Adam. He was saying goodbye to Julien on the far side of the courtyard. He stood tall and erect, yet he appeared to be relaxed. He ought to be married, she decided. A man with his looks and education shouldn't have been allowed to go unattached all these years. Maybe he really was a cerebral bachelor type after all, content with his teaching and sabbatical digs out in the middle of nowhere.

Yet she doubted it. He was undeniably a red-blooded male, and he was at ease in society. Surely he had women friends, maybe even a girlfriend or a fiancée. She studied his face as he spoke to Julien; she could look at him forever.

"Robin," came Christina's voice at her shoulder, "I thought you'd gone to bed."

"Not yet."

"You must be exhausted, dear." Then, before she could stop her, Christina was calling Adam over and chiding him gently for leaving Robin unattended. "See her to the guest house, Adam, she's very tired."

Robin's cheeks flushed as she stood and felt Adam's hand encircle her arm.

"Oh, that's all right, I can find my way," she managed. "Really, I can . . ."

"Nonsense," he said. "Mother's right."

It was all so polite between them, so artificial. Feeling foolish, Robin let him walk her along the paths while silence seemed to ring in the cool night air.

They passed the bench. The image of Cassandra flashed without summons through her brain; the woman was crushed to her Indian's smooth bare chest, her back arched, her lips hungrily moving against his. Robin felt dizzy and weak, almost able to hear their soft, forbidden moans of passion.

Why wouldn't Adam hold her like that, or kiss her? But his hand fell away as he pushed open her door. "Good night," he said, his deep voice uninflected.

She felt ashamed then, knowing how much she longed for an intimate touch, a word, a warm glance from him. But she wasn't going to get it. Not from this man, Adam, the man who walked far and—apparently—alone.

CHAPTER FIVE

IT WAS A DAY of frustrations.

Robin woke up with the sun, far too early, still tired but unable to sleep any longer. It was her obsession with Adam Farwalker, the anticipation that she would soon see him, that was making her jittery, as if she'd had too much coffee.

He was a strange, alluring man. Partly because he was Indian, and she admitted to herself that his heritage *was* terribly intriguing, but also because she could sense something powerful and significant behind his reticence.

It was pointless lying there. She rose, showered and dressed in white leggings and an oversized bright red shirt that hung practically to her knees. Of course, after cleaning up her shop she'd be filthy, but she couldn't show up at the Farwalkers' breakfast table in jeans and a work shirt.

She found her way along the paths to the main hacienda and entered quietly. Was anyone up yet? After last night...

She half expected to find Adam having coffee or already eating when she poked her head into the kitchen. But it was empty. Even Christina Farwalker was nowhere to be seen, although a fresh pot of coffee sat on a hot plate. She helped herself.

It was curiosity that propelled Robin to wander through the main rooms of the house. This was Adam's birthplace, the place where he'd run and played as a child. But it was hard to picture Adam young and carefree; it was as if the man had always been tightly contained.

As she explored, that ever-present sense of being an outsider struck Robin with a heavy hand. Since the loss of her parents, she'd often felt left out when confronted with a warm family scene, a large, inviting house that was occupied by loving parents and lots of squabbling children. And this house, this hacienda, impressed her with those feelings of close family ties.

It was a charming old place, in typical Santa Fe style. It had the casual plainness of architecture, the sharp contrasts between light and shadow and massive solidity of walls, doors and heavy, dark ceiling beams. There was a spareness in decoration and furniture, and an integrity of materials: smooth adobe and clear, polished pine, natural wool rugs and bright tiles. Each piece of Spanish colonial furniture, each stylized Navaho rug and graceful Pueblo pot had been placed by a loving hand.

Robin was fingering a three-foot-tall intricately woven basket that sat next to a corner fireplace when Christina found her. "And how do you like our house?" she asked cheerfully.

"I love it," replied Robin. "It's so... so warm."

"Would you like to explore—or perhaps you're hungry?"

"I already looked around," she admitted. "And I *am* hungry, thank you."

Adam, she was told, was not yet up. She felt a small stab of disappointment but forced it aside while Christina served her a plate of *huevos rancheros*, eggs on tortillas, smothered with a piquant sauce of tomatoes, peppers and onions.

"So, my son tells me you indulge people's fantasies," said Christina, leaning her elbows on the pale wood of the table.

"Oh, did he really?" Robin wasn't sure how she felt about Adam having discussed her with his mother—good, she guessed. Then she had to explain about her portraits and costumes and tell her stock of funny stories.

Christina was laughing over what Robin called the Lady Godiva incident when Adam walked into the kitchen. He hesitated when he saw her, as if he'd forgotten she was there and was chagrined to be reminded. She had to admit that his rebuff hurt. But she couldn't be so ridiculously sensitive, she told herself, and besides, Adam looked so darn handsome that morning, she could forgive him almost anything. He was dressed casually in jeans and a red and black plaid shirt rolled up at the sleeves. And he looked younger somehow, well-rested perhaps, or at ease in his parents' house. She glanced at him and nodded and smiled, but in her mind's eye she couldn't help imagining him on a horse with a lance in his hand and a bright band holding back his thick black hair.

"Did you sleep well?" he asked.

She gave a self-deprecating shrug. "Oh, sure."

Christina dominated the conversation. She had an easy, affectionate relationship with her son. She made him smile and joked with him; she bullied and meddled, Robin guessed, and gave advice a little too freely. But Adam took it in stride, indulgently, towering over his small mother, letting her think she was in control.

It would have been nice, Robin thought, to have Adam that free and open with her. Of course, she didn't believe in miracles, but still, he *could* give her one of those rare, white-toothed smiles of his, couldn't he? Instead, he made her feel as if she were the outsider, the intruder.

Eventually Ray Farwalker joined them for breakfast. He was awfully kind to Robin and she was made to feel very much at home. "Did you find the coffee I made?" he asked Robin and then told her about his morning, how he and some ranch hands had found a stray calf. The conversation turned to family stuff then, Christina reminding Adam about his sister's birthday.

"I'll try to make it," replied Adam, "but the team out at the dig has to be back in school soon and we've got a lot of work."

"An afternoon won't kill you, Adam," Christina pointed out.

He gave her a smile and downed the rest of his coffee. "I better be going," he said, getting to his feet. "Robin's got to get back to her shop, and I've got work to do, too."

Christina walked them to the door. "Robin, you phone anytime, I mean that. And you're welcome to stay here whenever you like. Really, I want to hear more about your clients. You bring her out here again, Adam, you hear me?"

Did Christina notice that Adam didn't answer her? Did she feel the abrupt prickle of strain in the atmosphere? But Robin said something inane, talking too much as usual, to cover the uneasiness, and followed Adam out to his car.

"That was quite an affair last night," she commented.

Adam pulled his big Land Rover onto Canyon Road and turned it toward Santa Fe before answering. "My mother loves doing it. She gets to see everybody she's missed during the year."

The vehicle was headed east, and Robin put on her sunglasses as the early morning sun glared right in her eyes. The wide valley, from the Sangre de Cristo Mountains in the east to the Jemez range in the west, was bathed in brilliant, clear light, striped with the long shadows of hill and tree and fence post. Robin's fingers itched for her camera; the light was perfect. She could possess these images forever.

The city took shape as Adam drove into it; the streets narrowed, the buildings crowded in, the walls and trees created privacy where it had no right to be. "You can drop your stuff at your place," he said. "Then we'll head to the shop and put it back into order."

"You don't have to," Robin protested. "I can call Ericka and we'll manage just fine."

He only glanced at her as he pulled up in front of her building. Of course, Adam checked the apartment, then, satisfied, told her to come in. "I wish you'd stay at the ranch," he said. "At least consider it, Robin."

She put her overnight bag in the bedroom and called, "Thanks, really. But I have too much work to do and honestly, we can't be positive that the mess in my store has anything to do with your forged pot." He said no more about it, but Robin could tell, by the way his brows drew together in a dark bar of concern, that Adam was not pleased.

They brought along what few tools Robin owned, a hammer and two screwdrivers. Then while she began to sweep up the floor in the front, separating damaged goods from still usable ones, Adam scavenged the alleyway for old boards, which he used to nail over the broken window in her office. Robin savored the early morning time they had together without his family or her customers constantly interrupting. As she glanced around her shop and assessed the damage, she decided something good had come out of all this. She could spend a few more hours with Adam.

"You better save the damaged frames and film," he called over his hammering, "for the insurance adjustor."

She made a sign, Open at Noon, and then the hard work began. The trouble was, the streets were filled with eager shoppers, Sunday being the last day of Indian Market. Faces kept peering through the front windows and hands continually rattled the doorknob.

Adam came into the front of the shop once he had the window temporarily repaired. He stood, hands on hips, and surveyed the place. "I still can't believe someone had the nerve to do this," he said grimly.

"Oh, come on," said Robin, trying to be cheerful, "it could have been worse." As they worked together, straightening, rearranging, tossing out, she decided to press him, to see if he would open up a little and satisfy her curiosity. "Tell me about your sisters," she said while they picked up film cases and cameras and lenses.

"They're both younger than I am." He paused, studied a coil of ruined film pensively. "Married. Felice has two children and Amanda has three."

"Oh, so you're an uncle. What fun. I would love—"

Someone was pounding on the door. Irritated when the person would not leave, Robin went over and unlocked it. "Mrs. Hartmann, well, hello."

"Are the proofs back?"

"I said Monday, Mrs. Hartmann."

"Monday? But…" Mrs. Hartmann thrust her face into the shop. "What happened here?"

"Burglars," said Robin swiftly, to forestall a long story. "Now, about those proofs…"

"Tomorrow. All right, I'll be back."

Robin locked up again and turned to Adam. She started to ask another question about his sisters, but someone else was knocking on the door.

"Lady, I need some film," called a man. "You opened up for that woman there."

Trying to be polite, Robin unlocked for a moment. "I'm closed till noon. I don't have any film. Can you come back—"

"Honey!" The man's wife had sidled in past Robin. "Look at that photograph! How much is it?"

It was a study of some buttes against a rainbow. Robin liked the picture herself, but right now its glass was broken and it was lying on the floor. Nevertheless the lady stepped daintily over the clutter and studied it.

"How much is it?" the man asked.

"Fifty-nine ninety-five with the frame. But the glass is broken..."

"How much without the glass?"

Robin gave up. "Oh, say fifty even."

"It's a deal." The man looked around. "Say, what happened here?"

"A burglary," replied Robin.

"Huh. Terrible mess." He looked down at his feet. "Hey, there's some film. I need just that kind."

She picked up the photograph and film and made her way to the counter. "Sorry, Adam, I'll just be a minute," she said over her shoulder. She started to remove the few remaining glass shards from the frame. She must not have been paying attention, because she felt the cold, numb slice of the glass across her finger and, before she realized what it was, a line of blood was welling up in bright ruby droplets.

"Oh, darn, I've cut myself.

Adam was at her side immediately.

"How dumb," she said. "I don't want to touch the picture; I'll ruin it."

"I'll do it," Adam said. "Just tell me..."

"Are you two married?" asked the man. "Nice shop you've got here. I'm a meat wholesaler myself. Pittsburgh."

Adam was wrapping his handkerchief around her finger, his dark head bent over her hand. Robin felt her cheeks redden. *Married.* How could this be happening? "We're not married," she said quickly.

"Young folk these days," the man went on. "Don't say a word, I got it. Listen, do you folks know beef—"

"Adam, could you ring up the purchases?" She felt really flustered now. Her finger was throbbing; the man was going on about how nobody ate meat these days; his wife was sifting through the mess on the floor, examining photographs and cameras.

Robin told Adam what to do, and he managed quite well, even remembering the sales tax. He wrapped the photograph, smiled at the people, thanked them and deftly got them out of Robin's Nest.

Then he turned to Robin, who was still standing behind the counter, her wrapped finger in front of her. "I wonder if the sale was worth the cut," she quipped.

"Let me look at it."

She felt quite foolish standing there with Adam unwrapping her finger as if she were a child. Then he was going into the back for a Band-Aid and she stared after him, her embarrassment transforming into a kind of floating elation. It had been ages since a man had taken care of her. She'd lost her father so early and her uncle, with whom she'd lived, had been a salesman always on the road. Robin had been forced to maintain her independence, to rely only on herself.

What woman wouldn't want a big strong man taking care of her once in awhile?

Adam was coming back, peeling away the paper on the Band-Aid, very businesslike, very quiet. Yet there was an energy to him that seemed to fill her small shop, a strange but soothing power that held her silent. Was it the Apache in him? Was that why he was so mysteriously attractive to her?

He looked up then and caught her studying him. For an instant there was a kind of communication in the glance, as if he were about to tell her something, to let himself go.

"Hello!" came a voice at the door and the handle rattled. "Hello in there, Robin!" Then a man's face appeared, pressed to the glass.

"Julien," said Adam. "Shall I let him in?"

"Sure," replied Robin, taking the Band-Aid herself and wrapping her finger.

"Oh, my, oh, my, what happened?" asked Julien, his high, intelligent forehead creased in concern. "*Dios mío*, what a mess!"

Robin sighed and put a smile on her lips. "We're not really sure."

"My brother told me some crazy story," he said, "about this being connected to that counterfeit pot. What is going on, Robin?"

She told him the whole story again while Adam interjected details here and there. She wondered if Julien was ever going to leave, to let them finish their work. Julien was a kind, sweet man, caring and concerned, but didn't he know it was still Indian Market?

"You must let me help you," he was saying. "What can I do?"

"We're managing," replied Adam as his eyes met hers over Julien's head.

"Yes," said Robin taking the cue, "we'll be done soon."

"Well, then... But tonight, Robin, at the association meeting we simply must discuss this matter."

"Of course," she answered, casually ushering him to the door. "See you then, and thanks, Julien."

Julien took one last look around and frowned. "A pity," he said, "truly a crime..."

By noon Robin's Nest was sufficiently back in order so that she was able to open the door to customers. Adam was in the back still putting a few things on shelves, but she knew he was anxious to leave. She hated the thought of his going; he'd be so far away. She'd probably never see him again.

He emerged slapping dust off his hands.

"Can I buy you lunch?" she offered.

"No, thanks, I've got to get going. I want to drop by San Lucas again. Maybe I can find out something more." He hesitated. "Look, Robin, I'm not trying to run your life, but I'd feel a lot better if you stayed out at my folks' at night, for a while, at least."

"I couldn't, really. Adam, I'll be fine. Obviously these creeps pulled their stunt and they're done. And besides, Detective Cordova knows about it now."

He stared at her, as if he wanted to say something else, but the moment passed. "I can't force you, of course," he finally said.

"No, you can't."

"But you will let Rod know if anything at all peculiar happens?"

Dutifully she nodded.

He began to move toward the door. *So this is it,* she thought. *I'm never going to see him again.*

For a moment Robin was about to ask him when he was going to be back in town, to tell him she'd like to hear from him sometime. But she didn't. If he'd wanted to see her again he would have said something already.

"Well," she said as they stood together beneath the cottonwoods, "thank you for last night and helping me clean up today." She held out her hand, feeling foolish and strangely shy. "It was nice meeting you, Adam."

"Yes," he replied taking her hand awkwardly, "it's been an interesting twenty-four hours. Well..."

"Well," she said as the tense handshake ended, "guess I'll see you around."

"Oh, Robin! There you are!" It was Shelly Dalton. She was hurrying along the street toward them.

Oh darn, thought Robin.

"Oh, my gosh," Shelly was saying, "Ericka had this call from the police about your shop being wrecked or something..." She glanced at Adam. "Oh, excuse me, I didn't realize..."

Robin sighed and made the introductions.

"So nice to meet you, Mr. Farwalker," Shelly said. "I believe I've met your mother."

They shook hands. Robin could have strangled Shelly for the coy looks she kept flashing at Adam then at Robin and for the inordinately long time she left her hand in his.

Then Chuck came out of the gallery and also had to be introduced. "Your mother does the auction every year, doesn't she?" he asked Adam. "Terrific idea."

Adam glanced at his watch as Shelly was saying, "You've *got* to tell me what happened! Ericka was telling us about the police thinking teenagers were involved or something. Anyway, I got busy."

"Just a second, Shelly," Robin said quickly, "and I'll fill you in."

Adam was anxious to leave, she could tell, and it made her nervous. Maybe if Shelly hadn't come over she would have pressed him a little to see if he planned on ever contacting her again. As it was...

"I do have to go," he said, "and take care, Robin, I mean that."

"Oh, I will." Then, aware that her voice had an edge of urgency, she said, "If you find out anything more you'll let me know, won't you?"

"Of course."

Then he was gone, his tall, dark form disappearing into the crowds. Shelly and Chuck were both talking at once, and Robin guessed she was giving the right answers but she could barely concentrate, her eyes still futilely searching the throng as if he'd reappear—her devastatingly handsome Apache Indian.

"And he helped you clean up?" Shelly was asking. "Robin, are you listening?"

She was and she wasn't. A part of her was wondering if she could find out more about the counterfeit pottery. Wouldn't that be an excellent excuse to contact Adam Farwalker?

CHAPTER SIX

"THE MEETING WILL PLEASE come to order," Julien Cordova said at seven sharp, and the murmuring and shifting in the conference room of the La Fonda Hotel settled into quiet. "I apologize for calling this meeting on a Sunday, but as you all know, after Indian Market and the end of the summer season many of you will be out of town, and I wanted to get the association organized before that. Now, for the first item of business, will the secretary please read the minutes of our last meeting."

Robin crossed her legs and sipped the coffee that was still piping hot in its Styrofoam cup. She hoped the caffeine would keep her awake during the meeting, as she was feeling bored and sleepy and wished she could just go home, collapse in bed and forget the past twenty-four hours.

"I'm not sure it's prudent to spend ten thousand dollars on a full-page and in *Travel and Leisure*," Chuck Dalton was saying. "Everyone knows Santa Fe's here. It's overkill."

Robin sighed. The arguments were commencing and probably wouldn't end for hours.

Thad Mencimer, a heavyset, fair young man whose face was red with aggravation, shot to his feet. "That's assuming an awful lot! There are thousands of people out there who don't know what Santa Fe has to offer. We need to reach a broader market. Why, last month's figures show a drop in sales tax—"

"One percent," scoffed Chuck, "and that's because we had a week of lousy weather."

Someone else stood and shook a finger at Chuck. "One percent means a drop in my gross receipts. *I'm* not about to ignore it. Everyone always blames the weather..."

"Has anyone considered a half-page ad?" asked Chuck Dalton.

"Ridiculous!" retorted Thad, and Robin saw Thad's wife, Lorraine, pull at his sleeve. Poor woman, she was young and very pregnant and embarrassed by her husband's ill-considered comments.

Robin shifted on the hard seat. She wondered idly where Adam was—back at Chaco Canyon? She pictured him crawling into a little pup tent. How did he live out there? In a trailer? A cabin? She wanted to know so that she could think about him, imagine him in the correct setting. Had he found the potter at San Lucas? Would he let her know if he had?

"...good Indian Market this year," Julien was saying. "I think we all did as well as can be expected given the economic climate."

"Not good enough!" someone called out. Thad Mencimer, Robin noted. Sometimes the man was a pain. "A full-page ad is absolutely necessary," Thad repeated. He shook a handful of papers. "I have figures here on how many people an ad like that would reach."

"We've neglected the overseas market," someone else said. "Japan, West Germany. That's where the bucks are."

"The *New York Times* travel section. Can't someone do an article?" another member asked.

"You're all getting off the subject," piped up Thad. "I call for a vote on this issue right now!"

Robin drank the rest of her now lukewarm coffee. It was going to be a long evening.

"Now, ladies and gentlemen, we're all friends here and we all have the same goals in mind." Julien was holding out his hand. "I must beg you to speak one at a time. Let's not get confrontational." Then he grinned. "Don't you love that word?"

He got a laugh, defusing the situation neatly. Thad Mencimer, however, still glowered, while his shy wife whispered earnestly into his ear.

After a few minutes more of discussion, the motion to put a full-page ad in *Travel and Leisure* passed. Julien had convinced everyone there was enough in the treasury to cover it, and Chuck Dalton acquiesced gracefully. One hurdle over with, thought Robin, trying to decide whether she should stay or get up, go to the ladies' room and splash cold water on her face.

Shelly Dalton stood then and said she had an important announcement to make. "Do you all know what happened to Robin Hayle's shop yesterday, folks?"

Expectant murmurs rose from the group.

"Well, I think Robin should tell us the whole story and we better think about it real hard."

"Robin, come up here and tell the association what happened. I was going to bring it up myself," said Julien.

Thanks a lot, Shel, Robin said to herself as she rose dutifully and went to the front of the room to tell her tale. She tried to be quick and clear, but she felt a little presumptuous rehashing Adam's theory about a counterfeiting ring. "And that's it. I still don't know for sure who or why someone broke into my shop. Julien's brother, Rod Cordova, thought it could be teenagers, but I really don't think so. Anyway, I've considered installing a security system like some of the galleries have."

"It's a disgrace!" a gallery owner in the back of the room said bitterly. "We're not safe anywhere."

"My insurance rates are too high now," said another.

"What do we pay the police for, anyway?"

"All right, everyone," said Julien, frowning, "let's keep this orderly. Comments, please, one at a time."

Thad Mencimer popped up, a red-faced jack-in-the-box. "If there really is a person or a group making fake pots and selling them to collectors, every art dealer in Santa Fe is compromised. No big collectors will trust us. We have to do something about this!"

"How about your brother, Julien? Can Rod help us?" asked someone.

"No police," came a voice from the side of the room. A statuesque woman stood. "If the police get into this there'll be publicity. How will *that* look? It'll be all over the art world in a couple of weeks. I can just hear it now, Santa Fe inundated with fakes. Then watch your business go downhill!"

"Madeline's right," said Shelly Dalton.

A voice came from the corner of the large room, "I can see our ad in *Travel and Leisure*," said the man. "Come to Santa Fe and get ripped off!"

"Right on!" called out a woman. "We *can't* let the police in on this. My God, every newspaper in the state will file a story."

"No police," agreed Julien. "Any other suggestions?"

"But Rod already knows," Robin pointed out. "Although he was skeptical about the reason for the break-in."

"I'll make sure Rod is discreet," said Julien. "He'll understand. But I think we should discuss methods of dealing with this problem, just in case you were being warned off, Robin."

The discussion was hot and heavy. Suggestions ranged from a vigilante committee to a registration system for each piece of artwork. Robin got herself another cup of coffee, sat down and wiggled her toes in her shoes. So far nobody had come up with a practical idea.

Julien stood, elbow cupped in his hand, fist to his chin, listening, soothing, directing. He was the perfect president for the association, intelligent, cultured, familiar with every facet of the city's business, history and people. He'd been elected unanimously at the first organizational meeting, and Robin thought he was doing a terrific job.

"All right," Julien finally said, "I'm beginning to see a pattern here. What we need is more information. We can't decide what to do until we have all the facts. I suggest we form a special subcommittee of, say, five or six people, to go into this matter. I make a motion to set up said committee. Any seconds?"

A hand rose. Thad Mencimer's. "I second."

"All in favor."

The ayes had it.

Before Robin knew what was happening she had been volunteered as a member of the subcommittee along with Chuck Dalton, Thad Mencimer, Madeline Lassiter and Ben Chavez, a longtime art dealer. Julien himself would also attend their meetings to help out.

It crossed her mind then, the promise that she'd made to Adam, her word that she would bow out of this forgery business. Now here she was, albeit innocently, involved again. Deeply involved. *Darn*.

"Well," Julien said, "I think we've made great progress. The new committee will meet three times a week—how about in the library of the Governor's Palace?—and will report back its findings to the association at the next meeting. Meeting adjourned."

Robin grimaced. Three times a week. Oh, well, maybe this committee she was on would actually come up with some ways of guarding against forged artwork, or at least find out for sure if her shop had been wrecked as a warning. So many questions still remained to be answered.

"See you Tuesday night," Madeline said. "Bring that photograph of yours, the one with the pot in it."

"Sure, see you," Robin agreed, smothering a yawn.

She walked back to her shop, where her car was parked, with Chuck and Shelly.

"Boy, am I beat," she said, letting the yawn finally take over.

"I bet," said Shelly. "Why didn't you bring your friend Adam with you tonight? I mean, he's involved, isn't he?"

"Oh, Shel, he has to work. It's a long drive out to Chaco Canyon. He can't indulge himself in the luxuries of civilization very often. Besides—" she yawned again "—I really don't think he was interested in me."

"Why not?"

"How should *I* know? Heck, I hardly know the man."

"Okay, okay, but what if he calls you again?"

She shrugged in the darkness. "I'm not holding my breath."

"What a guy!" said Shelly. "And tall, wow, is he tall."

"He certainly is that," muttered Robin.

"Oh, to be young and single and sexy again." Shelly sighed.

"The only one of those that applies to me is single," said Robin dryly.

As they approached the Sena Plaza, a thought flashed through Robin's mind: what if the blinds were drawn again when she reached her shop, what if they'd broken in again, smashed everything all over again? What if...

But Robin's Nest sat undisturbed, blinds up, window displays intact. She breathed a sigh of relief and swore to herself to get a security system installed no matter the cost.

Shelly and Chuck got into their green van and Shelly waved out the window as they passed Robin. "Night," she called. "See you *mañana*!"

Robin walked to her own car, a sporty white Japanese import, and started it up. When she flicked the lights on, they caught a shadowed movement under one of the spreading trees. Robin felt her heart leap, but it was only a tomcat, a big, gray one, who was calmly patrolling his territory, stalking from tree to tree with unhurried dignity.

"Oh, boy," she mumbled to herself, "are you a nerd. Jumping at shadows." Then she turned her car toward home and sped through the empty streets, whistling loudly to herself.

She hated to admit it, but she was a little nervous as she opened the door to her building and looked up the dim flight of stairs to her apartment. Last night she hadn't even thought about the possibility of danger, but last night Adam, big, strong, capable Adam, had been with her and had gone up there first.

She hesitated at the bottom of the stairs, fingering her keys. She could hear the television from one of the downstairs apartments. Well, somebody was home. She could knock on their door, ask to use the phone and call Christina Farwalker. It would be safe out there at the hacienda, safe and secure and . . .

Forget it, kiddo, Robin told herself angrily. She couldn't live her life jumping at every sound, every shadow, every locked door. She took a deep breath and started up the steps. Her heart pounded a little too hard, and she felt shaky. What if someone were waiting for her inside? That was ridiculous. How would they get in? She could see her door, and it was untouched, closed, just as it always was. Even that silly note she'd tacked to the door was still in place. Everything was fine.

She clenched her teeth and climbed doggedly to the landing. *Oh, Adam,* she thought, *where are you when I need you?*

The doorknob didn't turn; it was still firmly locked. Robin felt an enormous sense of relief wash over her. She unlocked the door and stepped inside, reaching out to turn the lights on. As Adam had done last night.

Light flooded the living room, glinting off the white walls, the tile floor, the familiar posters. "Whew," said Robin. No one had been there, no one had broken in to steal or make a mess. She'd been silly to even worry about it.

She threw her shoulder bag on a table, kicked off her shoes and took a deep breath to relax. Suddenly she realized she was starving. Wasn't there a package of cookies in the cupboard? And a glass of milk. That sounded good. Then she'd go to sleep; she always slept better on a full stomach. Oh, boy, she was sleepy.

She opened a cupboard door. Yes, chocolate-chip cookies. She popped one into her mouth, chewed, turned toward the refrigerator.

She froze.

From that angle she could see around the corner to her sofa and coffee table. There was something on the low, glass table, a pile of jagged pieces. What?

Slowly Robin approached the coffee table. Her eyes shifted around the room, her heart pounded again. What was on the table? What?

It looked like black and red pieces of something, scattered, broken. And when she was closer she could see that there were fragments all over her floor and her sofa and rocking chair. Red and black fragments all over, like spots of blood flung from an explosion.

When she finally stood over the mess she knew what it was, and then her heart nearly stopped and she gasped and felt sick to her stomach.

It was a red and black clay pot that had been smashed onto the table and broken, deliberately broken, so that shards had spattered all over. Yes, a pretty red and black patterned pot, an Indian pot—but not hers. Robin didn't own a pot like that.

Someone had brought that piece, gotten into her apartment and deliberately broken it on her table.

Why? *You fool,* her mind answered, *to warn you.* Adam had been right.

She backed away from the table, trod barefooted on a sharp fragment, hardly felt the stab. Someone had been in her apartment. How? Who?

"Oh, my God," she whispered.

She ran into the bedroom. The windows were shut. Nothing was disturbed.

The roof. Robin's apartment had a roof patio with stairs that led up from the living room. But that door, too, was shut and locked, just as she'd left it.

She sank into a chair and noticed that she was still clutching the bag of cookies. Her hands trembled. What should she do?

She tried to think. Whoever had done this knew everything about her, where she lived, when she was out. Had they picked the lock? Hadn't the neighbors noticed? But the intruder might have looked like a deliveryman or a friend.

She should have listened to Adam. Should she call the Farwalkers, pack a bag and drive out there? It was too late, she didn't have the nerve; she hardly knew them.

Rod Cordova.

But the association didn't want the police involved. Damn the association. Someone was *after* her!

Rod Cordova wasn't on duty on Sunday night. Of course not. A nice young officer with a faint Mexican accent spoke to Robin. "Miss Hayle, please explain to me again, what crime do you say has been committed?"

"Someone got into my apartment and broke a pot on my coffee table."

"Someone broke a pot that belonged to you?"

"No, not *my* pot. I don't know whose pot. But they got in . . ."

"Is there damage to your door?"

"No."

"I would send someone over, Miss Hayle, but my report must say what crime has been committed. Is it breaking and entering? Burglary? Destruction of property?"

"Breaking and entering, I guess," said Robin. "I'm frightened. Somebody got inside here and I don't know how."

"All right. I'll send someone over."

Robin paced nervously until the officer arrived.

"See," she said, indication the fragments of pottery, "someone got in here while I wasn't home and smashed it on my table."

"Do you have a cat, ma'am?"

"No, darn it, it isn't *my* pot. Someone brought it here."

"Someone brought you a pot and then broke it?"

Robin felt helpless. No one would understand. It sounded crazy. She tried again. "I made a report to Detective Cordova yesterday. The same thing happened in my shop. Someone got in here, too.''

"Did you have a fight with your, er, boyfriend, ma'am?''

"I don't *have* a boyfriend," she said too loudly. "I don't know who did this!''

"Yes, ma'am, I'll let Detective Cordova know about this when he gets in first thing tomorrow morning.''

"Thank you, but what about tonight? What if this person tries to get in again?''

"I'll tell the officers on duty to swing by here every hour or so. You lock your doors and windows now, ma'am.''

"They *were* locked.''

"Yes, ma'am.''

Just before he left, the officer looked over his shoulder at the pile of broken pottery on her table, shook his head and commented, "Too bad about your pot, ma'am.''

It was almost funny, *almost*. When the polite policeman had left, Robin wedged chairs against both her doors and checked every window. She went into the bedroom, put on her nightgown, brushed her teeth and got into bed, the usual nightly routine, except that tonight she lay there in the dark with her eyes wide open.

The night was utterly quiet. Only occasionally, outside, was there the sound of a car passing on Bishop's Lodge Road. She counted each one. The glow from their lights would hit the far wall of her bedroom then crawl slowly across the smooth paint. Then it would be dark again for a minute or two. In the corner of her room was a brass hat rack, which she could just make out in the blackness. When the car lights crossed the wall, the spindly object cast a skeletal shadow, creeping along with the lights. To top it all off, she'd left her closet door open; a childish fear made the roots of her hair tingle.

After fifteen minutes of desperately trying to calm herself, Robin sat bolt upright and turned on her bedside lamp. Purposefully she reached for her telephone and pulled it into her lap, dialing information. She felt better already.

"Chaco Canyon Visitor's Center," she said firmly into the mouthpiece.

They wouldn't be open this late. She dialed, anyway; clicks sounded in her ear. It rang five times. A recorded voice came on. "This is Chaco Canyon Visitor's Center. We are open to the public from nine to five every day. If necessary, you may leave a message at the sound of the beep. Thank you for calling the canyon."

Robin waited, tapping her short nails on the bedside table, her heart beating furiously. Sleep—sure, she'd get some sleep tonight... *Beep.*

"This is Robin Hayle," she began, "and I have an urgent message..."

CHAPTER SEVEN

ADAM WAS LOOKING OFF into the distance in the photograph. She'd caught his face at an angle, so that the artfully sculpted line of brow and cheek and jaw was made manifest. He was leaning against the adobe wall in San Lucas Pueblo, hands in his trouser pockets, frowning slightly. Not award winning, she thought, but even on paper that sense of mystery was present in his carriage, in the pitch of his dark head, and Robin formed in her mind the word *Indianness* to describe it, because that's what it was to her. She and Adam were of the same human mold, but there were vast dissimilarities between them.

She looked once more at the picture she'd secretly snapped. What had Adam been thinking just then; why was there that distant look to him?

Robin could have sat in the back of her shop and studied the image of Adam all night. But it was nearly six, almost time for the special committee meeting to begin.

Adam was coming to the meeting. Knowing that in a few short minutes she'd see him again made her stomach feel queasy. Of course, she'd phoned Chaco Canyon on Sunday night in a state of panic. Then, when Adam had gotten hold of her Monday, she'd been relieved to hear that he wanted to help, to at least address her special committee meeting. He'd sounded genuinely concerned and anxious to be involved. And he'd seemed worried about her, and angry over the broken pot. But now she was beginning to feel foolish. It was a long drive into town from the canyon; surely this was a terrible inconvenience for Adam. Even Rod Cordova, when he'd finally gotten in touch about the smashed pot, had told her not to worry. "Keep your doors locked and leave the forgery business to the police," he'd said, "and I'm sure everything will be okay."

She could have called Adam again and told him not to bother coming into town after all. She *should* have. But she wanted to see him again.

Robin went into the bathroom and brushed her hair. She smoothed her short black denim skirt and tugged at her pink and gray striped top. Not that Adam would notice, but she couldn't help wanting to look her best. A little perfume, mascara, lipstick...

The harsh bright light above her head was not in the least flattering. She could see dark circles under her eyes, and the soft grooves framing her mouth seemed deeper. She was getting old. Thirty had come and gone and her youth with it. She'd never had a husband, not even a fiancé, really. Why not? Everyone loved Robin Hayle. She was lively and vital and *fun*. No party or gathering was complete unless she was invited and brought along her camera and told her crazy stories. But the men sensed that insecurity in her, that almost frantic need to belong. And they got scared off. Who wanted a desperate woman?

Adam also had seen through her carefree facade instantly and discounted her. He probably wouldn't even come tonight.

She snapped off the light and took a deep breath. She told herself that thirty-two was still young and that she had plenty of time to have a family. And she told herself that Adam was going to be there—he was probably already waiting, wondering where she was.

By six sharp all the committee members had gathered in the library of the *Palacio Real*. Julien announced that Adam Farwalker was expected and would make a presentation about prehistoric pottery and how to detect a forgery; there were a few murmurs and curious glances exchanged. "I'm certain Adam will arrive shortly," said Julien, but Robin wondered, and her heart beat a little faster.

She kept glancing at the clock: six-fifteen, six-twenty, six twenty-two. At six twenty-three, she crossed one leg over the other and pulled at her short skirt. Her palms were damp against her knee.

At six-thirty the library door opened and a cool breath of air swept in. Robin's head swiveled, a ready smile on her lips. But it was only a janitor, pulling his mop and bucket along. She turned back to the meeting and sighed.

It was six forty-three when the door opened again. This time Robin merely stared ahead. No point in revealing her disappointment. But then the empty chair next to her, the one she'd been saving, was being pulled aside and Adam was sitting down. "Sorry I'm so late," he whispered, "but something came up."

"Oh, that's all right," Robin said casually. "We're still hashing over old business. This will probably bore you to death. I shouldn't have gotten you into it."

"Nonsense," replied Adam. "I want to help in any way I can."

On the other side of her, Thad Mencimer nudged Robin. "Who's he again?" he asked loudly.

"My name—" Adam leaned forward and spoke across Robin's chest "—is Adam Farwalker."

Robin rolled her eyes and shot an annoyed glance at Thad.

"I think," Julien was saying, "that we should concentrate on suggestions as to how we can stop these counterfeit pieces from reaching the marketplace." He glanced around the table. "Any suggestions?"

So Adam had come after all, Robin mused, relieved and happy, a dozen pleasant emotions buffeting her simultaneously. She glanced sidelong at him, as if shifting naturally in her chair, a smile glued to her lips. He looked great. His strong features were set in an impassive expression, as if carved in stone, eternal and beautiful. Wearing a lightweight khaki sport coat with a yellow polo shirt beneath, he appeared relaxed and comfortable. Robin sighed.

Yet as happy as she was to see him, a part of her was ill-at-ease, feeling guilty for her alarmist tactics in getting him to come.

Now he had to sit and listen to the committee's problems. And he'd told her not to get involved in the question of the forgeries in the first place. He hadn't smiled at her or seemed pleased to be there; he was probably boiling inside. She could feel his body next to her as if it radiated heat, as if it were pressed up against her.

For all her obsession with Adam, it was not lost on Robin that the heavy lady, Madeline Lassiter, hadn't taken her eyes off him since he'd slipped into the room. Obviously Robin was not the only one who was captivated by him. But Adam himself seemed oblivious. Was he really so unaware of Madeline's attention—or Robin's?

Her anxiety grew. Maybe she shouldn't have called and left that message at Chaco Canyon. Maybe it would have been better if she'd never seen him again. She uncrossed her legs and sat there feeling brittle, as if she'd break if somebody dropped a pin. Everything was turning out all wrong.

Chuck Dalton was speaking. "The first thing we've got to do is lobby the state legislature," he was saying. Robin tried to concentrate.

"Lobby?" scoffed Thad. "Oh, *that's* really going to help. Brilliant idea."

Chuck shot him a look. "If you'd let me finish, I was going to say that the laws pertaining to the sale of artwork could be clarified and broadened."

"Oh, come on," piped up Thad.

"Now, Thad," said Ben Chavez, "I think Chuck's got a point."

On it went. There were some good ideas thrown up to the committee, and some outlandish ones. Thad, always argumentative, came up with the suggestion that the police check all the artwork on sale in the local shops and carbon-date it, and even Robin had to laugh along with the rest of them. Only Adam sat there, unspeaking, glancing from one member to the next, his face utterly devoid of expression. Was he amused, interested or bored silly?

"Robin," said Julien, "surely you have an idea or two."

Jolted from her reverie, she sat a little straighter in her seat, aware that Adam's head had turned in her direction. She'd love to come up with something really clever. She folded her hands on the tabletop and cleared her voice. "There is something I believe might work as a starting point," she began. "I've been thinking along the lines of gaining the cooperation of the Indian artisans themselves. You know, go to the root of the problem."

"Oh, sure," said Thad, interrupting. "We don't even speak their language!"

Robin gave him a sharp glance. "Listen, Thad, why don't you let me finish?"

"Hear, hear," said Chuck, grinning.

"My suggestion is," Robin continued, trying to ignore Thad's unpleasant stare, "that we try to get the Indian community to organize. They could form their own association."

"I get it," chimed in Ben Chavez, "they could *police* themselves."

"Great idea," commented Madeline. She swiveled with amazing grace in her chair. "Mr. Farwalker, what do you think?" She held his gaze for an embarrassingly long time.

"Robin's idea is a sound one," he stated. "The Indian artisans have never been organized before. And like she pointed out, it's a start."

"Humph." Thad was impatiently checking his watch. "Are these meetings going to take all night or what?"

"Perhaps," said Julien, "we should break for dinner. I'd like Adam to have enough time to address us. After we all get a bite, we can meet back here at, say, nine?" All but Thad were in agreement, but no one moved for a moment, unsure and uncomfortable with Thad's rudeness.

Adam stood, turned toward the man and said in a deep, smooth voice, "I believe, Mr. Mencimer, that the majority rules." Then he took Robin's arm and led her out onto the street.

"Well," Robin said, "you sure told *him*."

They were standing beneath the portal of the *Palacio Real*, deserted now that the Indian women had packed up their wares and left for the day. September was just around the corner and the evening air was already crisp. In the mountains to the east, there were a few aspens whose leaves had changed and the last rays of the setting sun struck them, making them appear to be ablaze. The sun caught Adam, too. Robin gazed at him for a moment, watching the last light of day play on his strong face, turning his skin to a deep copper hue, his eyes seeming to glow with fire.

She felt that guilt sweep her again. He didn't really want to be there; he was merely living up to what he believed was an obligation. "Look," she said, "I feel really rotten for getting you into this. And now you'll have to stay in town till God knows what time..."

"Robin, listen," he said, his dark eyes coming to rest on her, "I would have driven into town just to see that broken pot alone and make sure you were all right. Don't you understand, this was all my doing? I'm the one who should apologize."

"I guess we could argue that one all night," she admitted. "So let's just say we're both at fault. Still, you'll have to let me cook you dinner or I'll really feel awful."

"I'm not too hungry, Robin; you don't have to go to any trouble."

"Maybe you're not," she stated, "but I'm starved. As usual." And finally, as if she'd been waiting her whole life for it, Adam smiled at her warmly.

"That'll get you a three-course dinner," she said.

"What will?"

"Oh, never mind, let's just say you have a nice smile, Adam Farwalker, when you relax a little." She tucked her arm into his and led the way.

Of course, Robin had planned all along to fix a meal for Adam. She'd hurried to the store at lunchtime while Ericka had watched the shop, and she'd organized everything, even set the small table in her living room for the two of them with candles and dusty-rose linen, her good Lenox china and her mother's sterling silver. She unlocked her door and switched on the lights. Yes, the place was neat and tidy, the atmosphere intimate.

"Would you like a drink?" She tossed her purse on the couch and turned to face him, her hands on her hips. "I have some vodka and gin, there's tonic and some red wine, and, let's see..."

"A glass of wine will be fine," he replied. "But first, Robin, I'd like to see that broken pot."

She was sorry she showed it to him. On the walk over to her place he'd been almost jovial with her, talking about the meeting and even laughing once when Robin had asked if he'd noticed the attention Madeline had paid him. "I think the woman likes you," Robin had said, and he'd thrown back his dark head and laughed.

But now he stood fingering the shards of clay and looking grim. "You shouldn't be staying here alone," he said. "I don't like it at all."

"Oh, Adam, it's a warning, like you said. Nobody's going to hurt me."

"And now you're on that committee." He looked at her with a grave expression. "You should have told them no."

"I couldn't. I'm just not the type to turn tail and run."

"Still..."

"Still, what's done is done. Let's forget it and have dinner. Come on, please, you'll spoil my appetite."

"I doubt that," he replied, his attempt at humor not in the least lost on her.

When Robin had the time, she loved to cook. While Adam sat on the couch and leafed through a book on Southwest Indians, she whistled and hummed and popped in the oven two individual casseroles of blue corn tortillas filled with beans and cheese and smothered in her own hot salsa. The lettuce and tomatoes were already chopped for the topping, and the bowl of sour cream sat in the fridge. Bread, swimming in butter and garlic, rested on a baking sheet.

She began to cut up a cantaloupe for dessert, wondering if he liked real whipped cream with it as much as she did. "Dinner will be ready in ten minutes," she called then glanced in his direction.

He'd been watching her; he looked down at the book too quickly and flipped a page. Her heart gave a glad little leap. *So he isn't totally impervious to me.*

She began to whistle again and glanced at him once more but this time he was buried in his reading.

Robin checked the casseroles: the salsa wasn't yet bubbling. She leaned her elbows on the counter and tapped her foot. "Do you think that book is accurate?" she asked.

"It's pretty superficial," he commented.

"So it doesn't catch the flavor?"

Adam shook his head. "It's what the tourists want to believe."

"What's it really like then?"

"Being an Indian or living in the Southwest?"

"Well, both, I suppose."

"I can only speak for the Apache, you understand," he said, "but for the last hundred years it's been a struggle."

"A struggle?"

"Yes. Between the old ways and the new. Very few of the young people make a success leaving the reservation. Many of them go off to college and find that they can't make it there."

"But *you* did, Adam."

"Not easily. The difference is that my family has never lived on a reservation. But the problems still exist. We have our tradition, our own way of thinking, and we like our freedom."

"But you're free."

"An Apache is free, Robin," he said, "when he can roam a land where there are no fences, no housing developments, no malls..." Adam smiled darkly. "It can never be the same again."

"You'd be happier hunting and fishing and wandering the hills?"

"Me? I don't really know. I can only speak for my race as a whole. We were far better off before the white eyes—" and at that Adam laughed "—came to the West. We're born hunters. We're closest to our true selves when out in the open. It's in our blood."

"Adam," she said carefully, "are you happy, then, you know, doing what you do?"

He thought for a minute, turning pages in her book idly. "I am happy, I suppose. I'm one of the few who has successfully bridged the two worlds. I don't think for a minute I could survive on the land as my ancestors did."

But she wondered about that.

"There's no easy solution," he added. "Time marches on, and the Apache as a nation are going to have to march with it or disappear as a race." He looked thoughtful for a moment, then continued. "An Indian feels as if he's betrayed himself and his people if he lives in the outside world, yet he can't have success in terms of that world if he stays totally within his tradition. Most opt for tradition. My family has tried to live with a foot in each. It can work, but sometimes it isn't easy."

"It must be challenging," Robin agreed, but he only nodded then went back to his book.

The candles were lit, the music turned low as Robin served her dinner. She sat down, put the fine linen napkin in her lap and gave Adam a smile. "I hope you like this recipe," she said.

Adam was pensive during the meal. Oh, she drew him out about his two sisters and their families and his uncle, his mother's brother, who lived on the reservation and was a "singer." He used the Apache word; Robin got the impression that it meant a combination of doctor and religious leader.

"A man's maternal uncle is a very important figure in his life. My uncle taught me a lot about myself and my clan," Adam explained.

"Do you have a big clan?"

A corner of his mouth lifted in amusement. "I think there are about a hundred in New Mexico, and that's just my mother's side, the turtle people."

"Wow," said Robin, "a family like that must be a real nice thing to have. Someday I'd like to have a big family, too..." When he said nothing she shrugged and went on. "So your uncle is sort of your mentor."

"I guess you could say that. He gave me my secret name, my war name."

"What is it?"

"I can't tell you."

"Oh."

"Only my family knows it."

"Now you've got me curious," she remarked lightly, but she felt the stab of rejection—she was the outsider again, not privy to the secrets that bound Adam's people together. It only brought home to her how far apart their cultures stood. She wondered what the odds were of two such different people ever getting together.

He had fallen silent and become contemplative. She certainly hoped that she hadn't been the cause of his withdrawal. Maybe she shouldn't have brought up the subject of Indians; maybe Adam wasn't adjusted to both worlds as he let on.

"So you studied archeology in Albuquerque?" she asked nonchalantly.

"A long time ago," he replied.

"Was it difficult for you? I mean, the change?"

"Sure. I had my problems. A lot of white kids do, too."

"Oh, I didn't mean..."

"I had to take all that my uncle had taught me, the myths, the stories of coyote men and ghosts and taboos, and reduce them to rational terms. Like the dietary laws of Jews and Moslems or the demons of Christianity. But educated people do that every day."

Adam went back to his meal. She'd tried and tried to get past the superficial conversation, but it seemed the more she delved, the more he fell back to lecturing, as if she were one of his students. It made her want to gnash her teeth. He wasn't this way with everyone, either. No, she'd seen him animated with others, even warm. Why couldn't she elicit that reaction from the man?

Robin looked up from her plate and once again caught him staring at her with those Indian-dark eyes. She felt her breath catch and was suddenly inclined to talk a mile a minute, but something in those expressionless eyes held her silent, aware only of the tension pulsing between them. What was she seeing in his face? Was it sadness? Pain?

The urge to come right out and ask him became overpowering. She had to swallow convulsively to keep quiet. She even reached for her wineglass and took several long drinks, hoping the urge to pry into his private life would pass. What had she thought to accomplish by asking him to dinner?

She glanced at the wall clock in her kitchen. Eight-twenty, it read. My God, how could it be so early? The minutes were crawling by, as if bogged down in a mire. Maybe if she broke a glass or pounded the table, it would break the sticky silence.

Robin sat there demurely, the food gummy in her throat, those horrible minutes slugging along at a snail's pace.

It was finally Adam who put down his fork and spoke. "Robin," he began, holding her gaze, "there's something..." But he never finished and she couldn't find it in herself to press him.

She must have been wearing her distress like a red flag, because several long moments later he said, "Look, I guess I'm pretty lousy company right now."

"Is something wrong, Adam?" she asked, her voice scratchy and dry.

"Nothing's wrong. Let's just say I'm worried about your safety."

"But I'm fine, honest, I am. If someone wanted to harm me they'd have already done it. You know that, don't you?"

"It may look that way," he said, "but I still feel you shouldn't be taking risks."

"I'm not."

"Just being on this new committee is risky."

"I don't believe that."

"Then you're only being stubborn."

Robin raised a brow. "Maybe I am, at that."

She did notice one thing, however; Adam had eaten his whole dinner, not to mention three pieces of garlic bread. For a not-too-hungry man, he'd done fine.

He even said, "You know, your tortillas are better than my mother's." Then, giving Robin one of those rare smiles, he added, "But don't tell her I said so."

"I won't. And thank you, I enjoy cooking." With another man, she would have quipped that the way to a man's heart was through his stomach, but Adam probably wouldn't appreciate her stab at humor. Instead, she poured herself half a glass more of wine and searched her brain frantically for an avenue that might lead to comprehending the man.

Over dessert he looked at her more and more; it seemed as if he was weighing something in his mind. It made Robin squirm restlessly and chatter too much again to ease that persistent feeling of discomfort. And yet, she slowly discovered, her tension was not entirely unpleasant; rather it was tinged with anticipation. Her stomach fluttered and her skin felt too sensitive, as if the air in the room was scraping it. And still he watched her, questioning now, deciding.

Finally, mercifully, it was time to clear the table and go. Adam helped. They each made several trips into the kitchen, back and forth, carrying plates and glasses, napkins and the bread basket. Robin dropped a fork, bent to retrieve it, and so did Adam.

"Here, I've got it," he said, and she found herself still stooped, staring directly into his eyes, their faces only inches apart.

For a flash of time she thought he was going to kiss her. It was in his eyes like a fire; it was on his parted lips and in the set of his shoulders. She held her breath, feeling a weakness in her limbs, a delicious pounding in her ears. And he did take her hands in his, but instead of drawing her to him, he helped her to her feet.

"Oh...thanks," she mumbled as he handed her the fork, "I could have gotten it," and she gave a nervous little laugh that was hideously transparent. She nudged past him and into the cramped kitchen where she hid her face for a moment, running water in the sink, busying herself.

She was wondering desperately how she was going to deal with her embarrassment when suddenly he was behind her, so close she could feel his breath in her hair. She shut her eyes, expectant, afraid, trembling. He was touching her lightly, his fingers on the curve of her waist, and she leaned back against him and drew in a ragged breath.

His other hand was in her hair then and he was lifting it to one side.

Robin felt his lips on the back of her neck, softly tracing a path to her earlobe. She could feel her breath quickening, and little stabs of pleasure deep in her stomach. He whispered something, but she barely heard it, wanting only for him to turn her around, to feel that sensual mouth on hers, to taste him.

She was never certain how long they stood there like that in her close kitchen or if she actually answered. The flow of time seemed to have paused, as if it, too, awaited Adam's decision. And Robin could only sag against his strong body and yearn to feel those arms around her, pressing her to his chest.

Somewhere she could hear the tap water running but his lips were still brushing her neck, and she only thought of Adam—he had taken over her senses, the space they stood in, time.

It must have been her confusion that kept Robin from realizing he had moved away from her. The running water was slowly coming into focus and there were the dishes just as she'd left them—hours ago, it seemed.

Feeling crept back into her limbs and she was aware of a strange, acute sense of emptiness. Where was he? But there he was, in her living room, standing at the window, gazing out into nothingness. She leaned her whole body weight against the sink and felt the cold stainless steel press into her belly.

Adam turned away from the window eventually and she heard him say, "It's almost nine, we better be going." Her heart sank like a stone to her feet.

He behaved in every way as if nothing whatsoever had happened back in her kitchen. He was polite, unerringly so, and proper to a fault as they walked together back to the library at the Governor's Palace. It took every ounce of strength Robin possessed to stride alongside him in silence. But she knew if she opened her mouth all sorts of things would come tumbling out—things she would surely regret.

"Ah, there you are," said Julien, who had waited out front for them. "Adam, I hope you didn't take offense at Mr. Mencimer's rudeness earlier."

"Not at all," said Adam.

"How glad I was to see you put him in his place! What a delight." Then Julien turned to Robin and took her hand in both of his. "You are such a clever woman, Robin Hayle, for thinking to bring Adam along. We are all most grateful and anxious to hear him. *Gracias*, my dear." He lifted her hand to his lips and kissed it.

When Adam stood to speak everyone was attentive, even Thad. Robin, able to be more objective again with Adam at a distance, was proud of him, childishly proud.

"Is anyone here familiar with the Archeological Resource Protection Act?" he began, and everyone was eager to comment. He had them eating out of his hand in short order. Robin was impressed. She sat without fidgeting, totally attentive, unable to keep from recalling the feel of his lips on her neck. She had an almost uncontrollable urge to lift her hair and touch the spot that still tingled, but he'd see, he'd know.

"A true Socorro pot in good condition," he was saying, "can bring up to twenty-four thousand dollars. Of course, anyone with skill can paint a black-on-white design over an unpainted antique that's all but worthless. And there you have a forgery."

"The paint's new," said Thad, "you'd think any idiot could spot it." He folded his arms across his chest and grinned.

"You would think so, wouldn't you?" countered Adam. "The trouble is, if the pot's been fired by a clever artisan, and aged with the right materials, it's very hard for even an expert to identify."

"There must be tests or something," said Madeline.

"Sure," put in Chuck, "there's acetone, for one. It won't take off really old paint."

"That's correct," said Adam, "and black light can be used to detect a forgery, but there again, it would take an expert. There's a lab at Los Alamos that tests a lot of artifacts. Unfortunately, it's time-consuming and costly."

"Maybe we could test our own stuff," said Thad.

"But," Adam interjected, "do you have the equipment for thermoluminescence testing, Mr. Mencimer?"

"Well, no, but . . ."

Julien stood for a moment. "I think Adam has a point here. Running our own tests on artifacts is impractical, and expensive, I'm sure."

"Well, I, for one," Chuck stated, "intend to stick with baskets and rugs. They're easier to verify as authentic."

"And the profit is better, too," Madeline said. "Gosh, a real old Navaho rug can sell for up to a hundred thousand."

"If you can get your hands on one." Thad made his humphing noise. "I say, let's get our artwork checked by a museum expert or something."

Robin saw Adam raise a dark brow. "I hate to put a damper on that," said Adam smoothly, "but there are very few true experts working in the museums. Maybe one or two in all New Mexico could spot or run tests on a forgery. It's an exacting science."

"So Adam," said Robin, "what *do* we do?"

He looked at her for a second and she thought she detected a softening in his expression. "There are positive steps the business community can take," he said, his attention back on the group. "For one, I would suggest a pamphlet be printed and distributed. On it could be a list of agencies and labs who run the tests we were discussing. And also I'd include a list of reputable independent art dealers, people who can be trusted thoroughly. The pamphlet," he went on, looking each committee members in the eye for a moment, "should also make broad suggestions that could be followed. Things like only dealing with licensed, reputable middlemen, and spending those extra dollars to have a so-called valuable antique tested for authenticity."

Adam's words flowed easily over Robin as she sat listening, almost transfixed. He was such a vital man, so efficient, so self-contained. It was the Apache part of Adam that made him so fascinating to her, so *different*. And it was, paradoxically, the Apache in Adam that made him impossible for her to reach. Was there a place they could meet, a common ground?

She couldn't take her eyes off his face, his strong brown neck, his capable hands when he made a significant gesture.

Body language, they called it. And Adam's was gentle but commanding. Even Thad had shut up and quit interrupting. Amazing. Wouldn't it have been wonderful, mused Robin, to have had Adam as a professor?

"Also," he was saying, "I think Robin's idea should be pursued. Help the Indian artisans to organize their own association. The majority of the artists are honest, hard-working people and have reputations to maintain. The few rotten eggs in the basket could be located and, once found out, no one would deal with them."

"Oh, excellent!' said Julien.

"It's an idea." Adam put his hands on the lectern, relaxed, casual, in complete control of the group.

He spoke until well past ten. And then, when the meeting was adjourned, Chuck and Julien both kept him tied up talking for some time out in front of the *Palacio*. Robin hung back; she'd said all she needed to at the meeting. In fact, her idea, along with the pamphlet, had gone over better than any. So she stood beneath the portal, hugged her pink and gray shirt around her and leisurely studied the man who, only a short time ago, had put a hand on her waist and kissed the back of her neck.

She could almost feel that sensual mouth brushing her earlobe as she stood waiting in the shadows. At that moment in her kitchen he'd wanted her. So what had stopped him?

"Adios," she heard Julien saying.

Chuck, too, was moving away. He waved at Robin. "See you tomorrow. Maybe you and Shelly can get up a tennis game now that the town's quieting down."

"I'd like that," replied Robin as she watched him head toward his van.

Alone at last, she thought. "Well," began Robin, "that was a long night. But productive. Don't you think so?"

"I hope I was of some help," he replied.

"Oh, you were," she said enthusiastically. She wondered just how long they were going to stand there on the deserted street and discuss business. Had Adam forgotten that brief, wonderful moment of intimacy between them? "Well," she said again, "it is getting late. I should probably..."

"Of course. I'll walk you home."

"You don't have to, I mean..."

"I want to, Robin. At least I'll know you're safely inside."

"You're not still thinking someone might be in my place waiting?" asked Robin, striding next to him.

"What I'm thinking," said Adam, "is that I wish you weren't staying there alone."

"But Rod is still sending a car around to check and besides, you know how I feel on the subject."

"I certainly do," he replied and because of the light tone of his voice, she could imagine that warm smile of his. He ought to smile all the time, she mused.

It felt *right*, strolling beside him in the darkness. It felt as if the most natural thing in the world would be to go home together and let their emotions have their way. In fact, she decided, everything just now felt exactly perfect. The brisk night air fanning her face, the sound of their footfalls on the brick street, that singular, embracing smell of Old Santa Fe, a mature aroma of aged adobe and century-old trees, of grass and dry earth. His hand touched her elbow as they rounded a corner, and her knees felt as if they were about to buckle.

"Are you driving back to Chaco Canyon?" Robin ventured. She glanced over at him and saw his profile, dark and shadowed, strong, evocative.

"No," he replied, "it's too late."

Her heart lurched in her chest.

"No," he repeated, "I guess I'll drive up to the hacienda instead."

"Oh."

Dutifully Adam unlocked her door and looked around inside. "Just in case," he said. Then they were standing in the entranceway—close. She knew that in a moment he would leave. She had to do something, to let him know, to hold him there somehow, even for only a minute more. To let him go, to see him disappear down that narrow staircase, was inconceivable.

She took a very deep breath. "Stay," she said. "Stay here with me." She knew her cheeks were flaming and her plea had been too bold—she didn't care. Suddenly, as if he'd only just registered her words, a tide of emotions played across his features: surprise, indecision, finally, amazingly, need.

He said absolutely nothing. But Robin barely had time to think before his hands came up and grasped her arms, urgently, almost painfully. Then, before her heart could beat again, he'd pulled her to him and was crushing his lips to hers. The bursting forth of his passion seemed to drain her of all emotion, all thought—she knew only a primitive urge to be possessed by him, to possess him herself.

Robin put her arms around his back and gripped his shirt with her fingers, feeling his muscles ripple beneath her touch, savoring him. The entire long length of her body was pressed to his, molded to it, fitting perfectly. She felt as if they were already in bed, locked together as one, and yet it was just a kiss.

Adam kissed her and held her and moved his strong hands along her hips, the curve of her breasts, into her hair. Her body quivered in anticipation, melted against his shamelessly.

She was lifted off her feet, held suspended by the force of his awakened passion, when abruptly she seemed to be falling, stumbling, reaching out for something to grasp onto, reaching out for Adam.

He'd let her go. Suddenly and without warning, he'd dropped his hold and backed away. She saw him as if through a haze, his big body seeming to sag, a look on his face she was helpless to decipher.

"Adam," she whispered.

When his voice emerged it sounded totally alien, a stranger's voice, strangled and in pain. "I have to go," he got out. "Robin...Robin, I'm so very sorry." And then he was gone, silently, swiftly, swallowed by the night shadows.

CHAPTER EIGHT

ROBIN STOOD STARING at the closed door. Tears welled up in her eyes—tears of want and need and frustration. The question hammered at her again: *why?* He'd wanted her. She knew that. A woman didn't mistake an outburst of desire like that. He'd touched her with a desperate urgency and then...and then he'd just turned off, as if a wellspring of gushing water had been quenched.

Why?

Slowly, painfully, she walked into her bedroom. She was ashamed and humiliated. Rejected. She wished she could feel angry; perhaps that would come later. Anger would be a step up from the misery that entangled her like a sticky web.

She turned off the lights and lay down in bed with her clothes on, staring into the darkness. Tears trickled out of the corners of her eyes, sliding into her hair. She hadn't the energy to wipe them away.

Sleep finally came, a relief, a sodden, restless time of forgetting.

Things, of course, looked different in the morning. The lemon-yellow sun slanted into her apartment, the weatherman called for another clear day in the seventies, and Robin whistled to herself in the shower: "I'm gonna wash that man right outta my hair."

"Good song," she said to herself staunchly, scrubbing shampoo into her hair.

She'd made up her mind. Life was going to be much simpler from now on. She was going to drop the whole subject of forged pottery; she wasn't even going to think about it again. She was going to quit that damn committee. They'd have to find someone else. Enough was enough.

And—above all—she was going to forget Adam Farwalker, erase him, wipe the slate clean and start over.

There were lots of men in Santa Fe. Tall ones, too, she'd bet. Men who appreciated a fun-loving, warmhearted lady and who communicated on her wavelength.

Sure.

She was still whistling as she drove to her shop and parked right in front in an empty spot, which never would have been there in the busy season.

She had an appointment after lunch. Ericka was coming in at noon to take over, as the portrait was going to be shot outside. Thank heaven for Ericka. Robin wondered what she was going to do when Ericka went back to college. Oh, boy. But then, it wouldn't be very busy, so she'd just manage on her own.

"I'm gonna wash that man right outta my hair!" she sang as she unlocked her front door and let herself in, turned on the lights and flipped the Closed sign to Open.

Things were definitely looking up.

Robin's appointment was with a man from New York who had bought a second home in Santa Fe. He was a small, pale man with tinted glasses, a clothing manufacturer, straight from Seventh Avenue—Gary Kahn.

He'd always wanted to be a cowboy. Robin had the outfit ready: chaps, plaid shirt, boots, rope, hat, even tattered long underwear. Gary wanted to be photographed on a horse, lariat in hand, rifle in the scabbard of the saddle. The works.

Robin had everything set but the location and the horse. The outskirts of Santa Fe abounded with dude ranches and stables where Robin knew she could rent a horse.

She had a better idea, however. She told herself firmly that the shoot would be more authentic this way, so she picked up the phone and called the Farwalkers' number.

Christina answered. "Robin, how nice to hear from you. Nothing's wrong, is it?"

"No, no, it's not that at all." Robin explained about Gary Kahn's portrait. "So I wondered if I could use one of your horses. I'd pay you, of course."

"Oh, what fun! Could I watch? Oh, Ray will be delighted. My dear, I must have you do a family portrait one day. Goodness, there won't be a charge for the horse. It's our pleasure."

And so it was all set up for one o'clock and Robin hung up with a ridiculous feeling of satisfaction, as if she'd put one over on Adam. Well, at least his mother liked her!

At noon Ericka arrived, adorable in a Western-style blouse with piping around the yoke and a full flower-print prairie skirt. "Wow," she said, "did Mom tell you I had a call from the police again?"

"Again? But I thought all that was cleared up."

"I guess not, Miss Hayle. This Detective Cordova still thinks teenagers broke in here. Why does everyone always blame teens?" Ericka pouted, two dimples appearing in her cheeks.

"I don't know," admitted Robin, "but when you're all grown up, remember this incident and don't be in too big a hurry to pin the blame on some poor kid."

"Boy, I'll *never* be as creepy as those cops," said Ericka firmly. "I can hardly wait until I'm out of here and back at college."

Robin smiled. "What about Shane?"

"Oh, Shane goes to the University of Colorado up in Boulder. It's only about fifty miles away from my school."

"Sounds like fun times ahead," said Robin and finally got a big grin out of Ericka.

Gary Kahn came in early, and Robin could tell he was excited. He changed into his cowboy outfit in the back of her store and emerged a changed man; he walked taller, his spurs clanked aggressively, his shoulders were squared. His shirtsleeves were rolled up negligently, allowing just a bit of ragged underwear cuff to show.

"This is great," he said eagerly. "Now, where's the horse?"

"The horse, Mr. Kahn, is a real working cow pony on a ranch run by some friends of mine. Shall we take your car or mine?"

Gary was impressed, but he handled it well with his newfound macho image. He shook hands gravely with Ray Farwalker, remarked upon the beauty of the weather and Santa Fe and expressed interest in Christina's yearly fund-raising dinner.

"Well, next year, Mr. Kahn, you and your wife will be on my list," said Christina. "You give me your address before you leave today. And be prepared to bid high."

"Oh, I will, Mrs. Farwalker. It's a worthy cause." Then Gary Kahn added, "And thank you, ma'am."

Robin spent about an hour taking photographs of Gary on horseback. Ray and Christina watched; a few ranch hands gathered around and gave Gary pointers on how to hold the lariat. One of them whistled so that the horse's ears would perk up nicely for the shots. Another adjusted the bandanna around Gary's neck just so.

"Great shots, Mr. Kahn," Robin said, folding up her tripod. "The proof's will be ready the morning after next."

"I'll be there. I'm flying back to New York next Monday, so I'd like to have them all picked out before then. What a kick. Say, do you think these folks deserve tips?"

"Well, not the Farwalkers, but I'll bet the hands wouldn't say no."

So Gary dispensed good cheer and twenties and Robin drove him back to Santa Fe while he grinned and slapped his Stetson on his knee like a pro.

"Robin," said Ericka, when they got back, "a lady was here looking for you."

"Mrs. Hartmann again?"

"No, an Indian lady. She was very sweet. I told her you'd be back about three."

"An Indian lady?"

"I guess so. She didn't say what she wanted. So, how'd the shoot go?"

"Great. I'm dying to see the proofs myself."

Gary came out of the back, a small, pale man with thin hair and tinted glasses on. A hint of his former expansiveness still remained in his walk and his smile. "See you day after tomorrow. Thanks, Miss Hayle." He shook her hand, grinned and left. Robin looked down; a hundred-dollar bill lay on her palm.

"Wow," said Ericka softly.

"Split it with you," said Robin, "and don't argue."

Ericka went home at four. The afternoon was as hot and still as summer—siesta time. Robin took out her copy of *Santa Fe Style*, a book of wonderful photographs of her adopted city, and began to study it.

She was examining a photograph of an old Santa Fe kitchen, white-walled, clean, spare, its typical corner fireplace raised so that the hearth turned into a bench, a bunch of ears of dried corn hanging from a post, when the bell tinkled and someone came into her shop.

She looked up, put a welcoming smile on her face and was about to say, "May I help you?" when something held her.

The woman stopped inside the door as if reluctant to go on. She was elderly, a Pueblo Indian, dressed traditionally in a calico skirt and blouse, a brightly colored shawl over her shoulders and many strings of beads and turquoise around her neck and wrists. Her thick, straight hair was streaked with gray, cut into blunt bangs, a Dutch-boy style that was immensely flattering on the Pueblo women. Her outfit, in fact, very much resembled that of Mrs. Hartmann, but this was no costume.

"Excuse me," the woman said. Her voice was slightly accented and timid, her sweet face creased with lines of worry. Was she lost?

"May I help you?" Robin asked, her finger still marking a page in her book.

"You are Miss Robin Hayle?"

"Yes." Robin cocked her head in question.

"You do not know me, Miss Hayle, but I know who you are."

Robin put the book down on the counter. "Oh, you're the lady who was looking for me earlier. I'm sorry, I was out on a job. Did you want a portrait done?" Somehow, even as she said the words, Robin knew this gentle Indian lady had not come to be photographed.

"Oh, no, please, that is not why I am here. I only wish to talk to you." She was shy yet dignified, proud, with a handsome bone structure under velvety, lined skin. Her hands, Robin noted, were small and square, work worn, with short fingernails and rough knuckles. Hands that had seen toil.

"Well, you seem to know me. May I ask your name? You know, you'd take a lovely picture. Are you sure you're not interested . . ."

"Oh, please, Miss Hayle." The woman held up a hand. "I have come to see you on an entirely different matter. My name is of no importance to you, but what I have to tell you may be."

"Okay. Come on in back and sit down and tell me. Would you like some coffee? No? Tea then?"

The woman followed her into the small office. Robin turned the hot plate on while her mind rattled with curiosity. "Please sit down," she said, indicating a chair, fussing with tea bags and cups. "I really am curious."

"You were in San Lucas Pueblo looking for a man," said the woman.

Robin nearly dropped a spoon. Her heart squeezed with sudden excitement. Casually she said, "Oh? You live there?"

"No, no. I live . . . somewhere else."

"I'm sorry, I don't understand." She handed the woman a cup and sat down facing her.

"Of course not. I will start at the beginning." Nervously the lady played with her spoon handle. She looked straight into Robin's eyes and her gaze darkened. "You see, I am a potter myself."

Of course, her hands . . .

"I know the man you were looking for," said the woman in her soft, apprehensive voice.

Deliberately Robin set her own cup down, afraid that she might spill it in her agitation. "Oh, I see."

"I have known this man for many years. He is a fine potter. He is very afraid now, because you and . . . a man were asking about his pot, one you took a picture of some weeks ago, and it is said his work is a copy of a very famous one."

Robin let out her breath slowly. It was hard to believe, but this stranger was telling her the whole story. She had to take great care not to scare the woman off.

"This friend of mine, he is innocent. He did not know the pot was going to be sold. He was asked only to reproduce it. Truly. He never knew he was breaking the law."

"I believe you," Robin answered.

"He is innocent, but he is very afraid that if he goes to the authorities they will not believe him."

"Yes, I understand." Robin pushed her hair off her shoulders. "But maybe he would talk to me."

"I don't know."

Robin drew in a lungful of air. "What is his name? How would I contact him?"

The woman looked down at her strong, blunt hands. Her voice was so soft Robin had to strain to hear. "He is John Martinez. He remembers you. He does not want any trouble, but he might talk to you."

"You'd tell him I mean him no harm? I only want to find out who asked him to make the pot."

The woman met her gaze and nodded slowly. "I want to stop these men, too. I told John . . . These people exploit us. It is not fair. But we are afraid to go to the police. So many years and still we are not always treated fairly . . ."

Robin reached out and put her hand over the woman's. "I know. I understand. Change comes slowly. But if you could tell John Martinez that I won't give his secret away. I can help. Please. I'd love to speak to him."

"I don't know. Maybe. I will tell him." Then she held her head high. "If you try to find him yourself he will disappear. You must wait. I will let you know."

"Yes, sure, whatever he wants."

"You will tell no one?"

Robin shook her head. "No, I won't."

"John is sorry he ever made those pots, and all the trouble he went to in order to make the firecloud appear in the right spot. He is afraid." The woman was growing perturbed, her fingers nervously plucking at the fringe on her shawl.

"Please, don't worry. You can trust me," Robin said fervently. "How do I get hold of you?"

The woman rose, shaking her head. Her heavy earrings, butterflies, swung gracefully under her curtain of hair. "No, no, please, you will wait."

"Okay."

"John does not know I am here." She started toward the front of the shop, striding quickly, wanting to be gone.

"Tell him not to worry, okay? I'm harmless." Robin tried a joke, following the woman out into the front of her shop. "Well, thanks for coming. I really appreciate it. You will get in touch again, won't you?"

But the lady never even turned around; she walked straight to the door, slipped through it and disappeared around the corner.

"Whew!" Robin said aloud, trembling in reaction. And then she realized in dismay that she had no idea who the stranger was or where she was from. She should have tried harder to find out.

Intrigue, danger, mystery. *Wow,* thought Robin, *I've solved the case.* Well, part of it, anyway.

John Martinez. She had a name now to put to the face she recalled from that first day at the pueblo. A middle-aged man of medium height, thin and sinewy, with the large, strong-looking hands of an artisan. His English had been accented, but he'd been proud of his work, and friendly. He must be innocent, Robin reflected. Otherwise, why would he have let her see that pot, much less photograph it?

So...who had requested John Martinez to make the copy? And how was she going to find out?

It occurred to Robin that she was being very naive. Perhaps there was no other party who had hoodwinked John Martinez into making counterfeits. Wasn't it much more likely that he was doing it on his own? That sweet old lady who'd just left could have been his sister or aunt or something, and might have been sent deliberately to throw Robin off Martinez's trail. Wouldn't that scenario better explain his fear and reluctance to show himself or go to the authorities?

The bell tinkled. Robin looked up. "Oh, hi, Shel. How's it going?" She had an urge to tell Shelly the story of her visitor, but something stopped her, some ill-defined, vague feeling that she better get it straightened out in her own mind before telling anyone else. Besides, she'd promised the woman not to talk about it.

"Slower than molasses. Chuck's reading magazines and I'm bored."

"Go home and get caught up on your housework."

"Are you kidding?" Shelly made a face. "You know, Chuck was really impressed by your friend's little talk last night. He checked every pot we've got in the store. He'd like to get them all tested at Los Alamos, but it'd cost an arm and a leg." She walked around, ostensibly studying photographs. "He said you and Adam went off together for dinner."

"You're fishing, Shelly."

"Unabashedly."

"Nothing happened." Robin turned away, not wanting to meet her friend's curious gaze. "I told you he wasn't interested. Now will you just drop it?"

Shelly held her hands up. "Okay, okay, sorry. I just have this awful urge to be a matchmaker. I can't help it. And you've got to admit that man is a catch if I ever saw one."

"Maybe for somebody else."

Shelly stared at her for a moment then came close and put a hand on her arm. "He hurt you, didn't he?"

"Oh, for goodness' sake, I hardly know him, Shel."

"Funny, he didn't strike me as a woman-killer."

"Oh, it's probably me. I have a tendency to be a little pushy. Men run screaming in fright from my attentions." She tried to be witty, to brush it off, her usual reaction to being hurt. Funny girl.

"They're all cowards. Never mind," said Shelly kindly. "They just don't appreciate a good woman."

Shelly's departure left Robin in a strange mood. On one hand, she wished Shelly had not brought up the subject of Adam again, because it brought back all the anxiety, focused and in sharp relief. On the other hand, her mind was still working on the problem of John Martinez and what to do about *that*. Restlessly Robin puttered around her shop, answered the phone and went through the motions of closing up at five.

On the drive home, Robin toyed with her choices. She could report John Martinez to Rod Cordova. But that thought was dismissed as quickly as it came; Rob would think her a lunatic by now. Martinez would disappear; there would be no proof of her story. No, that was not the thing to do. Besides, she'd promised the woman. What if she convened her subcommittee? The one she'd decided that morning she was going to quit, she reminded herself. But what, really, was she able to tell them? And what could they do about it? After all, she had no way of getting John Martinez to show up and give them his story, did she?

She had to do *something*. She had to get some kind of help, advice on the next logical step.

It came to her suddenly, as she pulled up in front of her building and parked. It hit her with logic and clarity and no small measure of spite—she'd dump this problem right where it belonged, in Adam Farwalker's lap.

CHAPTER NINE

THE LAND GRADUALLY FLATTENED, growing browner and drier, a stark, barren expanse of high mesas slashed by jagged arroyos. Off to the north a large bird—a hawk, a buzzard?—circled ominously, hunting.

Why was she doing this?

To solve a crime? To see that justice prevailed? To protect innocent people? To see Adam Farwalker again?

The sun pressed heavily on the parched land; Robin wondered how hot it must have been in midsummer. How did people live here? Yet there was a harsh beauty about this bleak corner of the world, a beauty of clean lines, of spareness, of wide vistas, of subtle colors and sharp-edged shadows.

She sped along the empty highway toward Chaco Canyon in her car. It was farther than she'd thought, nearly two hundred miles. Checking her road map, she calculated that she'd be there in an hour or so.

What would Adam do when he saw her? Would he smile, or would his face close, rejecting her, uncomfortable with her presence? Well, she told herself, she had a darn good reason to seek him out this time.

She stopped for gas at a lone station in Pueblo Pintado.

"Goin' to Chaco Canyon?" asked the bearded old-timer, as he cleaned her dusty windshield with a stained cloth.

"Uh, yes, how did you . . . ?"

"Yer from the city. What else would you be doin' out here?" he said, chuckling. "It's forty-five minutes from here, that is if you don't stick to the speed limit too close."

Although Robin was anxious to get going, she couldn't resist an opportunity. "I wonder," she began, "if you'd mind doing me a favor?"

He raised a bushy gray brow. "And what would that be, miss?"

"Well, as you can see, I'm new to the area and I'd love to get a picture or two..."

"There's plenty round these parts to photograph, miss. You can leave your car right here, if you like."

"Well, I was hoping I could take *your* picture."

"Me?" He poked himself in the chest with a grimy finger.

He had that kind of lived-in face, Robin knew, that went with the land, that had been weathered and lined and turned to leather by a lifetime under the Southwestern sun. She shot an entire roll of film, using the mesaland to the south for the background. He was quite a subject, puffing up for Robin, posing, tugging on his old sweat-stained brown hat for her. Through her lens she saw at least two great shots, which was a blessing, because a truly good photo might only come at the rate of one in a thousand.

"That it?" he asked when they headed back toward her car.

"That's it." Robin pulled out a twenty and forced it on him. "Take it," she urged, "you earned every penny of it."

"Well, okay, then. Now you drive careful and enjoy the canyon, hear?"

When Robin started her car up she was tempted to turn around and head back to Santa Fe; it was only the old man's cheerful smile that kept her headed northwest. The truth was that she was too embarrassed, after their conversation, to make a fool of herself and turn around.

Was she disgraceful, she thought once again as she raced along, only using the Indian lady's visit as an excuse to see Adam? How could she so easily have forgotten her promises to him to play it safe, to not get involved? How could she have forgotten the warnings she'd already received?

At times she wondered if there were someone watching her, following her. She glanced in the rearview mirror; the road stretched for miles behind her, ending in a shimmering mirage, as if a lake had appeared where seconds before there had been only dust and rocks and clumps of mesquite.

Adam. He was like a mirage. Sometimes he was there, a welcome, refreshing sight, and then he was gone and all that remained was emptiness, barren ground.

Why?

To the west, a line of pewter-colored storm clouds moved along the horizon. Perhaps there would be one of those late afternoon thunderstorms that were so common in New Mexico, although it was so perfectly, exquisitely blue overhead it was hard to imagine rain. But the clouds could rush in like a conquering army, drop their loads and hasten on, leaving a rainbow and an incredible sunset behind.

Nothing could survive on this sun-baked terrain, thought Robin. Yet it did: brush, mesquite, sage and bunchgrass. Squat twisted trees grew along the dry river beds and piñon on the hills. There were no animals that Robin could see, not even a prairie dog or a rabbit, nothing but the occasional snake carcass making a question mark on the road, sizzling in the unforgiving sun.

It was a relief to drive up to the visitor's center. A sign announced that she was entering Chaco Canyon National

Historical Park, under the auspices of the National Park Service. A pleasant-looking man answered her question: "Oh, Adam, yes. They're working at Pueblo Bonito. Just follow the road. It's a few miles, on your right. You can't miss them."

Getting in her car again, Robin noticed a butte off to her left, a tall column of eroded rock standing all alone like a sentry guarding the entrance to the canyon. She was momentarily tempted to get out her camera but then smiled to herself ruefully. If there had been one shot taken of the rock column, there had been two million. Santa Fe postcard stands abounded with good photos of not only this unique site, but of all Chaco Canyon. She might as well leave her camera right in its case.

It was hot, in the high eighties, she guessed. She felt wilted and tired, grimy and more nervous by the second as she followed the road up the canyon. The sand-colored walls rose on either side of her, not close, but still there, delineating her world, reflecting heat onto the dry river bottom.

Some ruins appeared at the base of the canyon walls, but the signs still directed her onward. Pueblo Bonito, pretty village, she translated. That, of course, was the name given the place when the white man discovered it, but what had the Anasazi called their town? And why had they built it here in this godforsaken wilderness?

Adam. He would know. He knew this broad canyon intimately, far better than he knew Robin. He was committed to his work here, he *belonged* here. Jealousy shot through her, then quick self-reproach. Jealous of a *place*; how ridiculous.

Ahead of her Pueblo Bonito loomed into view, a huge, semicircular area enclosed by walls made of stone, the afternoon light etching each square, picking out the neat patterns of the masonry. The city rose from the valley floor, sitting patiently in dignified decay, crumbling slowly, inevitably in the sun. Hundreds upon hundreds of cube-like rooms, desiccated husks now, piled one upon the other, their collapsed roofs open to the sky like empty eye sockets.

Robin stopped her car next to a pickup truck that was parked near a break in the walls. She could hear voices in the distance, and a sort of tent city had been set up to one side. Adam's Land Rover was parked in front of one of the tents. She stepped out of her car, taking a deep breath. The wind was hot and strong, whipping her tan skirt against her legs, lifting her hair off her damp neck. An eerie feeling settled in her bones, as if the wind carried on it the whisperings of others who had walked this land before her, an unthinkably long time ago. The Ancient Ones.

They'd built these walls and rooms, worked, sweated, laughed, died here. And something was still left of them—a spirit, a memory, an intangible presence.

She walked inside the walls, fighting her feeling. *Superstition doesn't suit you,* she told herself. People visited this place every day. It was just a pile of rocks, an archeologist's playground.

And yet . . .

The ground was rough and strewn with stones, so she had to watch her step carefully. The voices grew closer, and she saw a stable set up containing broken pottery. A roped-off area appeared; two boys crouched on the ground.

She saw Adam then and stopped. He was resting on his haunches in a trench, a small brush in one hand, an artifact in the other. His concentration was total. His shirt was off, his hard, lean muscles glistening darkly with sweat. He wore shorts, and the muscles in his legs glinted like molten copper in the sun. His jet-black hair was held back by a strip of cloth. Just as in her imagined portrait . . .

He hadn't seen her yet. An overwhelming urge struck Robin to run, to hide from her feelings for this man. He could never belong to her; he was a part of this time-worn land, and an insurmountable distance stood between them, a million miles and a thousand years.

But his head turned. She could see his body stiffen; he'd spotted her. It was too late to retreat. For a moment he remained unmoving, the object in his hand forgotten, his eyes boring into hers while she stood there helpless and self-conscious. His torso was coppery, hard-muscled, practically hairless, gleaming with decisiveness and strength in the harsh sunlight, and she couldn't take her eyes off him. The wind was gone, yet those ghostly whisperings of the past, of a people long gone, still sang in her ears, making her sway with dizziness. Maybe Adam himself wasn't even real . . .

He straightened then, his muscles bunching fluidly; he said something to one of the boys, handed him the brush and artifact and came toward Robin, dusting off his hands against his shorts. There was no welcoming smile on his lips.

"Adam, I'm so glad I found you," she babbled, nervously taking off her sunglasses. "I . . ."

"What are you doing here?" he asked quietly.

Her courage fled, her anxious energy drained from her body as if a plug had been drawn. She averted her face. "I came to tell you something, about the counterfeiters. I'm sorry, I shouldn't have disturbed you, but I thought . . . It's important, Adam."

For an unbearably long time he stood contemplating her, his hands on his hips, his black Indian eyes pinning her. Wild, uncontrollable thoughts flew around in her head. For a moment she felt terrified of him, like a pioneer woman of a hundred years ago confronted by an Indian warrior. But that was absurd; Adam was perfectly civilized; it was just her crazy imagination playing tricks.

She heard him sigh, a long, deep expulsion of breath escaping him. She shouldn't have come.

"Okay," he said, "let's go someplace a little more private. Are you thirsty?"

"Yes," she managed to say gratefully. "It's a long drive."

He took her arm and led her over to a couple of chairs and a water cooler that sat in the shade of a curved wall. A faded blue shirt was flung over one of the chairs, and Adam picked it up and pulled it on, leaving it unbuttoned so that his sun-bronzed skin showed in a smooth vertical stripe. Silently he handed her a paper cup and she sat down and drank the cool water.

"So you drove all the way out here to tell me something," he began.

"Yes." A small anger flared in her. *He'd* started this whole thing! "You certainly aren't making this easy for me. I thought you'd want to know..."

"I do want to know. You'll have to excuse me. I was a little surprised to see you," he said carefully.

"I know who made the pot," she blurted out. "His name is John Martinez and he does live at San Lucas."

His black eyes rested on her, unsurprised, expressionless. She turned the paper cup in her hands. "A woman came into my shop yesterday. She never told me her name, though. An older lady, a Pueblo Indian. She said she was a potter. She knew all about us looking for this John Martinez and the pot and everything."

Adam folded his arms across his chest and watched her unflinchingly. "Go on."

"Well, she said this Martinez is innocent, but he's afraid to go to the authorities. He doesn't want to be involved. Neither does this woman, but she wants the forgeries stopped. She said maybe, *maybe*, this John Martinez would talk to me. You see, it's whoever asked him to make the pot that we want. They're the guilty ones."

Adam walked a few steps, as if thinking, then turned to her in a sharp motion. "This woman, the one who told you this, you have no idea who she was?"

"No. But she was very sweet and gentle and scared, I think. About sixty, dressed in a pueblo dress and shawl. She was well-spoken and wore some beautiful jewelry. She had silver earrings, butterflies, that were lovely."

Adam rubbed his jaw with a long-fingered hand. "How are you to get in touch with her again?"

Robin shook her head. "She said she'd get in touch with me, that I shouldn't go back to San Lucas. I got the idea that if anyone looked for this Martinez character he'd disappear again."

"This woman, was she from San Lucas, too?"

"No, at least she *said* she wasn't. She didn't say where she was from, though. Then she left, in a hurry, like she'd changed her mind about talking to me."

Adam was staring beyond her, arms folded. His face showed nothing, not interest or curiosity or triumph. Yet Robin had the distinct impression he knew something more than she did, something more about the Pueblo woman. Perhaps it was his lack of surprise that made her think so, or the slant of his questions.

"John Martinez," Adam said, half to himself.

"Do you know him?" Robin asked quickly.

He looked at her. "No, of course not."

"What, what do we do now?"

"We?" Adam stepped toward her, his brows drawn into a frown. "I'll take care of it from here, Robin. I don't want you involved."

"But I *am* involved. That woman may come back. Maybe Martinez will talk to me. I can't just tell her to forget it, can I?"

"I'll take care of it, Robin. I know enough now. The proper steps can be taken. I promise you, you won't have to be involved at all."

She stood quickly. "But I *want* to be involved. You got me into this and now, just like that; you say I have nothing to do with it. I can't just drop it. I want to know what's going on, and what's going to happen. Adam, I can't just forget about it!"

She stood facing him, their eyes practically on a level. For a moment Robin thought he was going to relent, to tell her something, but his glance shifted to a place beyond her, and she knew he'd decided against it. "Adam . . ." she began.

"I do appreciate your driving all the way out here to tell me this. It was good of you." He smiled at her for the first time then, but it was forced, deliberate, signaling an end to the conversation. "As long as you're here, would you like to see what we're doing?"

"Oh, I'd love to but—"

"As a photographer, you'll be interested to know that William Henry Jackson photographed these ruins in 1877. Unfortunately the film was ruined, but he publicized the existence of Chaco Canyon."

She gave up. Adam obviously had closed the subject of her mysterious visitor and her own involvement. How easily he switched his moods, as if he were a TV set with remote control. On this station was Adam, aloof, private, self-contained. And on another was Adam, friendly, suave, the perfect gentleman and host. Then there was Adam the enigmatic Apache. And now he was the professor, archeologist, highly intelligent, well-versed and eager to educate.

Luckily Robin was interested. She had to admit she could listen to him forever—and stare at him like an infatuated coed.

He was still gazing a little past her, as if readying his thoughts. "As you can see," he said, finally catching her eye, "I'm hardly the first to work here in the canyon. There were excavations as far back as the twenties, funded by the National Geographic Society, and then there was the Chaco Project in the seventies. A lot has been done, but there're thirteen sites just in Chaco Canyon itself and thousands all over the Southwest."

"Thousands?"

"For some decades around 1000 A.D. there was a relatively wet spell in this area, so the land supported a larger population. Drought set in and eventually the Anasazi from all the settlements left, migrated."

"So they're all gone? The Anasazi died out?" she asked, following Adam out to the great semicircular central plaza of Pueblo Bonito.

"They were the predecessors of the Hopi and Zuni and Pueblo tribes of today," he said. "You know, the modern descendents of the Anasazi have kept many of their ancestors' customs. When an anthropologist or an archeologist has a question, say, about what a certain prehistoric artifact was used for, they go to the present-day tribes and ask. Often they get an answer to the puzzle, too." He looked at her. "Are you up to a walk?"

"Oh, sure. Where?"

He pointed. "Up there, to the top of the canyon wall. There's a great view. You'll understand the overall plan of the ruin better."

It was a tough climb. But Adam was always ready with a hand, in case she slipped. They scrambled up the rocky path, climbing over boulders. It was hot, too, but Robin didn't mind; it was an adventure, and Adam was talkative now, a different person, both the professor and a thoughtful companion. Every time his hand touched her arm or her back or her shoulder, she felt that jolt again, that exciting heightening of her senses. She could see rivulets of white salt on his skin where sweat had dried, and she smelled the man scent of his body.

"Whew! I feel like a mountain goat," she said once, stopping for a moment and breathing hard.

"There used to be stairs up here. Look, you can still see some of the stones."

She saw them, stones placed by ancient hands to make the climb easier. It touched her somewhere deep inside.

They reached the top. The high mesa stretched away from them in undulating brown waves; below, Pueblo Bonito lay in its precise semicircle, spread out for examination. Robin got her breath back and turned around slowly in a circle. "How did they *live* here?" she finally asked.

"They were experts. They built a sophisticated water-collection system, ditches, dams and holding tanks, on these canyon walls to collect every drop of moisture that fell, and diverted it to their fields on the canyon bottom. It was a highly organized society."

"How many people lived here?" she asked, seeing the other pueblos scattered along the canyon floor.

"Well, there's a debate about that going on. At first it was believed the population ran to the tens of thousands, based on the number of rooms in the pueblos here. But lately a new theory is being considered, that these huge pueblos with their many kivas, the ceremonial rooms, were not actually dwelling places, but centers of religion and trade. In other words, a kind of ancient convention center, nearly empty except during ceremonial occasions."

"So the Anasazi people came from all over to attend these, uh, services?"

"Probably. They built roads—" he pointed out over the land to the north "—all centering here, on Chaco Canyon. Thirty feet wide, straight as arrows, cut through hills and across valleys. You can just see a faint trace there. It was called the Great North Road."

Yes, she could see lines on the arid earth, faint markings, as straight as any surveyor could lay out. "Oh, my goodness. But I can't believe they could have undertaken such huge projects."

"They must have had skilled labor groups. Like I said, it was a tightly structured, highly organized society. There's still so much to find out. I could spend a lifetime here."

"What about your classes?" she asked.

"Yes," he said wryly. "Well, my grant only lasts until the end of this semester. And most of these kids working for me have to leave soon to go back to school."

"I can understand why you're so fascinated by all this," Robin said, gesturing out over the canyon. "It's so...so mysterious, so beautiful."

"Yes."

They stood together in companionable silence for a time, looking down at the ruined city. A sudden breeze plucked at Robin, a cooling caress at this height, molding her skirt to her. It ruffled Adam's hair and made his shirttails flap against his sun-bronzed skin.

"A storm," he said, shading his eyes and gazing off to the west. "But it may pass by us."

The thunderheads Robin had seen earlier were advancing toward them in a distinct line, pushing the wind before them, whipping up dust devils and bending the sparse yellow grass. They both watched, fascinated, as the black clouds billowed and grew, like a speeded-up film.

"Will it rain on us?" Robin asked. "Should we get back?"

"I think it's going to the north," Adam said. "It usually does."

The sky turned dark and brooding; dust blew into Robin's eyes. Thunder growled distantly, and she could see jagged flashes of lightning far away.

"Are you afraid?" Adam asked. "We can go down."

She glanced at him. "No, it's exciting. I'm not afraid. I wish I had my camera set up, though." She smiled. "Shouldn't we be doing a rain dance? Wouldn't the Indians have been praying for rain at a time like this?"

He gave her a sharp look, as if measuring her, seeing if she were poking fun. "Probably. I know a few words of a Navaho chant, but I'd rather you heard it from a real singer."

"Oh, I'd love it. Sometime," she said, holding her hair out of her eyes. She felt free up there on the rim of the world, the wind buffeting her, a strong, handsome man at her side, a man who belonged to this time and place. "This land is owned by the Indians now, isn't it?"

"Not according to the Department of Interior," he said dryly. "There are Apache reservations, two in New Mexico and one in Arizona. But when the Spanish came to New Mexico there were Apache herders all over the state."

"Here?"

He shrugged, the wind tugging at his shirt. "Probably. The Navaho and Apache are very closely related and got here about the same time, in the 1400s. They found these ruins here. As a matter of fact, the name Anasazi is a Navaho word."

"And what did they think of these ruins when they saw them?" Robin asked.

"They knew a very powerful race had lived here. They respected the Ancient Ones and stayed away from their dwelling places. They never molested the ruins, or lived in them." He paused and scanned the sky. "Yes, it's going to the north. It won't rain here, not today." Then he continued: "There's a legend about Chaco Canyon that explains how the People came to live here in Dinetah."

"Oh, please tell me."

"It seems that when my people, the Navaho and Apache, the Diné, found Chaco, the Ancient Ones who lived here were slaves of a supernatural gambler they called Never Loses. The Ancient Ones bet everything they owned against him and lost, so they bet their freedom and lost that, too. The spirits of the Diné—Wind Boy, First Man, Coyote and the rest of them—devised their own games full of deceit. They won the Chacoans their freedom and sent an angry Never Loses into exile."

"What a great story. But how did your people explain the disappearance of the Ancient Ones?"

"They simply said that they went away. That's all. And so far, that's all we can say."

"An interesting mystery," said Robin.

"I like to stand here and look down and wonder. Here's an insignificant valley in the middle of nowhere. Civilization flourished here on a grand scale and then was lost. What did the last group of people who deserted this canyon see as they straggled along, burdened with their belongings? Where did they go? What did their gods tell them about their leaving?'' His voice faded away on the wind.

Suddenly there was a closeness between them, a new and joyful sharing. It was as if Adam had opened that closed door of his for a precious moment, so that she could see inside his mind to the Aladdin's cave of treasures he kept so well hidden. The wind was dying, and a shaft of late sunlight speared through an opening in the storm clouds. A rainbow formed on the far side of the valley, a lovely refraction of light and color. A moment later the brooding clouds seemed to swell and part, and sunlight spilled into the canyon, illuminating the rim with a bright golden light that was washed clean by the rain. It shone on the hard chiseled lines of Adam's face, on his glowing copper skin. He was so beautiful, Robin thought, like one of his ancient Indian gods.

"Adam,'' she said after a moment, "I want to help you find the counterfeiters. Please let me help.''

He studied her for a long time, and her heart pounded too heavily. "It could be dangerous,'' he finally stated, "but there's no putting you off, is there, Robin Hayle?''

CHAPTER TEN

ADAM TURNED HIS FACE to the west, toward the setting sun, where streaks of light blazed across the valley beneath the fading rainbow and struck him with their warmth. For a moment he closed his eyes, searching for equilibrium, summoning the enduring bounty of nature to enter him and fill his spirit with harmony. When he opened his eyes she was still there, tall and long and lovely, soft and womanly. The last light reached out for her, too, and her windblown hair caught the rays like threads of yellow-gold.

She was strikingly beautiful, but she was more than that. She had an openness of mind, a sensitivity that most white people lacked. Perhaps it was due to her photographer's eye, which saw more deeply into things. And he sensed a vulnerability in her, a too-ready smile, a tenseness. He would love to scratch her surface and find the source of her discord.

What was he thinking? Why in the devil had he told her she could help? Had he forgotten the danger to her, the risk? He could easily have taken the information she'd given him and contacted Martinez himself. Or he could have insisted on calling in Rod Cordova to have the police handle it, in spite of the promise Robin had made to her mysterious visitor. So why hadn't he?

Adam knew the answers already. Despite the fact that nothing but ruin would ever come of a relationship be-

tween them, he could not quite let her go. He'd walked out
on her the other night—because then he'd still had the
strength to do so. It had been a cruel act, selfish and cow-
ardly. If only she'd stayed out of his life. He hadn't the
strength to let her go again; the spirits of his forefathers
had stripped him of his powers and left him helpless and
alone to face this woman.

"It's getting late. We better go down now," he said.

They were both quiet as they began the steep descent.
He'd deliberately withdrawn into the reserve and silence,
his cloak of aloofness, afraid that he'd revealed too much
of himself to Robin. For a moment, he'd let his true self
show, and he knew she'd recognized it. *Careful,* he warned
himself, watching her long slim back in a silky turquoise
blouse as she walked down the rough path ahead of him.

Something else was bothering him, too: the Pueblo
woman who'd visited Robin. There was little doubt in his
mind who it was—Josefina Ortega. He was angry with her
for dragging Robin back into this affair. Why in hell was
Josefina meddling in it?

"Can I see more?" she asked then.

"More?"

"Yes, of Pueblo Bonito. There's still plenty of day-
light."

"Sure. Yes. Have you ever seen a kiva?" He knew he
was distracted, and that his thought of a moment ago
about Josefina was unkind. She was a wonderful woman,
a lifetime friend of his mother's, in fact. She was also one
of the great Southwestern Indian artists of this century, her
pottery proudly on display in homes and galleries all over
the world.

It hadn't taken Adam more than a few seconds to guess
the identity of the woman when Robin had described her.
The earrings alone had been a dead giveaway. Her visit to

Robin was completely out of character for Josefina; she'd always been timid and retiring, finding fulfillment in her pueblo, her family and her craft. Going to Robin with her knowledge had shown great courage.

Of course, surmised Adam, his very own mother was no doubt the cause of Josefina's visit to Robin. Who else had known about the forged pot in San Lucas Pueblo, and also of Robin's involvement? Yes, his mother must have spoken to her friend Josefina, and Josefina in turn had found out about John Martinez. The trouble was, Josefina should have come to *him* and kept Robin out of it.

"A kiva," Robin was saying. "Isn't that a ceremonial room?"

"Yes, it's where the Anasazi and the modern-day Hopi men hold their religious ceremonies. They're often dug into the ground, to allow the initiates to get closer to the Mother Earth. Women were never allowed in kivas."

"Well, let's hope they don't find out about me," she said lightly.

He helped Robin over a pile of rubble, his big hands spanning her waist, half lifting her. And as he touched her in the waning light that was turning her eyes the color of wild violets, he felt that ache in his groin again. How he would have loved to feel the curve of her soft bosom against his chest, to savor her full lips and twist his fingers in that heavy mass of spun-gold hair...

He must have hesitated too long, because she stopped, still in the curve of his hands. "Adam," she began, her voice a whisper, "I..."

"Let's go," he said quickly, snatching his hands back. "It'll be too dark to see soon."

How was he supposed to think with Robin around? Yet he welcomed her presence, as if he were a dying man whose thirst was being miraculously quenched. But she was young and vital; surely she was looking for marriage and children. She *should* be looking for that, for God's sake.

Damn Josefina. It was her fault he was faced with this uncomfortable situation. Had his mother's friend really believed she'd stay anonymous? Highly skilled, sweet and kind and endearing as she was, Josefina was nevertheless painfully naive. And eventually, if indeed Robin stayed involved, she would have to be told everything. So much for Josefina's anonymity.

What *was* he thinking? *If* Robin stayed involved? Was he crazy?

"What were these rooms?" Robin was asking, and he had to drag his attention back to reality.

"It's believed they were family dwellings," he answered. "The women would have cooked over here—" he pointed "—and there, through that doorway, they probably slept."

"How do you know all that? I mean . . ."

"The earth tells us." He stooped and picked up a handful of loose pebbles. "If I found, say, a fragment of straw here, then I'd look for more in the area. It takes a microscope, sometimes, to determine what's there, but eventually the earth would give up its secrets."

"And if you found enough straws?"

"I'd surmise that women wove baskets in this area, you understand?" He let the dirt sift through his fingers.

"And in a kitchen area, do you know what they actually cooked?"

He nodded. "With the sophisticated techniques available to us now, we can tell exactly what they ate."

"That's amazing," said Robin, running her long slim fingers across a smooth stone seat. "I can almost see a woman sitting here, grinding corn."

"You can see all kinds of things here," he replied. "That's what my job is all about, to breathe life into these cold stones."

They passed the worktable containing the day's find of pottery shards. Robin stopped by it momentarily to look at the pieces then lightly fingered a sharp-edged fragment that lay there. "This is from a pot?" she asked.

"A very old pot," he said, "from around the tenth century." Then he put a fingertip on the surface of the shard and felt its familiar smoothness. "It's what we call a black-on-white. You see the lines here? This one had geometric designs on it. You can make out the corner of one here. I think this piece was from a mug. See? There's a part of the handle." He picked it up, turned it over in his fingers and showed her the design.

"Will you find the missing pieces and be able to put it together?" she asked, touching the black lines with a pink fingernail.

He shook his head. "Probably not."

"What a shame," she said.

"See this blemish?" he asked, pointing to a round black smudge on the curve of the shard. "It's a firecloud. Prehistoric pots commonly have them. They come from the pot being imperfectly fired. Just like modern Pueblo potters, the Anasazi fired their work in animal dung. The mark is from an incompletely burned fragment."

"Is this spot like the one on John Martinez's pot?" she asked.

"Yes. The blemish makes a piece less valuable to a collector."

"Oh, I think it makes it even *more* fascinating," Robin said, cocking her head. "I imagine an Indian lady and how mad she was when her mug came out of the fire with that mark on it."

"That's a minority opinion," he replied, watching her stroke the black smudge on the shard. And he couldn't help comparing that ancient piece of clay to himself: Changing Man, fragmented, imperfect, blemished. Quickly he turned away from her and began to move on.

That night at her apartment, Adam recalled painfully, he'd left and driven away and promised himself that he wasn't going to see her again, that a relationship between them was fair neither to him nor to her. There were so many reasons: their different cultures and beliefs, his own inadequacy, fear for her safety. But here he was again, allowing her sweet stubbornness to bulldoze him, permitting her to believe she could help uncover the counterfeiters.

He indicated a recently excavated set of steps that led up to a wide, flat stone platform. "Climb on up," he said, pointing the way, "but take care, the stones might be loose." He followed her closely, unable to take his eyes from her slim ankles as she held her full skirt aside with a hand.

"Oh, Adam, this is the kiva, isn't it?" She sounded so excited, so truly interested, that he hadn't the heart to bring up the subject of the black marketeers just then. But he would, and soon.

"Yes, this is it. One of many, in fact. But this one happens to be under excavation right now." Inadvertently he touched the small of her back, feeling the cool fabric slip over her warm skin. He suggested she approach the opening in the ground. "You'll be one of the first to see it."

"Me?"

He couldn't help it. He smiled. "Yes, you. Other than a few of my workers, no one's been in here for centuries."

"God, how spooky," she whispered, craning her neck to look down into the inky black pit, where countless centuries ago mythical rites had been performed by the Ancient Ones.

The kiva, which sat below the platform of stone, was not entirely excavated yet. There was loose masonry on at least one side of it, and Adam wasn't too certain of the ceiling. "Here," he said, leaving her side for a moment, "I'll get a lantern and you can look down inside."

"But can't I go in?"

He stopped and glanced at her for a moment. "It's not all that safe, Robin. I really would rather you..."

"Oh, please. There's a ladder and everything. Just a quick look. I promise I won't touch a thing."

Ordinarily Adam would have stuck to his guns. Ordinarily. But she looked so lovely, so enthusiastic, standing there in the fading golden light. "Well, I guess if I go down first... But just a quick glance, Robin. It's not in great shape."

As the deepening shadows reached across the twisted land, Robin held the lantern over the pit while Adam descended, then she handed it down and climbed onto the ladder. He was instantly aware of the cold in the kiva, a dry cold, and the odor of crumbled stone and dirt that was distinct in the air. There was even a faint, aged smell of dung left from the long extinguished fires of dried droppings that had once illuminated the pit.

Even to Adam the place was eerie. He had never entered a kiva without feeling the touch of the long dead who'd once performed their secretive, magical rites there with the firelight blazing in their dark eyes. If he stood very still, he could almost hear their chanting, a song like his uncle could sing: sensual, primitive, filled with the call of the spirits and the flesh.

"Wow," Robin said as Adam held the lantern shoulder high, bouncing its light off the aged walls and the fire pit in the center of the chamber. "So this is a kiva," she said, her voice a reverent whisper. "It's so strange, so mysterious."

He stood close, aware of the new scent in the lamp-reddened kiva—Robin's scent—fresh, womanly, very much alive. The stirrings began in his belly again and his head rang with the chanting, but this time it was his own song and was undeniably real. His senses had never been so charged with life, so in tune with the powerful force of the place. He wanted Robin with a kind of mindlessness; he wanted to possess her in every way, to own her body and soul, and he wanted to perform his rite in this haven, this magical place.

Adam felt her hand touch his arm. The pain was excruciating, tender and burning at the same moment. She said nothing, but he could hear her swallow, and the pulse in her fingers where they lay on his arm quickened, steady and strong. The blood began to pound in his head. He turned toward her, his eyes dark and shining in the lamplight, filled with his overpowering need. He placed the lantern on the hard earthen floor and cupped her face with his hands. There were only the two of them in this ancient kiva, on this lonely planet.

It was then that he became cognizant of the dust sifting down from the curved ceiling. He was confused for a moment, then he saw Robin look up and blink, and the air was filled with dust.

He heard it a split second later. Immediately he snatched Robin to him and dived for a corner of the chamber, covering her body with his. The ceiling seemed to crash down on them, dust and rock battering his back and head, suffocating, painful. Then suddenly, as quickly as it had begun, it was over. He could hear a few loose stones strike the floor, and dirt was still drifting down onto him, but it was over.

Robin was gasping and terrified beneath his weight. He shifted quickly, pulling her to his chest, rocking her. "It's over now. It's over," he said, coughing, his shallow breathing matching her own. "Are you all right?"

"I think so," she said weakly. "Oh God, what happened?"

"The ceiling. Part of it caved in."

"Can we..."

"Yes, I can see the hole. I don't know where the ladder is, though. Will you be okay for a minute?"

"Sure, yes, I'm okay."

He came to his knees, testing for injuries, and then to his feet. It was pitch black, and he had to feel his way over the fallen rock, stumbling once, finding his way like a blind man.

"Adam," he heard her say. "Where are you?"

"Over here." He coughed hard then, the dust choking him, gritting against his teeth. "I can't find the ladder." A moment later, he tripped against it. It was lying on its side near a wall. "Here, I got it," he called, rasping. "Hold on, I'll set it back up. You all right?"

"Yes."

By the time Adam had the ladder up again, he could hear footfalls on the stones above them. His workers. Then someone, it sounded like Jack, called into the opening.

"Mr. Farwalker! You down there? Adam!"

"Here! Help me with this ladder, grab the end of it."

In only a matter of minutes he had Robin on the surface, her weight leaning against him; she was still trembling and shaken, but unhurt, thank God. The student workers by now had all gathered around, asking questions, stunned by the sudden, unaccountable cave-in.

"Here," one of the girls offered, "drink this." It was Linda, holding out a plastic water bottle. "Oh, Mr. Far-walker," she said, "you might have been killed!"

"We're both okay," he assured her. Then he looked at Robin, who sat close to his side, hugging her knees to her chin. "I never should have taken you down there," he said in a hoarse voice. "When I think what might have happened..."

She gazed at him then gave a weak smile. "I *wanted* to go down there, Adam. I made you do it."

"Yeah, Mr. Farwalker," said Jack, "it's not your fault. Why, we've all been in there. Lots of times, in fact. It just happened."

The six young people stood around, obviously wondering, thinking about their own safety. Adam couldn't blame them. He'd worked on digs for many years, though, and had seen some cave-ins. Yet he'd thought this kiva was relatively safe.

He felt Robin's hand on his shoulder. "Come on, Adam, stop blaming yourself," she urged. "I'd have sneaked in there when your back was turned, anyway. Come on." Then, amazingly, he heard her giggle. "Besides," she said, "I look pretty good compared to you."

He glanced at her dirt-smudged face then down at himself.

"See?" said Robin, "you look like a chimney sweep. And your hair's gray."

A few of the students laughed nervously while Robin sat smiling and expectant. He had to give in. Adam, too, smiled. She was right, of course; no one was really at fault, and they were both unharmed.

"And excitement makes me hungry," Robin said sheepishly.

It was good, walking beside Robin, her lean body molded to his in the dusk. He kept his arm around her shoulder—merely a protective gesture—but he could imagine the silky softness of her bare skin. He'd bet her whole body was velvety smooth, and warm, yielding.

"You're not still feeling guilty, are you?" she asked as they made their way toward the students' campsite.

"I should be," he replied, wiping his mind clean of his thoughts.

"You know, guilt is such a wasted emotion. I mean, anger, now there's an acceptable one. Or happiness."

He stopped and looked down at the path, trying hard not to smile. "You're something, Robin Hayle," he found himself admitting. "Nothing ever daunts you, does it?"

She was quiet for a moment then said, "Some things get me, Adam Farwalker, you bet they do," and there was that insecurity again, that wistful tone of voice.

Nancy and Linda had been cooking dinner when word of the accident had spread throughout the camp. The students took turns over the stove. Too bad, Adam thought, because it was Jack and Craig who were the good cooks of the group.

So packaged macaroni and cheese it was, with a can of tuna or two thrown in. "Why, this is delicious," Robin said kindly, and a few friendly arguments broke out among the crew.

The talk finally turned to the cave-in. Adam sat quietly and listened to the reactions of his students. Nancy said, "I think we should begin restoring the kiva first thing tomorrow."

Craig concurred with Jack's statement: "It's going to have to wait for spring next year. We'd only get about half of it cleared out before it snows."

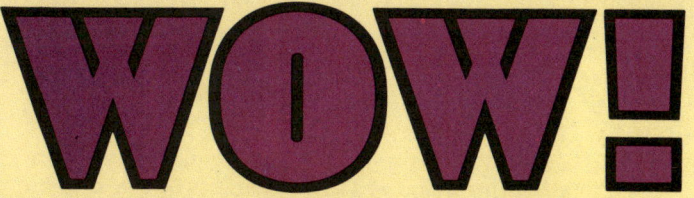

WOW!

THE MOST GENEROUS
FREE OFFER EVER!
From the Harlequin Reader Service

GET 4 FREE BOOKS WORTH $11.80

Affix peel-off stickers to reply card

4 FOUR FREE BOOKS 4
4 FOUR FREE BOOKS 4

PLUS A FREE ACRYLIC CLOCK/CALENDAR

AND A FREE MYSTERY GIFT!

NO COST! NO OBLIGATION!
NO PURCHASE NECESSARY!

Because you're a reader of Harlequin romances, the publishers would like you to accept four brand-new, never-before-published Harlequin Superromance® novels, with their compliments. Accepting this offer places you under no obligation to purchase any books, ever!

ACCEPT FOUR BRAND NEW

YOURS

We'd like to send you four free Harlequin novels, worth $11.80 retail, to introduce you to the benefits of the <u>Harlequin Reader Service</u>® We hope your free books will convince you to subscribe, but that's up to you. Accepting them places you under no obligation to buy anything, but we hope you'll want to continue!

So unless we hear from you, once a month we'll send you four additional Harlequin Superromance novels on free home approval. If you choose to keep them, you'll pay just $2.74 per volume — a savings of 21¢ off the cover price. There is *no* charge for shipping and handling. There are *no* hidden extras! And you may cancel at any time, for any reason, and still keep your free books and gifts, just by dropping us a line!

ALSO FREE!
ACRYLIC DIGITAL CLOCK/CALENDAR

As a free gift simply to thank you for accepting four free books we'll send you this stylish digital quartz clock — a handsome addition to any decor!

Crystal acrylic case looks good in home or office setting.

Changeable month-at-a-glance calendar pops out, may be replaced with a favorite photograph!

Quartz movement for exceptional accuracy.

Battery included!

WE EVEN PROVIDE FREE POSTAGE!

It costs you *nothing* to send for your free books — we've paid the postage on the attached reply card. And we'll pick up the postage on your shipment of free books and gifts, and also on any subsequent shipments of books, should you choose to become a subscriber. Unlike many book clubs, we charge *nothing* for postage and handling!

"And it snows in October around here sometimes," Linda was quick to point out.

"Plus we all have classes in Albuquerque," put in Jack.

"I don't," said Nancy, "I graduated, remember?"

"Well," said Robin, coming to her feet, "this has been one heck of an afternoon, but *I've* got work tomorrow. Bright and early."

Adam stood quickly, confused. "But you're not driving back tonight?"

"Of course I am."

"Robin—"

"Hey," interrupted Craig, "be careful driving that highway alone at night. There've been some strange people around here today."

It was only a small alarm, but nevertheless a bell sounded in Adam's head. "What people, Craig?"

"Oh, this Indian I saw. He was drinking or something, stumbling around in one of the roped-off areas." The young man shrugged. "Then he got into a junky old pickup truck and drove off like a demon."

"Roped-off areas?" asked Adam, the bell sounding louder.

"Yeah. It was right before the cave-in, I think. Or maybe..."

"Right *after* it?" asked Adam in a quiet voice.

CHAPTER ELEVEN

ADAM STOOD ALONGSIDE Robin's car and frowned. "I don't like you making this drive tonight," he said as she started up the motor. "You won't be back in Santa Fe till midnight as it is."

"I have to get back," stated Robin, "I've got appointments tomorrow. Work calls."

"I still don't feel right about it."

Robin gave him one of those big bright smiles of hers and turned on the headlights. "I'm going to be fine. Just because one of your students saw some man nosing around doesn't mean he had anything to do with the cave-in."

Maybe she was convinced of that, but Adam had his doubts. No, more than doubts; he felt there was a connection. But Robin was putting the car in gear...

"Well," she was saying, "I'll let you know the minute I hear anything more about this John Martinez. I honestly believe my Indian lady will be back in touch. Goodbye, Adam," she said, "I hope I see you soon."

He put his hands in his pockets and watched grimly as she pulled away, her tires kicking up loose gravel on the road. At that rate, Robin Hayle would be back in town well before midnight.

Why hadn't he tried harder to stop her? Was it because she was getting to him, chinking away at that armor he'd so calculatingly donned ten years ago? Or maybe Robin was as resilient as she seemed and not in the least vulnerable. Maybe she didn't need or want a strong man telling her what to do. He wondered about that, though. In certain respects, they were very much alike despite their different backgrounds.

It was an utterly cloudless night. Above the canyon walls the immense canopy of stars gleamed with a pristine beauty, the air so rarefied and clean that the Milky Way seemed to be made of white gauze. Adam could almost reach out and touch it. As he stood there, hands still in the pockets of his shorts, he felt a closeness to nature that steadied him, that made him feel whole again.

He was ready to turn, to walk back up the stony path to his camp, when some vague apprehension held him. His glance followed the curving road below. He could see where the dark highway flowed with the land's contours, and yes, there were Robin's lights, glowing, turning the pavement to silver ribbons in front of her car.

He stood immobile, watching for a moment as the twin tunnels of light grew smaller. A part of Adam's mind said she was okay, driving a bit too fast, but all right. Another part, that nebulous place in his brain that reacted purely by instinct, noting anything out of order, any dissonant element, argued against complacency. Everyone had that place, but it was the Indian who was trained to listen to it.

And there it was, the cause of Adam's disquiet. His heart pounded heavily as he watched another set of headlights pull onto the highway just behind Robin. At this time of night, in that isolated part of the canyon, the car tailing her was far too coincidental . . .

Suddenly he was all muscle and bone and nerve reacting. Crossing the parking area at a dead run, Adam was in his Land Rover in seconds, backing out onto the highway, stripping the gears, forcing the sluggish vehicle to leap forward like a scared cat.

He pounded the steering wheel with a fist. Damn it! Why hadn't she listened to him? Why hadn't he insisted she stay?

Catching up to Robin would be impossible. At best, his Land Rover could do fifty, and it was a nightmare at that speed on the sharp curves. The road dipped and twisted, sometimes climbing, sometimes dropping down to the canyon floor where his lights picked out roadside objects eerily from the shadows.

Fifty, fifty-three miles an hour—the vehicle's motor strained like a beast of burden hauling too heavy a load.

For a moment the road straightened on top of a rise. He could just make out the two sets of lights, far ahead of him, as they disappeared in tandem around a sweeping curve. Robin must have been aware of the car following her, Adam decided, and probably had the gas pedal to the floor. He'd never catch up in time.

Images floated unbidden through his head. Robin lying along the roadside with a gunshot wound to her breast. Robin in her burning car, a pillar of orange flames reaching to the heavens. She was screaming for help, her deep blue eyes filled with terror.

For several miles Adam could see nothing whatsoever ahead. Only the huge, massive humps of rock stood on either side of the road, dark, forbidding sentinels. His engine was beginning to heat up now, waves of acrid-smelling heat radiating from the metal floorboards. The vehicle couldn't be pushed this hard . . . It occurred to Adam that he was about to crack the engine block but that it made no difference. He was never going to reach her in time, anyway. A horrible, wrenching sadness gripped him, a sadness for what they could have had together. He recalled with strange clarity her last words: "I hope I'll see you soon." There had been promise in her voice and expectancy in her eyes. He'd chosen to ignore it then, but now it seemed the most important thing in the world.

Several miles before the main highway, Adam thought he saw the cars but perhaps that was only fear and wishfulness.

He came around a sharp bend in the road then and definitely spotted taillights in the distance. They seemed, however, to be sitting, unmoving, at an odd angle. Robin's?

The red lights grew in his vision as the temperature gauge in the Land Rover rose into the danger zone. Then, as he neared, the taillights took on an otherworldly quality, as if a primitive animal was staring at him with glowing, fiery eyes; he pushed on the gas pedal even harder until he thought his foot was going to go through the floor. God, if that was Robin's car... He could make it out now, tilted onto its side in a ditch, its headlights turned skyward, askew, crazily searching the night.

Adam pulled up and came to a stop. The car was Robin's, all right. His chest tightened, and he was vaguely aware of his racing heartbeat, as if he'd been running to catch up to her. Leaving his door swinging, he was tugging on Robin's within seconds, calling out her name, yanking on the handle.

She was inside and moving, although moving as if she were drunk, moving very, very slowly, her head lolling from side to side. He heard her moan when he finally jerked the door open, and he crouched, putting his hands on her shoulders gently. "Robin, it's Adam," he said, his voice a harsh whisper. "Come on, Robin, we've got to get you out of here."

Again she moaned.

"Come on, there... Okay? Can you stand?" But she couldn't. She sagged against him, dazed, hurt, but he couldn't see an injury.

He scooped her up in his arms and saw it then in his headlights, the blood that had spattered her turquoise silk blouse and matted her spun-gold hair. Carefully bending down onto one knee, he propped Robin against the back of her car where he could see better in the light. She was pretty well out of it but still breathing steadily, though very deeply, and moans escaped her.

"I'm going to get the first-aid kit out of my car," he said softly. "Just sit here." Of course, she wasn't going anywhere, but he felt so protective toward her, so worried, that he didn't care how foolish he sounded.

The blood was coming from a beaut of a gash on her forehead above her right eye. The deep cut still welled blood, though with gentle but firm pressure, Adam soon had it stopped. "Robin," he kept saying, "can you talk? Can you understand me?"

He did the best he could to clean up the wound; then, holding back her damp hair, he placed a wad of gauze on the cut and taped the edges. It was all he could do for now. "You need stitches," he said. "Robin, please, can you hear me?"

"I can hear you," she said after a frighteningly long time.

He whispered something that could be translated as "thank God" in his native language.

"What?" she mumbled.

"Nothing." Adam smiled and felt tension drain from his body. He was crouched in front of her, knees splayed, his hands on either side of her head. "Do you think you can make it to my car?"

"Oh... sure."

She was not at all steady on her feet, but she was coming around. She even said, "Aren't you supposed to ask me what day of the week it is or something?"

"What day of the week is it, Robin?" He helped her into the passenger seat of the Land Rover.

"It's Monday," she said groggily.

"Try Thursday."

"Okay, Thursday then. And my name's Robin Hayle. I got that right, didn't I?"

Adam closed her door and touched her shoulder with his hand. "You're doing great. Now hold on a minute and I'm going to get your car keys. Okay?"

"Oh, my car..."

"It'll be all right. The tire rim's bent, you've got a flat. The driver's door sticks."

"It always did." Then, when he was finally in the driver's seat, she said, "Where're we going?"

"To Cuba. There's a doctor I know there."

"Cuba? I've never been there."

"Cuba, New Mexico, Robin. It's right up the road."

"Oh." She turned in her seat and grimaced. "Do I really need a doctor?"

"Yes. And that's the last word on it. Don't try me again, lady."

Dr. Ernest Lopez was that rare commodity known as a country doctor. He still made house calls, although he did urge the Mexican and Indian population of Cuba to come into his clinic. Sometimes they did; mostly they didn't.

Adam pulled up in front of his small adobe home. The lights were on in the living room. "Hold on," he told Robin, "and I'll find out if Ernest can see you here or at the clinic."

"Adam," she said, "about how I got off the road back there..."

"We'll talk about it when you're fixed up, okay?"

"Okay, I guess."

Robin was semi-brave as she sat in Dr. Lopez's kitchen and was stitched up. "Oh, I hate this," she complained, squeezing her eyes shut as Ernest injected Novocain around the wound. She put out her hand, groping for Adam's, and he found her fingers and gently held them. "Ouch," she said. "Good thing I have bangs. I'm going to look like the bride of Frankenstein."

"Oh, I don't think you'll look *that* bad," he offered.

Adam forced Dr. Lopez to accept payment for his services. "If you don't, Ernest," he said as they were leaving, "then next time I'll take my business elsewhere."

"And where else would you find a clinic, Adam, around here?"

"Good question."

Soon Robin was seated in the Land Rover, Adam's old blue jean jacket, which he kept in the car, around her shoulders. "My blouse is done for," she said lightly, but he could see her glance down at the blood stains and tremble in reaction.

He turned on the cooled-down vehicle. "I'll buy you a new one."

"But you don't—"

"Yes, I think I do."

Even though he drove slowly, watching the temperature gauge, they were halfway back to Santa Fe before she wanted to talk about the accident. "You know my car's stuck way out there," she began, "and I don't know how I'll get along without it."

"Don't worry about your car," said Adam, "I'll take care of it."

"That maniac." Her hand went gingerly up to her forehead.

Adam wanted to be very careful how he approached the subject; after all, Robin had damn near been killed tonight. "What do you remember?" he asked in a soft voice, and he looked sidelong at her for a moment.

"Not much." She shrugged then held the folds of the jacket together with her fingers. They were shaking. "He followed me, you know. It was no accident."

"Yes, I know."

"Of course you do... He even bumped the back of my car a couple of times."

"Robin, if you'd rather not—"

"It's okay. I'm starting to get mad, actually. Can you believe it? That guy would have killed me! And, Adam, it *was* an old pickup."

He said nothing.

"He kept following and following. So close I couldn't even see his lights in my mirror... And then, oh, hell, he pulled alongside in that old, souped-up truck and forced me into that ditch."

Anger flared within Adam, red-hot and boiling. "He's going to pay," he said between clenched teeth.

He could feel Robin's gaze on him, questioning. "And just how is he going to pay? We don't even know who he is."

"Oh, I'll find out."

"You seem very sure of that."

"I'm calling in Rod Cordova," Adam said firmly. He heard Robin's intake of breath.

"You can't," she protested. "I gave my word to that woman, Adam. I *promised*."

"I understand. But do *you* understand, Robin, someone tried to... to kill you tonight? Do you realize that?"

She only nodded.

"I'm sure your visitor, that Indian lady, would understand."

"I don't know... I really don't."

"Well, I do." He knew his voice had risen and that he was no doubt scaring her. "Look, I'm sorry. I didn't mean to shout. I just know what has to be done. Someone knows every move you're making."

"But how?"

Adam shook his head. "If I knew that... And I have to guess the reason you were attacked tonight is because of that special committee you're on."

"That's crazy."

"I don't think so. Why else would someone still be after you?"

"I don't know."

"The other possibility is that you're being watched every minute of the day. If someone saw your visitor..."

"The Indian lady?" asked Robin.

Adam nodded. "I've got a very bad feeling about her visit. It was unwise, to say the least."

"But she couldn't have known I was being watched."

"Maybe," he said pensively.

"Oh, my gosh!" cried Robin suddenly. "My committee meeting was tonight!"

"I'm sure," said Adam, "they'll understand completely why you missed it. And I think that you're better off out of it now. It's time to hand this over to the police."

"But calling in Rod..." Robin said doubtfully.

"I'm *going* to call Rod. He can locate your John Martinez and maybe come up with some leads."

"And if Martinez won't talk to him?" asked Robin slowly.

"Then I'll talk to him myself."

"Adam, I don't think—"

"The subject's closed." For an instant he regretted his authoritative tone, but then when she fell silent he decided not to relent.

It crossed Adam's mind as he drove to tell Robin about her mysterious Indian woman—Josefina Ortega. To let her know that Josefina would probably call the police if she knew the trouble her visit had caused. But maybe the less Robin knew right now, the better.

"I want you to stay at my folks' for the next few days," he said as the lights of Santa Fe illuminated the horizon.

"It's so inconvenient," she replied. "Not just for me, but for them, too."

"Actually," put in Adam, "I'm not asking. I'm telling." Again, taking command seemed to work. It was amazing, he reflected, how incredibly protective he felt. And over a strange woman, a white eyes, a foreign creature. And yet, how quickly she had gotten under his skin, like sand fleas. Always there, always making him itch.

Maybe, he thought suddenly, as he steered up Canyon Road, she didn't even like him and all these mental acrobatics were for nothing. But no, a man did not mistake those signals that had been running between them since that first day when she'd come from the back of her shop and their eyes had met. And at dinner that night, at Maria's, with the setting sun striking her golden hair and catching in those blue eyes... Yes, it had been there since the beginning, and, damn it all, he'd done nothing whatsoever to stop it.

"I'm afraid we're going to upset your mother," Robin was saying. "It's really late, Adam. This is unfair to them."

"Nonsense. My parents would have a fit if I *didn't* have you stay out here."

"I can't stay forever, you know. I mean, I have my own place and I can't go around like a scared rabbit. I won't go—"

"Robin," he said, pulling up in front of the hacienda, "let's take it as it comes. Tomorrow Rod may be able to get to the bottom of things."

"Do you really believe that?"

He didn't. But he merely said, "Here we are. Wait, I'll come and get your door."

Adam was careful not to awaken his parents, as it was nearly one o'clock. Of course, they were relatively used to his coming and going at odd hours; whenever he was in Santa Fe during the summers, he used his old bedroom at the hacienda. Christina and Ray would find out everything in the morning, anyway.

He led Robin along the dark twisting path to the guest-house complex. She was still not entirely steady on her feet, and Dr. Lopez had suggested strongly that she see her local doctor. Concussions were nothing to fool with, but Robin, Adam surmised, would no doubt ignore his advice.

"I'll turn up the heat," he said as he swung open the door and switched on the lights. "It gets downright cold up here in the beginning of September."

"Thanks," she replied. She plumped herself down on the side of the bed, then looked at her hands and blouse. "I'm a mess. I look like a creature out of a horror movie."

"I better find you something to sleep in," he said. "Maybe you could, um, rinse out your blouse or whatever while I'm gone. Mother's clothes will never fit, I'm sure."

Robin only nodded tiredly, looking like a lost little girl sitting there.

He hesitated at the door. "Will you be all right while I find something for you to put on?"

"I'm fine. Just pooped."

He made his way along the path and quietly entered the main house. His sisters, he knew, had long since moved all their clothing out of their old bedrooms. So what was he going to get for Robin to sleep in?

Adam walked silently down a long, narrow hall and entered his own room. He could give her a shirt to wear, but didn't he have pajamas somewhere—a Christmas present, never worn? Sure he did. In the bottom dresser drawer.

For some reason it was terribly awkward pulling them out of the drawer. He always slept in the buff, but standing there dangling the blue pajamas from his fingers made him feel foolish. Robin could have slept in her underwear or whatever. This was absurd and embarrassing.

Yet he could see her in them. The V at the neck would hang low because she was really very skinny. And the waist would droop down over her lean hips. Inadvertently he wondered how the new, stiff cotton would feel against her soft skin.

"God, man," said Adam, grumbling at himself, "they're only pajamas!"

He knocked on the guest-house door when he returned. But there was no answer. Was she asleep already? He opened the door quietly and heard the sound of running water coming from the bathroom. Crossing the room, he tapped on the door, clearing his throat. "Um, Robin, here's something to wear."

"Oh, thanks," she called and the door opened a crack. Her hand came out. "I'll be right out."

"I, ah, better get going," he said.

"Hold on, I'm almost done."

He sat in an armchair, feeling ridiculous. He ought to get back to the main house and get some sleep. Yet a part of him refused to move, envisioning Robin in those pajamas. What a desperate old lecher he was becoming.

When she came out she was holding her crumpled wet blouse in one hand. "I need a hanger."

He was on his feet in a flash. "Here, there's some in this closet. Go climb into bed," he offered, "I'll get it." Hanger in hand, he took her blouse, shook it out and hung it near the heater to dry. It seemed so small to him, so feminine, so damp and smooth, silky cool to the touch... Robin was pulling up the coverlet when he turned around and, just as he'd imagined, the neckline on his pajamas was far too large, exposing her neck and the faint swell of her breasts.

He took a deep breath.

"Thanks for your pajamas," she said, smiling, looking absolutely beautiful to him.

"They've just been sitting in a drawer," he managed to tell her. "You know, Christmas stuff. I never wear... Oh, well, they're new."

"Oh," she replied and he could see a twinkle of amusement in her tired eyes. She yawned then, and he forced himself to remember the late hour. He had a lot of things to do tomorrow, not the least of which was to contact Rod Cordova. Adam would have loved to have questioned this John Martinez himself, but he didn't trust himself not to murder the man. It was, after all, an Indian whom his student had seen nosing around near the kiva and then driving off in a battered pickup.

"Adam," said Robin, breaking into his dark thoughts, "I wonder..."

"What?"

"I wonder if you would stay here awhile. I mean, just to be here, nothing...nothing else..." Her usually bold glance fell to her hands, which held the coverlet.

He felt himself swallow hard. He shouldn't stay—God, he didn't have it in him to stay and not touch her. But to just leave...

As if an unseen entity, the Apache trickster Coyote, propelled him forward, Adam found himself sitting on the side of her bed and then Robin's golden head was on his shoulder and she let out a contented sort of purr. "Thank you," she whispered.

He had to get out of there. In a minute he'd do something they'd both be very sorry for, and Coyote would yip in laughter.

Somehow he managed, though. And when her deep rhythmic breathing reached his consciousness he rose carefully and turned off the lights. When he sat back down on the bed, he put his feet up and gently rested her head in the crook of his arm, his fingers softly moving through the hair that he had been forbidden to touch for such a long time. Yes, it was like silk, yellow-gold silk.

Several times over the next hour he lowered his head and his lips brushed the hair that his fingers caressed. His senses, in spite of his weariness, were acute. He was aware of the scents filling the room, the rough wool of the Navaho rug, the clean sheets, the powder-scented soap in Robin's laundered blouse. And of Robin herself, a warm, earthy, womanly scent. His eyes, adjusting to the dark, stared out through the parted curtains, and he could see the pinpoints of light in the night sky, the star warriors that guarded the world until Father Sun came out again to rule. The heater groaned quietly, almost in tune to his own breathing, and Robin's chest rose and fell softly.

Regret sat in his stomach heavily. He wished he weren't
so keenly aware of his surroundings or so honest with
himself. It was, of course, the Indian blood that pounded
through his veins. In many ways, his heightened senses
were a curse. He'd prefer to run from himself at moments—like now, as he held this woman to him, all the
while knowing he could never really have her. When this
was over, when the police found the counterfeiters and
Robin Hayle was safe, and she was gone from his life, he
would have his uncle, his mother's brother, the singer, sing
him a cure and set his mind at rest. When this was over.

He closed his eyes for a minute then opened them and
looked down at Robin's peaceful face. She was so brave.
So perfect. And the only thing he could do for her was to
protect her from this terrible situation he had gotten her
into. It seemed too little.

He must have slept then, because when he again opened
his eyes the moon had passed overhead and dawn was a
promise in the eastern sky. And he knew he'd slept, because Robin was in his arms now, her firm breasts pressed
to his own chest, her mouth dangerously close to his.

CHAPTER TWELVE

THE ROOM WAS EMPTY when Robin awoke. She knew that even before she opened her eyes, but there was still the impression Adam had made on the bed and, in the air faintly, his scent, male and erotic.

He'd left silently sometime in the night. She lay in the bed, stretching voluptuously, and remembered the feel of his arms, the warmth of his skin, the hardness and smoothness of his body. She wondered where he was and when he'd knock at the guest-room door to say that breakfast was ready. He'd no longer be closed to her, not after the intimacy of last night—he couldn't be.

Sitting up, Robin felt her head throb; automatically her hand went to her forehead. "Ouch," she said, feeling the sore bump under the bandage.

She climbed out of bed and padded barefoot across the floor to a mirror. The white square of adhesive should have been a sobering reminder of her accident, but somehow she couldn't muster up angry sentiments, not this morning. She felt filled instead with cheer and optimism, as if the sun were always going to shine in a cloudless sky and never, never again was there going to be a drop of rain to spoil a perfect day.

Of course, it was Adam who had done that to her. And how crazy it seemed that it had taken a brutal jolt to awaken him. An accident was nothing to take lightly, but nevertheless Robin was smiling. What a changeable man he was, she thought again. It seemed miraculous that suddenly he'd opened that door to his private world. It was miraculous and glorious, and she felt warm all over—warm, and she knew now, decidedly in love.

Where *was* Adam? Oh, probably sleeping in. They'd both been up late last night. Wonderful Adam. She imagined him asleep—oh, if only she'd seen his room in the hacienda so she could really picture him. His face would be relaxed and young-looking, his body stretched out—those lovely long, muscular thighs and calves. The hard flat stomach, the broad, hairless, coppery chest.

She'd never met anyone like him. He was quiet about his feelings, careful with them, but when he decided what he wanted, he was gentle and caring. He'd be a passionate, considerate lover. They'd talk. Oh, how much they had to say to each other! How much they could learn from each other.

Robin took a shower, careful not to get her bandage wet, and dressed in the same clothes she'd worn yesterday: the full tan skirt, the dry, stained turquoise blouse. But they'd have to do. Looking at herself in the mirror again, she decided the white adhesive was not the least bit becoming, so she tore it off.

Her face two inches from the mirror, she examined the cut. Four neat stitches. Big deal. Experimenting, she discovered that her bangs covered the stitches up nicely. That was much better; she didn't need to look like a wounded veteran. Thank goodness she at least had some makeup in her purse. She *was* looking a little pale—nothing that blush wouldn't remedy.

It was almost nine o'clock. Was Adam still asleep? She'd love to just go on into his room and wake him up. But Christina wouldn't exactly condone that, Robin decided. She was dying to see Adam again, to bask in that loving expression on his face, to hear him say her name. Would he kiss her good morning? Well, maybe, if his folks weren't around...

He was old-fashioned; he'd care what his mother thought. He was overprotective and old-fashioned, but it was only because he'd been alone too long—like Robin—and somebody, something had hurt him once. She'd find out what it was, and she'd love him, adore him so much that she'd cure his hurt and he'd be happy all the time. Whatever happened, however different the worlds they came from, now that she knew he cared, she was going to move heaven and earth to bring them together.

Christina was in the kitchen, reading the arts section of the Santa Fe paper over a cup of coffee.

"Good morning, Robin. Are you feeling all right?"

"Oh, I'm fine. Is Adam—"

"Let me see that cut. Adam told us what happened." Christina stood and pushed Robin's bangs aside, stretching up to look. "Oh, it's not too bad. No one will ever see it." She shook her head. "This is terrible. Adam says you're going to stay here."

"Is he up yet?"

"Oh, he was hours ago. He drove back to Chaco to get your car fixed. He said for you to wait here."

"Oh." He was gone already. She felt absurdly disappointed. "He didn't have to do that."

"He didn't want to wake you. He'll be back this afternoon. Now, don't you worry, just relax and enjoy yourself and eat. You're so thin."

Robin made an effort to smile. Christina was handing her a cup of coffee. "Oh, thanks. As a matter of fact, I'm starving."

"I knew it," said Christina.

There were eggs and refried beans, soft, tasty home-made flour tortillas and strong coffee. "This is great," Robin enthused. "I'd recommend this restaurant to my friends."

Christina laughed. "Ray likes a big breakfast."

"This is all very gracious of you," said Robin, "but I really do have to get back to my shop. It's Friday, and I've got to get to the bank. And Ericka won't be coming in till afternoon."

"Adam said you should wait here until he gets back with your car."

"My car." It struck her then. "But what's he going to do with *his* car if he drives my car back?"

Christina shrugged. "Now, don't you worry. He'll probably get one of his students to drive it. He'll figure something out. He also said he's going to see Rod Cordova and he doesn't want you wandering around alone until he talks to the police."

"It's so crazy," said Robin. "I don't believe any of this is happening." She stared at a rolled tortilla in her hand and shook her head. "Maybe it's a dream. Or maybe it's all a series of strange accidents."

"Adam doesn't think so."

"Well, anyway, I've got to get back to town. There's a man coming in this afternoon for a shoot."

Christina frowned slightly. "My son will be very angry with us if we let you go alone."

"Oh, I feel awful, putting you out like this. I'll call a taxi..."

"You wait until Ray gets back. He'll figure something out." Christina leaned her elbow on the light, clear pine table. "What fantasy does your client have? Can you tell me?"

"Let's see." Robin closed her eyes and thought. "Oh, yes, today's the man who wants to be photographed as a Confederate officer—up on Glorieta Pass. Oh, my goodness, I've got to get his costume!"

Christina clasped her hands. "I love your stories!" she said. "Of course, you have to meet this man. Ray will take you."

"I couldn't ask—"

"Nonsense. Now you get the man's uniform lined up."

What else could Robin do? She phoned the rental agency about the Confederate Army uniform and arranged for a horse, complete with cavalry saddle, to meet her at Glorieta Pass at five. All the time she was aware of Christina, moving around the kitchen, tidying up. Adam's mother. And what, exactly, did Christina think of her—the strange white woman whom her son had to keep rescuing as if he were a knight on a charger?

Ray came in from work and had a roll and coffee. "So, more adventures," he said to Robin. "My son seems to have turned your life upside down."

If only he knew, Robin thought.

Christina told her husband that Robin had to get into town. "She shouldn't go alone. You'll take her, Ray, won't you?" Then she called him a strange, caressing word that Robin guessed was Apache. An endearment. She wanted Adam to say that word to her, to explain its meaning. She'd ask him when he got back.

"I can take her into town."

"She can't be left alone," said Christina.

"Fine, let me get a few things done around here first. Give me an hour or so."

"Mr. Farwalker, wouldn't it be easier to lend me a car?"

"What if something happened?" He shook his head soberly.

"Oh, for goodness sake," said Robin, "I hate being a burden."

"My dear girl, relax and let yourself be a burden, just this one time. Enjoy it," said Christina kindly. "That's what families are for."

Whose family? Robin wondered. *Adam's family?*

"Can I phone Ericka? Just to open the shop until we get there?" asked Robin. "Then I'll relax."

Shelly answered. "You're *where*? And I thought you said he wasn't interested! Naughty girl."

"Shel, his *parents* are being very nice to me. His *father* is driving me in later."

"Oh, I get it. Mom and Dad are there. I won't say another word."

"Listen, tell Chuck I'm real sorry I missed the committee meeting last night. I was out at Chaco Canyon until late."

"Chaco Canyon? What for?"

"Uh, photographs. Yeah, I got some great shots," she lied. "Is Ericka there?"

"Still in bed. You need her at the shop?"

"Well, yes. I can't get in for a while."

"Okay, I'll roust her out and send her over there."

"That'd be great. Tell her she can have the afternoon off."

"Sure, will do. And, hey, you better talk to Chuck about the meeting. He came home raving about Thad Mencimer. Seems there was some sort of argument..."

"Terrific." Robin groaned.

Ray drove her into town in his big, roomy air-conditioned pickup truck. He had the radio tuned into a station from Gallup, New Mexico. The commercials were all in English, but the news was in Navaho, a curious sibilant language to Robin's ear.

"And you can understand Navaho?" she asked.

"Enough," he replied.

"I wonder how many people know there's a Navaho radio station?" Robin mused.

Ray Farwalker took his role seriously. He accompanied her to her apartment, which he insisted on checking out first. At last, she could change her clothes—to something deliberately frivolous, a blue denim jumpsuit with rhinestone snaps down the front. He went with her to the bank, to the rental shop to pick up the officer's uniform, to the grocery store for tea and bread and meat for the sandwiches that Robin fixed for Ericka and Ray and herself for lunch. Adam's father didn't say a whole lot, but he was a comfortable man, quietly competent, and he had a subtle, dry sense of humor.

There were practically no customers all afternoon; Ericka went home, and Robin perched herself on the stool behind the counter to pay the first of the month bills. By four, she was done and went back to see how Ray was doing. He'd gotten through *American Quarterhorse* and *Cattle Breeding* and *Western Rancher*, so they had a cup of tea together.

"I hope you aren't going out of your mind sitting around," said Robin. "You know, you really could go home now. Obviously I'm perfectly safe here."

"I'll wait for Adam. He wants you to stay out at the ranch again tonight, so I can just drive you on out there."

"Your son certainly does like to manage things," she replied, exasperated.

Ray looked at her, his dark eyes giving nothing away but, she knew, judging her according to some inexplicable Apache standards that she could never understand. "And you are a little the same, I think," was all he said.

The bell over her front door tinkled. "Oh," she said, "a customer. Thought I'd never see one today. Excuse me."

It was Adam.

He looked hot and tired and impatient. Her heart went out to him—he'd gone to so much trouble for her. "Adam..." she began, but something in his expression stopped her, some unfathomable anger.

"Is my father here?" he said in a curt tone, dismissing her, making her shrivel up inside. And all she could do was gesture with her head toward the back of the shop.

What had happened? Her mood swung abruptly from cheerfulness to anxiety and all she could think was that she'd said or done something terrible. But what?

In a few moments both men appeared from the back; they had their dark heads bowed and were speaking in Apache. Robin pressed her lips together, refusing to give into paranoia. Finally Adam met her gaze.

"I talked to Rod Cordova this morning," he told her.

Robin sighed. "I still wish you hadn't. I promised that woman and..."

"You promised her," said Adam sharply, "before you were damn near killed."

There wasn't much she could say to that. "So I suppose you told Rod all about John Martinez."

Adam nodded slowly. "I had to. And I *am* sorry about the promise you made to your Indian friend, Robin, but making you swear to keep quiet was...frankly very childish of her."

Robin felt her cheeks flush with irritation; even Ray Farwalker put a hand on his son's arm. "She wasn't being childish," said Robin, "she was just scared."

"Sorry," said Adam, running a hand through his hair, "it's been a long day."

"Okay, I understand. What did Rod say, anyway?"

"He was very upset about your accident last night and when I drove out to Chaco, he went up to San Lucas."

"Did he find John Martinez?" asked Robin anxiously.

"Yes. I just got through talking to Rod again, in fact. It seems he got nothing out of Martinez, though. The Indian said he's never heard of you or the pots or an old woman with butterfly earrings. Rod even checked where Martinez was last night. He was home, according to everyone in the pueblo." Adam made an angry gesture with one hand. "But, of course, they would say that, whether it's true or not."

"You mean, you think John Martinez was out at Chaco Canyon yesterday and . . ."

"He has an old pickup truck."

"But so do most Indians—and a lot of white ranchers, too," put in Ray.

"I know, I know," said Adam. "It was worth checking out. But it didn't amount to anything. Damn."

"Adam," said Robin, "don't you think, now that you're here, your dad can go home?"

Adam raised a hand and tiredly massaged the back of his neck. "There's a small problem. Dad, I need you to drive me back out to Chaco."

"Today?" Robin asked.

"I've got to be out there tomorrow morning. And my car's still there."

"I can do that," said Ray. "Why don't we drop Robin off at the hacienda on the way? And your mother will want us to eat something first."

What a bother she felt, Robin thought. She absolutely couldn't bear the trouble they were going through for her. "Wait a minute," she said, putting her hands on her hips. "This is turning into an awful mess. Adam, *I'll* drive you out to Chaco. It's the least I can do."

"Robin, it's a long drive and your head—"

"My head is fine. Ask your father. I didn't pass out once today."

He watched her for a moment. "I'm not sure it's a good idea."

"Why not? Look, I'll just stay at a motel somewhere near Chaco and drive back here first thing in the morning." She looked from one man to the other. "Hey, I'm a big girl, you know."

Ray seemed noncommittal, but Adam was frowning.

"My car's fixed, isn't it? The only problem is that I have a five o'clock appointment. Could you wait a couple hours?"

A corner of Ray's mouth lifted in amusement. "Son," he said, "there's an old Apache proverb that says when a woman speaks wisely, even Coyote must listen."

"Well," said Robin when Ray was gone, "I have a great idea."

Adam quirked a brow.

"You need a nice, relaxing drink. I'm going to close up here, and we'll go over to La Fonda until my client meets us back here."

"I won't argue with that," Adam replied.

The atmosphere in the Conquistador Lounge was old world, very Santa Fe. The decor consisted of wrought iron, Indian adobe and bunches of bright red dried chili peppers; Anglo service and business acumen provided the rest.

Adam took a long swallow of his frosty margarita and sat back with a faint smile. "Not a bad idea, at that."

"You must be exhausted. Your mother told me you left very early this morning." She was being careful, speaking only of impersonal subjects. The man sitting across from her was not the same one who had held her tenderly last night. She didn't know what had gone wrong, what she'd done, to cause this drastic change in him; she only hoped it was due to his long day.

"Um," he said.

Julien came in just then, accompanied by Madeline Lassiter. They seemed to be looking for a table in the crowded lounge. He saw Robin and waved, then the two of them, an odd couple, made their way over to Robin's table. "*Buenas tardes, amigos.* Robin, you weren't at the meeting last night."

"Uh, no, sorry I couldn't make it."

"There was quite a row," Madeline said, eyeing Adam. "Why, Mr. Farwalker, how nice to see you again. You know, I wanted to ask you about a pot I have, a Hopi polychrome. The dealer I bought it from told me it was sixteenth century, but I have my suspicions it's newer than that."

"The laboratory at the university would be glad to help you, Miss . . ."

"Lassiter. Madeline Lassiter," she answered, beaming at him.

"I'm afraid I just don't have the equipment with me to help you," Adam said sidestepping gracefully.

"Is this the same fight that Chuck told Shelly about?" Robin asked Madeline.

"Oh, boy, it was hot and heavy there for a while. We discussed your plan to organize the Indian artists. Well, Thad—you know Thad—made a disparaging remark about Indians." She shot a glance at Adam. "I apologize for him, Mr. Farwalker. Anyway, Ben Chavez got up in arms. His grandfather was Navaho, you know. It was ugly, I'll tell you. So we left with nothing accomplished."

"Thad, dear boy," put in Julien, "is hasty and misguided, but he's not a bad person."

"Oh, no?" commented Robin.

"He'll come around," replied Julien.

"Don't you think the committee would be better off without Thad?" asked Robin.

"My dear, we can't just kick him out of the group. That wouldn't be fair. We'll convince him."

"I hope so," murmured Madeline, eyeing Adam again. "What did you think of Thad, Mr. Farwalker?"

"I really don't feel qualified to make a judgment, Miss Lassiter," said Adam.

Robin looked from Adam to Madeline and back again. Her head was cocked, her brain working. "You know," she began, "maybe your mother, Adam, could speak to the committee. She'd be such a good liaison . . ."

"You'd have to ask my mother *that* one," remarked Adam dryly. "The Indian community, as I'm sure you know, is very closed. Your idea, like I said at the meeting, is sound, but getting the Indian artisans to organize may not be so easy."

"But it's certainly worth a try, isn't it?" put in Julien.

"Of course it is," replied Adam.

"Well," said Robin, "it can't hurt to ask your mother. The worst she can say is no."

"Splendid idea," Julien was saying. "Well, we'll leave you two. Madeline and I are meeting a dealer here. Enjoy yourselves."

"Good night, Mr. Farwalker, or may I call you Adam?" Madeline said.

"My pleasure," Adam replied, rising and taking her hand.

"Well," said Robin, shaking her head, "I think you have a new fan in the form of Miss Lassiter."

But Adam only finished his drink, pointedly not taking the bait. Yet he was pleasant company, despite his reticence and his weariness, and all the women in the bar noticed him. Robin liked the feeling of being with such a handsome man. She could pretend that they were a couple, that she belonged to him and to Santa Fe, that there was a place for her, a home.

"It's almost five," Adam said.

"Is it? Oh." She finished her margarita. "Back to work, I guess."

"Your head's okay?" he asked.

"Just fine."

Her client was Ted Butler, a shy, bone-thin Texan from Houston with such a strong southern accent Robin had trouble understanding him. He changed into his officer's uniform in her shop and strutted out to show them. "Ah shirley dew look shop," he said, which Robin translated as, "I surely do look sharp."

"You certainly do," she agreed, cocking her head, checking him for authenticity. His breeches were snug, his gray tunic flattering, his tall leather boots elegant. His hat brim was rolled precisely, with the emblem of the Confederacy in front.

Adam drove Robin and Ted the thirteen miles to the spot on the highway marked Glorieta Pass, the site of a Civil War battle. It was a place of broad vistas, rolling hills dotted with stands of evergreens, dry and brown this September day. The horse trailer was already there, and a sullen-looking driver leaned against the fender of the truck smoking a hand-rolled cigarette.

"Could you get the horse out of the trailer, please?" Robin asked the man.

"Not this horse, lady," he said. "She's nuts. I told my boss..."

"Oh, great," said Robin. And as if to punctuate her words, a loud blow came from inside the trailer—a hoof connecting with the wooden tailgate.

"Ah don't know," said Ted doubtfully, his brows arched. "Ah'm no great rider."

"Let me," said Adam, "I've handled a couple horses in my day."

"Oh, could you?" asked Robin.

He backed the horse out easily, seemingly unafraid of the mare's rolling white eyes and quick hoofs. He spoke softly to her in his native language as he led her around. His big hands caressed her sweat-blotched neck and withers until she stood quietly. Robin watched spellbound. *If only he'd touch me with the same love and indulgence,* she thought. *If only he'd talk to me like that.*

"Mr. Butler, you can mount her now. She was just excited," said Adam.

Gingerly Ted Butler mounted the horse. Adam held the reins still, his voice and hands soothing, the mare's ears flicking back and forth, but she stood quietly.

"She'll be fine now," Adam said, moving away.

Robin dragged herself back to reality and set up her tripod. The sun slanted over the hills from the west, making interesting shadows on Ted Butler's rather ordinary face. If she caught him at a certain angle, he looked broader than he was, older and more commanding.

"Put your right hand on the hilt of your sword, Ted. That's it. Sit up real straight. Good."

Robin pushed her hair off her brow and looked through her lens again. "No, Ted, toward me. There. Okay." She waved a hand at him. "Just a little to the left. Good. Now, tuck your chin a bit... Good. Good." *Snap. Snap.* "Okay, that's better." *Snap.* "Now look past my right shoulder. Too high ... Okay. Perfect." In twenty minutes, her voice growing raspy from directing Ted Butler, the shoot was all wrapped up. Robin let out a long breath. Ted Butler wasn't the easiest subject, but she had seen a number of interesting shots through her lens.

"How'd ah do, ma'am?"

"Great, Ted. The proofs will be ready Monday."

Ted was grinning. "And just think," he said, "mah great-grandaddy sat on his horse right there, maybe on that very spot."

They drove Ted back to Robin's shop, stopped by her apartment for a few of her things and were on the road, supplied with a bag of fast-food burgers and milk shakes, by six-thirty.

"You were wonderful with the horse," Robin said, munching on a hamburger as Adam drove.

"It's only experience. The animals know." He glanced over at her, and she couldn't tell whether he meant to be serious or not. "They say Apaches were always good with horses. Maybe it's just in my genes."

For all practical purposes it looked like she was involved with her French fries, but Robin couldn't take her eyes off his hands as they grasped the steering wheel, the same hands that had gentled the mare as if by magic. Apache magic. "What were you saying to the horse?" she finally asked.

"Oh, the usual. Things like take it easy, calm down. But in Apache the words seem to reach the animals better. I can't really translate them."

"I think it's wonderful," she said, "I mean, that you have that kind of power with animals. Will you teach your children how to do that? Is it really difficult?"

He was so completely still that Robin looked over at him, wondering if he'd heard her. His profile was stern, his lips set. He pulled out around a truck, pressing the accelerator of her racy white car to the floor.

"Adam?"

"Um. Sorry, I was concentrating on driving. What did you ask me?"

Robin looked at her hands, closely examining a pearl ring that she'd worn for at least ten years. "Oh, nothing, it wasn't important."

His thigh swelled with muscle under the fabric of his pants as he drove. She watched it surreptitiously, itching to touch the smooth skin beneath the cloth, to feel the male strength of it. She sipped on her milk shake and tried not to stare at him, but it was just too tempting.

Finally Robin stuffed the crumpled-up burger wrappers, straws and napkins into a paper sack and turned to toss the trash into the back seat. She spied a pretty lemon-yellow bag from a downtown Santa Fe clothing shop lying on the seat. "What's this?" she asked, stretching to pick it up.

"Oh," Adam said, glancing over, "I forgot completely. When I got back into town this afternoon with your car, I stopped by this shop my sisters always use..."

But Robin was barely listening. She'd opened the bag and seen a lovely, pure silk blouse in it. A dark, shimmering blue color.

Adam was saying, "I hope you like the color. They didn't have anything in turquoise."

"But... Oh, Adam, you mean you *really* replaced my blouse? I don't believe it!"

"Of course I did," was all he replied, and she couldn't find a single thing to say in return—not one word in her abundant repertoire came to mind.

Robin knew not to make too much of a fuss; Adam would have been embarrassed. Yet she couldn't help fingering the silky material, touching the tiny round covered buttons. He'd gone into a woman's shop and picked this out all by himself. The enormity of the act was staggering. And she noted, as well, that the dark blue color of the silk nearly matched that of her eyes. She wondered . . .

"It's a very thoughtful gift," Robin said finally, putting it back into the bag and dropping the subject. But she still wondered, for a long time, about the color.

They left the foothills of the Jemez range behind as it grew dark. The vast, parched plateau stretched before them; they were heading right into the sunset, into a realm of purple and pink and orange that changed iridescently each second. A single small cloud, its silhouette black, hung unmoving in the sky.

"Beautiful," Robin commented.

"Desert sunsets, they say, are the best."

Silence fell between them, strained, expectant, too difficult to break. Finally Robin said, "I can drive, you know. I had a lot more sleep than you did last night."

"I'm okay."

"If you feel tired . . ."

"Sure."

She crossed her legs, cramped in the little car, her muscles unable to relax with Adam's proximity. "Do you think John Martinez lied to Rod?"

"Yes."

"How is anybody going to find out anything?"

"Sooner or later, either Martinez will have to admit to what he's done, or someone will make a mistake, give himself away."

"What if they don't? I mean, I can't camp on your doorstep the rest of my life."

"No, you can't. Well, if the authorities put enough pressure on the counterfeiters, the ring will either quit or move elsewhere. Your idea for an Indian association is good in that respect, too, because the crooks get pressure from both sides. We'll get them eventually."

The miles sped by; few cars were on the road. The sun sank below the horizon slowly, like a burning ship going down.

At Torreon, Adam pulled into a small gas station and topped up the tank. Robin went to the ladies' room and splashed cold water on her face. She wondered what Adam really thought of her. The constant curiosity nagged at her because she couldn't read him. Yet last night he'd cared; he'd touched her with gentle passion. What had changed between now and then?

When she got back he handed her the keys. "Your turn," he said.

She drove faster than he did, enjoying the power and control. It was pitch-black outside the beam of her headlights; the moon had not yet risen. Adam reclined his seat. "You okay if I catch forty winks?" he asked.

"Fresh as a daisy."

Robin was aware of the moment he slept, the very second his breathing became slow and cadenced. She glanced over at him but could only see shadows, a dark form lit briefly by a lighted sign in a village. She barreled on through the darkness of the ancient land toward an even more ancient rendezvous, the man she wanted for a mate sleeping beside her, their roles reversed. Odd, disconnected images flitted through her mind: the lights of the pickup truck approaching too fast from behind her, John Martinez handing her his pot, Madeline Lassiter batting her eyelashes at Adam, Adam's hands on the nervous horse's damp coat.

Adam woke up as they passed Pueblo Pintado. He rubbed a big hand over his eyes, looking out the window then checked his watch. "You driving or flying low?" he asked.

"Feel better?" she inquired.

"Probably will when I really wake up. You okay? Your head bothering you?"

She touched the cut with a finger. It was still tender. "Gosh, I almost forgot about it."

"I didn't."

It was past ten when they turned at the visitors' center.

"Pull up for a second, Robin," Adam said.

Dutifully she stopped on the shoulder of the road. "You want to drive?"

"No. Listen, Robin." He hesitated, and she knew he wanted to say something difficult. "It's late. There isn't a motel for miles. I don't want you driving off alone."

Her heart began a swift rhythm, knowing a decision was coming, anticipating it, before her brain allowed her the knowledge. "Okay. What do you propose I do?"

He was looking, not at her, but past her at the rising walls of the canyon. "Stay here with me."

She wasn't sure she'd heard right. He'd asked her to stay with him. Was it possible?

He reached out and touched her shoulder. "Stay with me," he repeated softly.

"I . . ." Her heart was pounding so furiously that she thought he must be able to hear it, to feel the glad, frightened beat.

"You realize what I'm asking?" he said with incredible tenderness, his fingers stroking her shoulder, moving up to her neck, her earlobe.

"Yes," she whispered, her throat closing over the word.

CHAPTER THIRTEEN

SHE FOLLOWED HIM along the dark, stony path, her hand in his, her heart beating so hard that it was almost painful. Powerful feelings gripped her, excitement contradicting terror, her whole body quivering with anticipation.

"Do you want to slow down?" he asked, stopping once. "The path is hard to see."

Robin could only shake her head. She was breathless—but not entirely from the walk.

Nothing could have been more foreign to her than following a man along an ancient trail beneath an immense, startlingly clear night sky—knowing where they were headed—longing for it, yet somehow afraid of what was to come.

What am I doing? she asked herself. She was embarking on a journey, a journey she had sought and craved. But Adam, like his fierce ancestors, was strange to her. Did she really know what she'd begun? Shouldn't she have played it safe and waited until she knew him better? The myriad questions flew elusively around in her head, but with each step her commitment became more solid and defined.

"Why don't you camp near the students?" she asked.

She could see his shoulders shrug. "They're young, and they don't want a chaperone."

His camp was big and inviting. There was a tent large enough to stand up in and a canvas lean-to across from it that covered a worktable. Papers, held down by rocks, were scattered on its top and books sat in negligent piles.

Beneath the lean-to was a Coleman stove; a fire pit sat in the center of the area, and nearby were a woodpile and kindling. Adam began to build a fire for warmth.

"Make yourself comfortable," he said as he built a tee-pee of wood in the pit.

Robin glanced around.

"Oh," he said, "there's a canvas stool in the tent, folded up."

"Okay." She pulled back the tent flap and, using a lantern he'd lit, she found the stool. For a moment she stood there, inside the tent, aware of his scent in the place, his own singular scent mingling with earth and canvas and wood smoke. Her skin tingled.

Then she saw the air mattress that he slept on, that *they* would sleep on, and her heart lurched. She came out of the tent quickly, feeling a little dizzy and a little intimidated.

He was crouched on his haunches, feeding a small red flame that coiled up from the fire. He gazed up at her for a moment, his eyes reflecting pinpoints of firelight.

"Don't you get cold here at night?" she asked.

"No."

There was so much of the Indian in this man that she had a hard time at that moment envisioning him at his university, living in an apartment, surrounded by creature comforts. She sat on the stool and put her hands near the fire, rubbing them together. "Do you prefer living outdoors?" she asked.

He gave her a sudden glance. "You're so curious, Robin. I get the feeling at times that I'm a specimen and you're studying me."

She felt her cheeks grow warm. "I *am* interested in you," she said, deciding absolute frankness was the only way to go. "You're a complete enigma to me."

"Because I'm an Indian?"

She looked down at her hands. "Yes," she admitted, "that fascinates me. But you shouldn't take it the wrong way. It's part of you, just like someone's shape or size or personality." She looked up and saw that he was watching her intently. "That's why you're attracted to a person, because of what he or she is, isn't it?"

"I admire your honesty," he said. "I'm afraid I've been taught to know myself but not necessarily to communicate it to others. An Apache trait."

"A person can learn to communicate."

"Yes, if he has a good enough reason."

She let that drop. Adam seemed willing to talk, and she wanted so badly to delve into his soul. "Does my being white make me an enigma to you?" she asked.

He smiled faintly. "No one's asked me *that* before."

"Well, does it?"

"Not really. Sometimes you do things that seem odd to me, but I can always figure out your reasons."

"Like what?"

"Like pursuing this pottery scam," he replied.

"Justice and the good ol' American way, huh?" she asked lightly. Didn't he realize that if it weren't for this pottery scam, they wouldn't be in this camp together? "You know," Robin said, "I really do envy you. I envy you all this." She made a sweeping gesture with her hand. "You're comfortable in what you do. With your family, your job, your *self*." And then she laughed. "Don't I sound well-adjusted?"

"You do to me," he replied, dead serious.

"Anyway," Robin continued, "we poor whites have been searching and searching forever for those qualities that come so naturally to your people. But we've never even come close."

"Most whites don't seem to notice the lack."

"But I do. I always thought that if I belonged to a big family I could find that harmony."

"And can't you belong?"

She shook her head then pushed her hair behind her ears, a pensive gesture. "The only way I can belong is to have a big family of my own."

"You deserve that then," he said, resting his arms on his knees and meeting her steady gaze. The firelight, now blazing, burnished his face and hands. "So you feel that you aren't comfortable with yourself?" he asked.

"Me?" Robin laughed again, too easily. "As much as anybody, I suppose."

He was silent for a minute, his stare pinning her. Slowly he got to his feet and stood there, tall and commanding, his eyes bronze in the eerie glow, his jet-black hair gleaming. Her breath caught in her throat. "I have no business probing into your life, Robin," he said quietly, "it's enough that you're here with me." Without hesitation he moved toward her, reached down and took her hands in his and pulled her to her feet.

She was face to face with him, with the man she'd ached to know for so long now. She felt she could hardly function, her thoughts spinning too madly, her pulse racing wildly out of control.

Gazing down at her, he released her hands, placing his own on either side of her face. "I want you," he whispered as his eyes searched hers. She barely had the presence of mind to nod and follow him into the tent.

He turned down the lamp then faced her. The tent flap was open and the firelight flickered on his face and chest as he unbuttoned his shirt and pulled it off. He stood there, big and powerful, dark shadows dancing on his beautifully coppered skin, his muscles moving as he breathed deeply and silently.

Robin drew in a breath. She felt as if all her senses had suddenly sprung to life. There was no existence other than in this small enclosed place with Adam. Civilization was stripped from her, and she let it fall away as her eyes half closed in expectancy. Her own hands reached up to undo the rhinestone snaps on her jumpsuit.

"I want to do that," came Adam's voice. She let him. His hands seemed to linger on each shining stone, his fingers brushing her flesh, leaving a blazing trail of sensation behind until her body trembled with yearning. Then he was slipping the suit from her shoulders and helping her to step out of it.

"You're very beautiful," he said softly as he unfastened her bra and it, too, joined the mounting pile of clothing.

Goose bumps formed on her skin as the cold night air enfolded her nakedness. It was not at all unpleasant, because she felt so alive, so uninhibited. Perhaps a young Anasazi couple had once stood on this spot near the pueblo and dropped their clothing to the hard earth...

Adam kissed her lips, her eyelids, holding her hair aside, turning her in his arms, kissing her shoulders and the nape of her neck while his hands moved along the curve of her hips and buttocks. He seemed to want to possess her entire body, to memorize each curve and hollow before they would lie down together. Her knees grew weak, so unsteady that she sagged against him and turned to put her arms around his naked back where her fingers began their own quest for knowledge of him.

Adam was all iron-hard muscle and sinew beneath that smooth, hairless skin. He was amazingly warm to the touch, warm and vital as her hands searched him, bringing life to his beautiful flesh. His lips met hers and she moaned gently as his tongue probed her mouth, slowly, luxuriously, as if time itself no longer had meaning.

Still in each other's arms, Adam urged her down until they were both on their knees on the mattress, holding each other, hands exploring more quickly now, more hungrily. Then Robin's head fell back and her spine arched; she clutched his shoulders as his lips found each breast and drew its cool silkiness into his mouth.

She felt a primitive need to join with him. It was primeval but human; her brain registered each touch, each nuance of body language, each breath. Each instant between them was burned into her memory deliciously.

He eased her onto her back and kissed her with exquisite tenderness, such loving, that she felt herself open like a flower. Then slowly, patiently, he filled her, moving on top of her in fluid motion, his body in control, beautifully tuned and in rhythm with her own.

It winged softly through Robin's consciousness that they were made for each other, that no other man or woman could come together this perfectly. But soon she was incapable of thought or reasoning as that place deep in her belly began to burn and seek release.

Adam's mouth moved against hers, lightly brushing it, his lips parted, his breathing shallow and quick. "Oh, Adam," she moaned and he knew she was ready. Her back arched, and her legs strained and together they cried out softly into the night.

For a time they slept. But Robin was restless. The fire outside dimmed and she awakened occasionally in Adam's warm arms inside the goose-down sleeping bag and listened to the crack of an ember or the chatter of a night creature in the canyon.

She wanted to awaken Adam, to tell him so many things, to listen to the sounds together, to watch the fire die out. But he was sleeping so deeply, an arm thrown over her breasts, a leg possessively over her calves.

It was dawn when Robin opened her eyes again. A faint pearl glow lit the land outside the tent and drove the deep night shadows back into their dens. She turned her head and met Adam's gaze.

"Good morning," he said quietly.

"Hi," Robin replied, smiling lazily, drugged with happiness as his arm moved across her chest and his fingers touched the side of her breast.

Their lovemaking was different this morning. It was slow and tender as it had been before, but now there seemed to be a kind of sadness to Adam's passion. He kissed her and loved her and stroked her as before, but in his touch she sensed a holding back, as if he gave all of his flesh but none of his soul.

That notion shot through Robin's head for only a moment, though, and then disappeared as pure sensation gripped her. Then there was only Adam, his superb body poised above hers, his dark eyes capturing her own as he entered her gently.

By the time their morning song had died down, Robin was covered in a fine sheen of perspiration, her thick curling hair clinging to her neck and forehead.

Adam propped himself up on an elbow and smiled. "God, you're beautiful," he said, pushing a damp lock from her eyes. Then he leaned over and kissed her brow.

He was so gentle and kind and loving, she thought, so very special. A joy filled her to bursting. Yet there was that *something*, that remoteness. Oh, she'd tried in dozens of ways to fathom it, but each time without success. It was as if he were trying to tell her something by holding back, almost as if he were issuing a kind of warning. But maybe it was only her imperfect understanding of him.

While she dressed, Adam brought her a pan of water. "It's freezing cold," he told her, "but I thought you might want to ah, wash up or whatever."

She smiled and took the pan and absolutely adored his shyness. He was old-fashioned, a true gentleman, a rare breed. She could spend the rest of her life with him, she dared to think.

To fend off the crisp morning air, Adam had built a fire. He was cooking breakfast, however, on the Coleman stove. She could smell bacon frying.

"They say this stuff's lousy for you," Adam said over his shoulder as he turned the spattering bacon strips.

"Totally rotten," Robin agreed, "but I adore it." She sat near the fire. The logs hissed and popped and warmed her. Over the rim of the mountain the first rays of sun were creeping across the canyon. In a matter of hours, the canyon would be blazing hot, baking beneath that relentless sun. Bitter cold at night, scorching by day. A cruel trick of nature.

"How do you like your eggs?" Adam asked. "Scrambled or scrambled?"

"Oh, scrambled, please." She watched him at the stove. He was wearing a green and black plaid shirt, blue jeans, work boots. His sleeves were rolled up and she couldn't take her gaze off those strongly corded forearms—the same arms that had held her so carefully only a short time ago. Her love was so strong at that instant that it was like fire running before a relentless wind, utterly out of control, unstoppable. She hugged her arms around her waist and smiled secretly.

"We have to talk about tonight," he said as he dished up the breakfast.

"Oh?" Of course, she couldn't stay there forever—Ericka had to take off for Denver, and the shop wouldn't run itself, for Pete's sake. But staying out at his folks', without Adam...

"There's the hacienda," he suggested.

She shook her head as she took the plate from his hands. "I suppose I'll have to ask Shelly. She has a guest room, two of them, in fact."

Adam shot her a grave look as he sat on the ground in front of the fire. "I hate to say this," he began, "but I'm not sure I trust you to stay at your friends'."

"Adam!"

"I'm serious. You take everything so lightly." He continued to study her face. "I'm not sure you remember what happened to you the night before last, Robin."

"Oh, I remember," she answered dryly. "I've got the stitches to remind me. I've learned my lesson."

"I hope so. Someone, somewhere, knows an awful lot about your movements."

"I'll think about it," promised Robin, "and I swear I'll spend the nights at Shelly's until this business is cleared up."

"Even if it takes awhile?"

"No matter how long. I could even get a room at a hotel; it's off-season, cheap, you know." She almost added that she'd gladly make the long, inconvenient drive to Chaco every night, but she deemed it best to take things more slowly.

And there *was* something in Adam's demeanor that morning. It wasn't anything she could quite put her finger on, but it was present nonetheless, just hovering below the surface of his calm expression.

They ate their breakfast in relative silence. Robin felt happy, though, content just to be near him in this marvelous place of his. She was certain he'd never brought anyone else there, too; a woman knew those things.

She wondered if Adam felt the same way about her as she did about him. Did he love her? She knew him well enough to suspect that he'd not had too many flings in his life, so last night must have been as special for him as it had been for her.

Contentment filled her, and so did a new, alien emotion, that of belonging, feeling comfortable, feeling wanted and needed.

"It's a lovely morning," commented Robin. "Not a cloud in the sky."

He finished the last piece of bacon and looked over at her. He seemed to be contemplating something. "What did you say?"

"Oh, just that it's a perfect morning."

"Yes, it is."

For a few minutes Adam straightened the campsite, clearing the stove, setting the dishes in a bucket of soapy water. He restacked the woodpile and hung the sleeping bag to air in the sun. Robin tried to help, but he didn't seem to want her to do anything.

"Leave the dishes to soak," he said when she tried to wash them. "I always do," he added as if to explain his curt tone.

"Well," said Robin, "It's already eight o'clock. I better get a move on."

"Oh," he said.

"And Adam, thanks, thanks for everything." She was picking up her big purse from the ground and then found herself saying, "For last night, too."

He didn't say a thing, not a single word. A faint alarm sounded in Robin's head.

"I'll, ah, walk you back to your car," he finally said.

"You don't have to."

"No problem."

He'd withdrawn from her. It was written in his closed expression; it was in his distant glance and in the set of his stride. She tried not to make too much of it, telling herself that he was preoccupied with his work, that maybe he was thinking about the cave-in at the kiva and trying to decide whether or not to work on it this fall. He couldn't be upset with her. He couldn't be.

Their vehicles were parked alongside each other. Robin stopped by hers and searched her bag for her keys. The sun was warm on her back already, and Adam stood with his hands in his pockets, his face catching the bright light, his expression hidden from her.

"Oh, here they are," she said, holding them up and rattling them.

"You will stay at Shelly's, right?"

"I promise," she replied, unlocking her door, tugging on it when it stuck. But Adam was there to help her, pulling it open. Then, when she was about to climb in, he put a hand on her shoulder, stopping her.

"Listen," he began, "about last night..." His touch was stiff. "Robin, I . . . Look, it was very special to me. And I do want to see you again." He paused for a long moment, his dark eyes reaching out to her, telling her something, something sad and frightening. Her heart began to beat furiously.

"What is it?" she asked softly.

He drew in a long breath. "I hope, Robin, that we can always be . . . well, that we can always be friends."

She stared at him in stupefied confusion for an eternity. *Friends?*

She knew that the blood had drained from her face and that her lips were quivering. "Is that what you call *friendship* Adam? I thought we made love."

His face tightened. "I'm sorry, Robin. I never meant to hurt you."

"Thank you for your good intentions."

"You deserve much better than I can give you. We're too different. It can't work between us."

"Is this some kind of *Apache* revelation?" she asked sarcastically, lashing out at him.

He shook his head. "Only human."

"Well; so that's that. And I liked you, Adam, I really thought . . ."

"Robin, don't . . ."

"Please." She shook her head in disbelief, desperately holding back tears. "I guess I better get going." Shakily she got into the driver's seat and somehow managed to start the engine. *Friends,* he'd said. She felt like laughing hysterically.

"You'll be okay driving alone?" he asked, his tone as strained as hers.

"Oh, sure, perfectly fine." She stepped on the gas, backing out with her tires screeching, then forced the gearshift into first and sped off down the road. In her mirror she could see Adam, still standing there, the dust from her tires settling onto him.

Friends. How could she have been so intolerably stupid?

CHAPTER FOURTEEN

THE WEEKEND DRAGGED BY. Adam classified dozens of pottery shards, relaid some masonry in the collapsed kiva roof and tried to read a new tome on Mimbres pottery discoveries. The physical work permitted him to forget Robin for a few relief-filled moments, but attempting to read turned out to be futile.

On Sunday afternoon, the students headed off for a restaurant meal in Farmington; Adam took a long walk. The clouds built up in the west and came rolling in, cutting off the sun, but this time it did rain. The heavy drops hit the dusty earth and bounced, then more came, and the ground turned damp; unable to drink anymore, it became muddy.

Still Adam walked, his head drawn between his shoulders, hands in pockets, rain dripping into his eyes, trying to realign himself with the earth's harmony, to walk in beauty, as the Apache would say. He was not very successful.

He should have told her.

He'd seen her expression Saturday morning, hurt, bewildered, begging for answers. *Friends,* he'd said. He couldn't blame her for running from him. He couldn't give her what she wanted, not emotionally or in any other way. He was a living lie.

His feet slithered on the muddy path; a trickle of water gurgled down the usually dry streambed of Chaco wash.

Nine hundred years ago this life-giving fluid would have been caught and diverted. It would have kept communities alive. Now it just went to waste, sucked up by the thirsty earth to nurture only snakeweed, mesquite and rabbit brush. A wasteland, as empty and desolate as his life.

Robin had loved him with her whole being, body and soul. Why had he led her on; why had he let himself give in? Because he couldn't help himself, because he was weak and lonely, because he wanted a woman. No, not any woman; he wanted Robin.

Well, it was over and if he had any damn sense, he'd leave it that way.

Monday wasn't much of an improvement. Odd flashes of memory bedeviled him: Robin in his arms, her head bleeding, Robin laughing, her hands touching his back, sending electric shocks through his body, Robin telling one of her funny stories, drolly, with perfect timing.

He had an irresistible urge to drive to the visitors' center and phone her shop. Was she safe? Was she staying with the Daltons? Had Rod come up with anything? But he didn't give in to the urge, because that would mean starting in all over again, hearing her voice, wanting her.

He didn't notice his students regarding him strangely, exchanging questioning looks. It was as if a tight band encircled his head, pulled tighter and tighter each minute.

"Do you think this hole is a ritual one or is it natural?" asked Craig, holding out a curved section of a bowl that had a small hole in it.

Adam looked at the piece, but he saw only Robin's face and her blue eyes, shocked, hurt. "Uh, let's see." He took the shard, felt its sun-warmed surface and recalled the silkiness of her skin. "Ritual hole? I'm not sure."

"The Mimbres people punch holes in their funerary pots, but did the Chaco people?" asked Jack.

"The hole could just be from your pick," Adam said, handing the young man back the piece and turning away.

Monday night he took his sleeping bag and lay out under the moon. He tried to relax, to open his mind to the mighty forces that pervaded the universe. The Apache way might bring him peace of mind, he thought, because, surely, the white man's way was not working.

The moon was nearly full, the silver disk slightly lopsided. The white man called the markings on the moon a face, but to Adam that night the bright globe in the sky was marked, flawed, like himself.

He wished once again he could go to his uncle on the reservation, undergo the ritual sweat bath, take part in a Blessing Way, invoke the spirits and be cleansed, healed. He didn't question the efficacy of the ceremony, nor did he judge it according to the beliefs of the outside world; he only accepted. But the ceremony was long and costly and needed weeks to set up. He would have to wait and bear his pain alone until a Blessing Way could be arranged.

Apaches despised a coward. Was he a coward? he wondered. Or was he merely a man trying to do the best he could under intolerable circumstances? He'd had no choice, either, none whatsoever, when he'd put off Robin that morning. Maybe if she hadn't told him so honestly, so adamantly, how important a family was to her, how she dreamed of one day having a *large* family. Maybe if she'd said she never wanted children—as some women nowadays professed—then he would not have felt the terrible necessity to distance himself from her.

But that hadn't been the case at all, had it?

He stared at the blotched face of the moon and craved the soothing Apache chants, the stamping dances, the fire and drums, the regalia of costume and mask, the intimacy with a world beyond the limited human one.

Could he exist without ever seeing or hearing or touching Robin again? His mind said yes but his heart cried out against the decision. He missed her already, more than he could have imagined. He missed her affection and warmth and the constant delight that emanated from her.

Did he really want to go through life alone?

A tiny dart of hope pricked at him. What if he told her the truth? If she loved him she'd accept him. Lots of couples had no children. As for the family, his sisters had plenty of children between them; one of his nieces or nephews would want Las Jaritas. It could work out.

But inwardly he shuddered at telling Robin of his infirmity. What if she pitied him? Or what if she stayed with him from a misguided sense of duty and resented him forever?

Adam rubbed a hand over his face. No, time would heal them both. It was better this way.

By Tuesday morning his mind had turned on him treacherously. He'd been taking it for granted that she was safe, that she was keeping her promise to stay with her friends. And he'd left the question of the forgeries up to Rod. He'd ignored the fact that Josefina Ortega knew what was going on and that perhaps he, as an old family friend, could coax more information from her.

How easy it had been to remain in the canyon and pretend everything would work itself out. But this passiveness did not suit his character. It was too bad, because by facing up to his responsibility, it would mean seeing Robin again. He'd have to pretend they were merely acquaintances, turn his feelings off, somehow see this business to its conclusion without causing either of them more pain.

He drove to the visitors' center and reentered the world of the living by phoning Rod Cordova. And as he'd suspected, Rod had come to a standstill with his investigation. "Sorry, Adam, but I came to a dead end with your pal, Martinez. I'll keep the file open, but it's going to be damn difficult even proving there's a counterfeit ring."

"Okay," Adam replied, but there was one more thing he was going to try, and he wasn't going to mention it to Cordova. "I'll be in touch," was all he said.

His next call was to his mother. When he told her to telephone Josefina and explain about the danger Robin had been put in, his mother hesitated. "Look," said Adam, "you're the one who told Josefina about the forgeries in the first place. Just call her and ask her to be cooperative when I get there. She trusts you."

Christina was uncertain, admitting to her son that her friend Josefina was scared of her own shadow, but eventually, reluctantly, she agreed. "You'll be careful though, won't you?" she asked.

And now there remained the question of Robin. She was the real key to Josefina's cooperation. Leaving the visitors' center, he looked up into the sun, closed his eyes for a moment and steeled himself.

ERICKA DALTON SAT ON THE STOOL behind the counter of Robin's Nest. She looked up at the tinkling of the bell and smiled. "Oh, hello, Mr. Farwalker."

"Is Robin in?"

"She's in back, doing a portrait." Ericka rolled her eyes, then whispered, "The lady is dressed up like Marie Antoinette. And she's got her two poodles with her. *French* poodles, get it? I think Robin's going to throttle those dogs."

From the back room came a sharp yipping and a lady's admonishing voice. Ericka giggled.

Adam glanced at his watch. "She'll be awhile then?"

"Another half an hour, at least."

He told her he'd be back then walked down the street and grabbed a bite to eat. The time passed in a strange jerky fashion; seconds dragged endlessly but minutes flew. He strode back into Robin's Nest before a half hour was up.

Robin was standing talking to a lady in full eighteenth-century costume: billowing satin skirt, low bodice, powdered wig. Two white poodles frisked, nipping and yapping, around their feet.

"So, I can see the proofs on Thursday?" the lady was saying.

"Yes, stop by at around eleven," said Robin, but her voice caught when she saw Adam standing in the doorway. She looked shocked for an instant then seemed to recover. "You can change in the back room, Mrs. Downing," she told the woman.

Robin was pointedly ignoring him. She had every right to. "Ericka," he heard her say, "why don't you go and get lunch now." The young woman glanced from Adam to Robin and back then quietly picked up her purse and disappeared.

With Ericka gone and Mrs. Downing in the back, the shop was suddenly, utterly quiet. Adam crawled with discomfort. "Robin," he began as she headed around behind her counter and started to sort through some papers. He tried again. "Look, I've got to talk to you."

This time her head came up.

"It's about the Pueblo Indian woman who paid you that visit. I'm afraid I've been keeping a few things from you . . ."

Robin listened silently, with an impartial expression. When he was done, she finally said, "I see." She pushed her hair off her shoulders in a familiar gesture. "Why didn't you tell me this before?"

"I wanted to keep you out of it, I guess. But now I have to ask you to help again."

"Well, I don't really see what I can do," she said, still standing behind the counter as if for protection.

"I'm going to see Josefina this afternoon. I'd like you to be there. If you tell her what happened to you, I'm sure she'll decide to cooperate. I'm hoping she'll take us to John Martinez."

"Why should she want to help us all of a sudden?"

"I asked my mother to call her, to persuade her."

She stared beyond him, held by her thoughts. He knew she was reluctant to go with him; he didn't blame her. He was stupid to have come.

Finally she spoke. "All right, I'll go with you. Just this afternoon, you said? I've got to get back by seven. Shelly and Chuck are having a dinner party."

"Good. I really appreciate your help." He hated himself for mouthing the meaningless words. "Why don't I come back for you at two?"

She looked relieved, probably glad to escape his company until she had to endure it. "That'll be fine," she said.

Marie Antoinette, now dressed as an ordinary twentieth-century lady, came out of the back with her nervous poodles. "See you Thursday," she said, "and I can't wait! Are you sure they'll be ready? Now, did you say Thursday morning or afternoon?"

At two, Adam pulled up to the front of the shop. Robin was already outside, waiting for him, a tall, graceful figure in a slim beige skirt that buttoned down the front and a stylish emerald-green knit top with shoulder pads. She struck him the same way every time he saw her—she was beautiful, full of life and love.

"I forgot to ask where we were going," Robin said, settling into the passenger seat.

"San Claro Pueblo," replied Adam. "Josefina lives there."

"Why didn't she go to you? After all, she doesn't even know me."

"She didn't come to me or my mother for the simple reason she wanted to remain anonymous. It's the Indian way not to get involved."

"She was so sweet. Did you think she'll be upset when we arrive out of the blue like this?"

"I hope my mother already phoned her."

"Um," was all Robin said before quietly turning her attention out the window. The tension in the car pressed on Adam heavily. It seemed that a hundred questions lay buried below the surface of the silence, like lava in a volcano, ready to erupt. It was on the tip of Adam's tongue to tell her everything, to relieve the agony, but what good would that do now? He couldn't change the facts of life.

He glanced over at her. She was still sitting there, stiff and removed—utterly without her usual exuberance. Yet there was no point in kidding himself. He wanted her as much now as he had that night in Chaco. It was almost unbearable to sit so near, to smell her scent, to know what secrets lay beneath her clothing, the velvety softness, the curves and hollows and taste of her. And he couldn't have them, not again. Not unless he was willing to tell her everything, and then he'd lose her anyway.

He switched his eyes back to the road and this time kept them there.

San Claro was one of the oldest continually inhabited pueblos in New Mexico. It sat nestled in a fertile valley between low, rounded hills. Tall cottonwoods shaded the old Spanish chapel in the plaza, and the houses were more scattered than in San Lucas or many of the other pueblos.

They found Josefina firing pots outside her studio. Her son was assisting her, building up the pile of sheep dung over the pots so that it would burn evenly, smothering the fire with ash to make the pots turn the lustrous black for which Josefina was so famous.

Adam helped Robin out of the Land Rover and approached the smoking fire. Josefina saw him and stopped her work, holding her rake still, staring from his face to Robin's, uncertain.

"Josefina," said Adam carefully. "I see we've come on a busy day. Do you have a moment to talk to us?"

"Your mother called me," she said, almost in a whisper. "I promised her I would help you."

"You know Robin Hayle."

Robin smiled, stepped forward and took Josefina's hand. "It's good to see you again. I'm so glad to know your name," she said with genuine warmth.

Josefina led them inside her studio. Although it had been several years since Adam had visited Josefina in San Claro, he smiled to see that nothing had changed. The big room held forty years of clutter from her craft: clay and unfired pots, brushes and paints, bundles of plants from which the paints came, tools, drawings, specially curved stones that were used to polish her work. And rows of exquisite finished pieces of all sizes and shapes, some in colors, but most the lustrous black-on-black style that had brought Josefina international acclaim.

"Oh!" breathed Robin, stopping on the threshold. "They're beautiful!"

"You like my work?" asked Josefina, obviously enjoying Robin's appreciation.

Robin went to a long table that was filled with pots, each one different, each one gleaming like a black jewel. She touched one with her fingers, stroked it. "Incredible," she was saying. "I've seen some like these in the galleries, but I had no idea you made them. I always wanted one, but they're far too expensive for me. How wonderful that you can create them."

"It has taken me a lifetime," said Josefina modestly. "But come, we can sit down and talk."

Adam could see that Robin had to pull herself away from the studio to follow Josefina's brightly clad form through a door into her immaculate house.

"So," Josefina began, putting a coffee pot on the stove, "Christina tells me that you are going to solve this crime of the false pots and that I am going to help you. But first, I want to apologize to Miss Hayle for not telling her who I was. I was only trying to help, but it didn't work out the way I thought it would."

Robin leaned forward, her elbows on the kitchen table. "Have you spoken to John Martinez since I saw you?"

The woman shook her head. "No. I left a message for him as he has no phone, but he has not replied."

Adam was relieved that Josefina didn't know that Rod Cordova had questioned Martinez; he knew she wouldn't like that at all. He felt vaguely guilty about using the harmless woman this way, but he had to find out more about John Martinez. "Josefina, we would like very much to talk to John. I'm sure he can tell us more than you know. He can help us nab these people that ordered the pots." *That is,* Adam thought, *if John himself isn't the guilty party.*

"I want to help. But I know so little. Perhaps I can convince John to see you. Perhaps not." Josefina brought a tray of coffee cups to the table. She looked tired and sad.

Adam felt another small twinge of guilt but suppressed it. "Josefina, let me tell you what happened to Robin last Thursday night, and then you decide if it's worth persuading Martinez to talk to us." He told Josefina about the kiva caving in, the suspicious Indian and the pickup truck that had pushed Robin off the road. He saw Josefina's face grow paler, her eyes wider.

The woman finally sank into a chair, visibly shaken. Adam took one of her work-worn hands in his. "The forgeries must be stopped. So that Robin is safe, but also because they'll ruin the reputation of all Indian potters."

"Like you, Josefina," Robin said softly. "What if someone copied *your* pots?"

"Oh," said Josefina, near tears. "What am I to do?"

"Take us to see Martinez. If you tell him we can be trusted, he'll talk to us, won't he?" said Adam.

"I don't know."

"We can try," put in Robin. "Isn't it worth trying?"

Josefina nodded, her hands clasped tightly in her lap, and Adam knew they'd won the first round.

Her son, Manuel, was left to watch the pots that were being fired. Nervously Josefina climbed into the back seat of Adam's Land Rover, and they began the short drive to San Lucas.

Robin turned around to say something to the older woman and Adam was uncomfortably aware of the way her skirt split and showed her long, lean brown legs. He stared straight ahead, following the winding road, half listening to the women talk.

"You're doing the right thing, really," Robin was saying. "Don't worry."

"John will be angry when he sees I have brought two strangers."

"But I'm not really a stranger," she explained gently. "I met him when I took those photographs. Remember? Now, don't worry, everything will be fine."

Then Robin started asking questions. Curious Robin, Adam thought, always wanting to know everything about everybody.

"So your whole family helps you?" she asked. "Those beautiful patterns, your daughter does them? Oh, she's *so* talented. I'd give anything to be able to do something like that!"

"I learned from my aunt," said Josefina, "but the black-on-black I learned myself. A professor digging up old pottery years ago found some black shards and came to me wanting to know how to recreate the black color."

"How did you do it?"

"Oh, I tried many ways. I found it was the kind of dung I burned and it was also the smothering of the fire with ash. I had many failures at first. And then, you have to rub the unfired pot with a special stone so many times, over and over." And Josefina made rubbing motions with her hands.

"Oh, I'd love to see how you do it," Robin enthused.

"I would be happy to show you."

"You know," Robin said, "you'd be the perfect person to organize the Indian potters. If you formed an organization, then all the members could be warned about people like the ones who had John making pots for them. You know what I mean? And if the police needed to be called in, your organization could do it, and you wouldn't have to go as individuals."

"An organization?" Josefina said doubtfully.

"Yes, it could work. All the pueblos could join. Like our association in Santa Fe. You'd be able to protect yourselves."

"I don't know..."

"It would be a great thing. Oh, Josefina, don't you see?"

"I wouldn't know where to start."

"I'll help you," said Robin enthusiastically.

"It's a good idea, Josefina," put in Adam. "The time is coming when the Indians are going to have to do it."

"I cannot think of such things. I am only one woman, a simple potter. I wouldn't know what to do. I don't think I could do anything like that," said Josefina.

"But you're so well-known. You're famous. Everyone would listen to you," pressed Robin.

"Oh, I don't think so."

Robin gave up then, wisely, Adam thought. Josefina needed time to get used to the idea.

Robin was wonderful with the older woman, warm and friendly, drawing her into conversation. There was so much love in Robin, and it showed in so many ways. But to Adam she was very stiff, very polite, very careful. It was best that way, he told himself. It was the only way. But it hurt.

At Pueblo San Lucas, Josefina directed them to Martinez's house. Parked in front was an old, rusty pickup truck with dented fenders. A pickup, reflected Adam, like the one that pushed Robin's car off the road. But how ridiculous to think that this could be the same one; there were probably twenty more just like it in San Lucas alone. Yet he saw Robin staring at the truck, too.

Josefina knocked on Martinez's door while Adam and Robin waited in the car. They didn't want to scare him off. This was going to be a ticklish situation as it was. It was possible, after all, that Martinez was guilty, despite what Josefina believed.

"Yes, that's him," Robin said excitedly when a man opened the door.

It took Josefina several minutes to calm John Martinez down. He kept glaring at Adam and Robin in the Land Rover and shaking his head and arguing. Then Josefina walked back to the car, looking very upset again. "He will see you, but he is angry, like I said he would be. I don't think he will tell you very much." She looked down at her feet. "I'm very sorry."

"You've done your best," said Adam. "Let's see what John has to say."

The adobe house was small and neat. John's wife grinned and nodded and served them all coffee, but she spoke only Tewa with Josefina and her husband. Then she left them alone, with a tortoiseshell cat curled up by the corner fireplace for company.

John was sinewy, about forty-five, Adam guessed. He was of medium height, with a weathered face and large-knuckled fingers, and there was clay still under his finger-nails. He smoked unfiltered cigarettes incessantly, obviously anxious. He spoke to Josefina in Tewa, an angry tirade, Adam suspected.

"He says," Josefina translated, "that the men he made pots for heard about people looking for him and threatened him. He can tell us nothing."

"Threatened him!" said Robin.

"Explain to him he can do more good by telling us who these men are. He won't have to go to the police. We'll take them the information," said Adam.

Josefina spoke to Martinez at length. Adam could see the man's eyes darting from face to face, belligerent, uncertain, afraid.

When Josefina stopped talking, Martinez said something short and harsh.

"Tell him," Robin said, putting her hand on Josefina's arm, "what happened to me." And she lifted her bangs to show the cut on her forehead, while Josefina told the story in Tewa.

Martinez appeared shaken. He stared at Robin, and Josefina patted his hand, speaking quietly and persuasively. Adam felt hopeful; maybe it had been a good idea to bring Robin along after all.

There was a long silence when Josefina finished. It was so quiet that Adam could hear the big cat purring in its corner. John Martinez finally turned to Adam and, in accented English, said, "When a woman is hurt I am at fault, too. I will tell you."

"Oh, thank you, Mr. Martinez," said Robin.

"I want you to know that I made those pots because a man who said he was from a museum came to me." Martinez inhaled deeply on his cigarette. "He wanted me to copy some pots in pictures he showed me. This was to learn how the pots were made in the past. I believed him, and I enjoyed the . . . how do you say?" He spoke a word to Josefina.

"Challenge," she answered.

"Yes, I enjoyed the challenge. Even to making the fireclouds appear in the right spots. I do not make much money from these pots."

Adam listened silently, not wanting to disturb the man's narrative. He was terribly aware of Robin sitting next to him on the plastic kitchen chair, her face full of concern. She felt sorry for John Martinez; she believed him. But could this seemingly innocuous Indian potter have tried to kill Robin? Was he lying?

"Two men come every month to pick up the pots. I do not know them."

"The same men?" Adam asked.

"Yes, but they wear hats and I think false...." He said a word to Josefina again, "Yes, mustaches. They leave me money. That is all."

"How do you get hold of them?" asked Robin. "I mean, if you need to."

Martinez stubbed out his cigarette. "I am given a number. But I have to leave a message. It is one of those machines."

"An answering machine," said Adam.

"But I only called it once because I have no phone. I must use the one in the plaza."

"Do you have the number?" asked Adam cautiously.

After a moment's hesitation, John thrust his hand in his pocket, came up with a wallet and pulled out several scraps of paper. "Yes, this is it."

Robin had already gotten a pencil and piece of paper out of her shoulder bag. She wrote the number down, checking it twice.

"You will not say who gave you the number?" asked Martinez anxiously.

"Not unless you want us to," Adam replied. "And I think it would be best if you go on making your pots, for now, anyway. Just in case, you understand. You *are* our only link to these counterfeiters."

"And they'll have to get in touch eventually, won't they?" asked Robin. "To pick up your pots."

John sat there with his eyes still shifting cautiously from face to face.

"Can you tell us anything more, anything at all?" Adam's voice was quiet, in control, gently urging.

"Please," coaxed Robin, and Josefina nodded at the Indian man.

Martinez sighed deeply. "They come every month in a different car," he began. "But one I remember more than the others. It was a van, very pretty. It was green and silver with a painting on its side, a picture of the desert." Wistfully he said, "I would like a van like that."

But Robin was rising from her chair, her eyes wide. "My God," she said in a horrified whisper, "I know that van!"

CHAPTER FIFTEEN

ROBIN FOLDED HER ARMS across her chest tightly and compressed her lips. She turned her head and stared out the window of the Land Rover.

"Listen," Adam said, "I didn't mean to knock your friends. Maybe they are good people. But I think you're going to have to face the facts. Martinez told us about this state-of-the-art green van and the Daltons have just that van."

"Then Martinez is lying," she shot back. "He's just trying to pin this whole thing on somebody else."

"You don't know that."

"I know Shelly and Chuck are honest. I'm not that bad a judge of character. I mean, heck, they've got two grown sons, both college graduates. They've got grandchildren, for Pete's sake."

"And that makes them innocent?"

God, he was making her mad! First he gave her that friend business up at the canyon, and now he was trying to convince her that the Daltons were heading a counterfeiting ring. Well, she wasn't buying it.

"Robin," he said, "listen to me a minute, will you? I'm not trying to start an argument—"

"I'd say we *are* arguing."

"Come on. Face it. There's no other van around like theirs. It's custom made. I've even seen it myself, that

night at your committee meeting when Chuck Dalton
drove off."

"So what? That only means that everyone's seen the van
around, including John Martinez. I say he's lying. I say
he's the one who ran me off the road." She crossed her
legs, feeling as if she were going to break in two. "And
what's more, Martinez is an Indian and your own students saw an Indian near that kiva. *And* he owns an old
pickup truck."

Adam let out a long sigh. "I know all that. I think we
ought to give Cordova a call and let him do some questioning—"

"Of the Daltons? I absolutely won't let you do that.
Adam," she said, turning toward him quickly, *"please.*
You just can't implicate them. It's too horrible. I abso-
lutely won't let you do this."

"He'd only question them." His voice had finally lowered. "I'm sure they'd understand."

"Understand what? That I've named them as suspects
who tried to kill me? I can't. They're my friends, Adam.
They're very special to me. My God, Ericka is practically
my protégée." She put her face in her hands for a moment
and then took a deep lungful of air, looking back at Adam.
"I only know one thing," she said, "someone tried to kill
me and no matter what else you want to believe of the
Daltons, it wasn't them. Neither Shelly nor Chuck would
be capable of it."

Adam was quiet for a long time. As they drove through
the outskirts of Santa Fe, she could see a frown creasing his
forehead. Did he believe her?

Whether or not he trusted her judgment, Robin knew
that she couldn't let him go to the police, not with what
little they had, and certainly not on Martinez's word. She
sat in silence, uncomfortable and nervous, knowing that

she had to go lock up the shop and face Ericka. But even more awful, she had to stay at the Dalton's, and they were even giving that dinner party...

And then there was Adam. Enigmatic Adam Far-walker. Her *friend*. What a joke! Maybe she *was* a bad judge of character, after all. She'd sure gotten him all wrong. And worse, ironically, pathetically, she still wanted him. Would it always be there, every time she bumped into him, that need to be held in his arms? She felt sick and afraid, as if she were in a tailspin with no hope of pulling out.

He stopped in front of the shop. It was nearly six o'clock. She had only a few minutes left to convince him not to go to Rod, not yet. She thought frantically, and then remembered. "The number," said Robin, almost desperately. "The phone number John Martinez gave us! We've got to try it, Adam. Maybe the phone company could give us an address."

He turned off the engine and nodded. "Okay," he agreed. "But I doubt we'll get a thing. The minute we started asking questions up at San Lucas last week, I'm sure the counterfeiters began to cover their tracks."

"You mean the number will be disconnected?" Robin was disappointed.

"Probably. And the address will turn out to be under a false name anyway."

"You're giving them an awful lot of credit."

"And I'm beginning to wonder," said Adam, "if they won't change the way they pick up the pots. They'll want to be really careful now. Unless the money's too good to pass up. Or unless they feel that they've scared us off."

Robin was quiet, thinking. If those men came this month to collect Martinez's forgeries... "Adam," she said, "*we* could be there. You know, when the men come

for the pots. We could watch John's place and see if anyone shows."

He looked at her for a long time before he answered.
"It's too dangerous."

"But it doesn't have to be. Not if we're just watching.
When we see who shows up—or *if* anyone shows up—we
call Rod. At least that way we'll be sure who the real crim-
inals are."

"Robin . . ."

"Look, it's the only way we'll ever know if Martinez is
telling us the truth."

"It would be a lot safer if the police were waiting," said
Adam.

"Oh, sure," she put in quickly, "except for one thing.
We can't tell Rod the story and keep the Daltons out of it.
And if we *did* tell him, and didn't mention the van, then
we'd be lying. We can't do that, Adam, don't you see?"

He was studying her face, obviously skeptical.

"What harm would be done if we hid and watched
Martinez's house? All we have to do is see if there really is
a pickup and if so, we get a license-plate number. We go
straight to Rod with it. It's foolproof."

"We'd need to know exactly when the pickup will happen."

"That's the only problem. John might not want to tell
us. And if he's the one behind the black-market pots, he
won't tell us. But if he's innocent . . ."

"Josefina might convince him to help us," suggested
Adam.

"Would she?"

"She likes you, Robin. She might do it on that basis
alone." He thought for a minute. "I'll talk to her. If she
can get that information from John she could let you
know."

"If," said Robin.

"I can try." Adam hesitated then asked, "And if it turns out to be the Daltons? Could you turn them in, Robin?"

It was a long time before she replied. "I could do it then, Adam, if I had to, if there was proof. But not now. Promise me you won't call Rod until we at least try this."

"I don't know. I suppose I could be at Martinez's myself..."

"No. I'm going, too."

Adam gave her a half smile then shook his head. "I guess we'll be debating that one again," he said, relenting for the time being.

"Okay," she answered, feeling much better. "Should we go let Ericka off and try that number?"

As Adam suspected, the number had been disconnected. He tried the telephone company but got nowhere as the number had been unlisted in the first place. Short of obtaining a court order, there was no way they were going to get an address.

"Darn," said Robin, "you were absolutely right, these crooks are sharp."

They were standing together in her office, their shoulders nearly touching. Deliberately she stepped back from him. "Well," she said, hesitant, "there's that dinner party..."

"Come on," he said quietly, "I'll drop you at the Daltons'."

Robin had to direct him. Their house was only a few miles southwest of the city, built into the side of a dry, red clay hill in an exclusive country-club suburb. Like all the homes on the private circle, the Daltons' was a one-story sprawling adobe structure with natural gardens of cacti and wildflowers behind its low wall. It was a showplace.

"Quite a house," commented Adam and Robin knew just what he was thinking: it took a lot of money to own a home like this. She hoped to God he didn't notice the swimming pool.

To make matters worse, Chuck was in the driveway, getting something out of the van—the custom-made green van with the desert scene painted on its side. Robin felt a surge of nausea as they pulled up alongside and stopped. "They have a very successful gallery," she whispered, realizing how ridiculous she sounded and how nervous she was bound to be around the Daltons.

"I'm sure," replied Adam laconically.

"Hi, there," Chuck was saying, poking his head into Robin's window. "Come on in, everyone's about to arrive. Good to see you again, Adam; I hope you can stay."

"I really..."

"Now, come on, Adam. Shelly's a great cook. At least have a cocktail and some of her pooh-poohs, or whatever she calls the stuff." He nodded as a car pulled in behind Adam. "There. Now you have to stay."

Robin had known that it was bound to be awkward staying with her friends. But she wasn't prepared for the doubts that plagued her mind. She kept remembering how shocked she'd been when Martinez had told them about the van, and the things that had flowed through her head.

How much money did the gallery bring in? Enough, really, for all this, and to send two sons and now a daughter through expensive, out-of-state colleges?

Shelly was dashing around, putting out plates and bowls of hors d'oeuvres, directing her maid. *Her maid,* thought Robin as she gave Adam a surreptitious glance to see if he was noticing.

"Oh, hi!" called Shelly from the sunny patio. "Come on out and fix yourself a drink. If you wait for Chuck, you'll die of thirst."

"Hi, Shelly," said Robin. "Everything looks delicious." She felt her heart sinking. She'd never be able to pull off this farce of friendship. Why had she let that business about the van get to her?

Adam crossed to the far side of the pool and fixed them both gin and tonics. Other guests were arriving, about a dozen or so of them. Julien appeared, and on his arm was none other than Madeline Lassiter. There were other familiar faces, a few acquaintances. Ericka's boyfriend was there, as well. Robin looked long and hard at the handsome young couple who stood by themselves, chattering away, totally engrossed in each other. What if Chuck were involved in this ring? What would become of his beautiful daughter if her father went to prison?

"Are you all right?" asked Adam as he handed her a tall, frosty glass.

"I can't do it, Adam, I just can't," said Robin.

"Do what?"

"Stay here."

"Then you'll have to stay out at my folks'. You can't go back to your place alone. Not until everything's cleared up."

"Great," she said. "But I can't stay with your parents. It's just too inconvenient for everyone concerned."

"Robin . . ."

"Seriously. I'll get a room in town."

"What will you tell the Daltons?"

Why should he care? she thought. "I don't know. Something. Anything. This is just too ghastly, having to face them like this."

Adam was studying her face. His expression mirrored hers; both were grim. "Do you want me to drive you into town?" he asked solemnly. She looked him in the eye. Why was he bothering? Was it his sense of duty, or did he still feel something toward her—something more than friendship? What had gone wrong? Maybe nothing at all; maybe he simply had had his fling and it was enough. At that moment she hated him.

"Do you want me to drive you?" he asked again.

Robin shook her head. "I'll get a ride later, with Julien or someone."

"Are you sure?"

"I'm positive," she said in a steady voice.

Adam did hang around for a few more minutes. He was obviously as ill-at-ease as she was, but Robin didn't know if it was because of her or the Daltons. And she couldn't ask.

"I simply love that sweater of yours," Madeline said in Robin's ear. "Where did you get it?"

"A catalog, I think," she replied distractedly. "I don't recall . . ."

"Doesn't Robin always look wonderful?" Julien put in as he approached, dipped his dark head to her fingers and shook Adam's hand. "It is so good to see you up and around," he said to Robin. "What a terrible, terrible accident you had."

"But how—" began Robin.

"Oh, my," Julien was quick to say, "my brother made a point of phoning me. Everyone has heard by now, of course, that your car was run off the highway. I've had nothing but calls from the association members. We were all very worried."

"That's right," agreed Madeline, staring at Robin's forehead where the stitches just showed beneath her bangs.

"And I'm betting it was no accident, either. It's got to be connected to those forgeries, doesn't it? I mean, things like that don't just happen."

"Well, we think..." began Robin.

"It's difficult to say," Adam interrupted smoothly. It was apparent that he didn't want to discuss what they knew.

Why? wondered Robin. Hadn't he said a dozen times that it was another warning to her? He'd told Rod Cordova that, so why minimize it now?

"It's a dreadful business." Julien's pale brow furrowed. "And Chuck tells me that you are staying with them for safety's sake. I am so glad."

"It's a smart thing to do," agreed Madeline.

Then Shelly joined them, carrying a silver tray of deviled eggs. "Hi," she said, "has everyone got a drink yet?"

The group talked at length about Robin's situation, and Julien promised to speak to his brother. "Rod must be made to understand the danger to our Robin here. I don't care if he *doesn't* have any leads, Robin should have twenty-four-hours-a-day protection."

"Absolutely," said Madeline, flashing Adam a smile. "That's what we pay the police for, isn't it?"

"Well, I think," interjected Shelly, "that Robin's perfectly fine right here with us." And it struck Robin then: could Shelly have an ulterior motive for wanting her to stay here? Was it to watch her activities?

Oh, Lord, she thought in shame, here she was believing the Daltons were guilty! The seed of doubt had been planted and no matter how hard she tried she couldn't escape her doubts.

"I, for one, don't think Robin looks very well at all," Madeline pointed out. "Why, you're so drawn. It's the strain. I know, when I had that bad season two summers

ago at my shop, well, let me tell you, I had one sickness
after the other. It's stress, Robin, and if I were you, I'd
drop this whole business about forgeries.''

Adam shifted his weight and took a sip of his drink.
"She *is* dropping it," he said. "In fact, both of us are. It's
up to the police now.''

"I'm so glad," Julien said, "for Robin's sake, of course.
I think in our special committee we'll come up with a solution to this problem. And we must band together. Like
an army, yes?''

"Exactly," said Madeline firmly, flashing Adam a winning smile.

It was at least another ten minutes before Robin and
Adam were alone again. She was sick to death of this
whole mess and only wished it could be erased, like chalk
from a blackboard. "Sorry about cutting you off earlier," Adam was telling her. "I just think we better keep
this Martinez business to ourselves. The fewer who know,
the more chance we'll have to get a look at the men who
pick up his pottery.''

"I see," Robin answered without enthusiasm.

"Of course," Adam put in carefully, "we can always
call Rod. This has been a nightmare for you." He sounded
so concerned. But why not, she thought dismally, they
were good friends, weren't they?

"I want to go through with it," said Robin. "I want to
prove to you it's not Chuck and Shelly.''

"All right.''

"And I want to be there, Adam, I don't want to be left
behind. Promise?''

"We'll see," was all he'd commit himself to. "Look,"
he added, "I've got to get going. And I'd like to take you
to a hotel if you're bent on leaving here.''

"I can't stay here," she said, "I'd feel like a traitor. Oh, I don't know..."

"Then let me give you a lift."

Robin gazed at her shoes. "I'll get a ride later." She was aware of their stiffness with each other, of the awkward moments as they stood side by side, not touching, surrounded by a dozen cheerful people. Suddenly she felt miserably alone. Robin against the world, she mused darkly. What had happened to that sense of comfort she'd once felt here in Santa Fe? She couldn't trust a soul, not anymore, except, of course, Adam. And where would that get her?

"Where will you stay in town?" he asked in a concerned voice.

"I don't know. I haven't thought about it. Maybe the Governor's Inn. Someplace close to my shop."

"Okay. I'll be in touch soon. And don't go to your apartment alone, Robin, I mean that. You just wait till we see who shows up at Martinez's place."

"Oh, sure. I hope it isn't too long." She knew she was sulking, childishly pouting. But she had a right to, darn it all—Adam deserved it. And she knew she'd much rather have him drive her to the hotel, but this was one way of showing him that she no longer cared. It was spiteful and devious, but it actually felt good.

He left shortly thereafter, promising to keep in touch as often as possible, expressing his belief that all this would soon be behind them. Robin hadn't the energy to respond. She never even said goodbye; she merely stared at him, undisguised pain in her eyes, her heart aching for what could have been.

"OH, BUT ROBIN, I WON'T HEAR of it," Shelly was saying. "You're staying right here."

"I appreciate all your concern *and* your hospitality," said Robin, unable to meet her glance. "But I just... I guess I need to be alone. I'm like that, you know, at times."

Shelly put her hands on her hips and frowned. "You are not like that, Robin, not one bit. I know what you're hiding, though. And it's absurd." Robin's heart stopped and she felt heat soar up her neck. Shelly knew about Martinez, about the van... "It's Adam, isn't it? He's got you so upset you can't think straight," her friend said.

Robin suddenly felt like laughing. She let out a breath she'd been holding. "You're right, Shelly," she said, "it is Adam."

"Well, you don't have to leave because of him. You could stay here, we could talk. Come on, Robin, this isn't at all like you."

She couldn't look at Shelly, she just *couldn't*. "No," she said, "it's better if I'm alone. I can sort things out in my mind that way. Honest, Shel, I need time to myself."

"Well..."

"I'll be fine. I'm going to get a room... in town," she said, realizing that she didn't even trust her friend enough to tell her where.

"You'll call me, though, won't you? We can talk?"

"Oh, sure, I'll call, and I'll see you at work."

"That rat," said Shelly under her breath, "he's nothing but a womanizer. You poor kid."

By nine, Robin was checked into the Governor's Inn. She would dearly have loved to have had Julien, who had given her a ride, stop by her apartment so that she could pick up a few things. And she would have, except she felt utterly drained. She wanted only to drop into bed, to sleep and to forget.

She showered and pulled on her nightgown and thought about what a traitor she'd been to the Daltons. Some loyal pal she was!

She tried the TV. There was early news on a local channel, all bad news. She switched to a *Magnum PI* rerun, but then his tall, dark good looks reminded her too much of Adam. She switched that off, too. She sat in bed and tried to watch a sitcom, but it was terrible, the jokes stale and old, predictable. Finally she turned it off altogether and lay there, tired and shaky, in the darkness.

How could she have been so blind? Adam had always played it straight with her, but no, Robin had bulldozed her way into his life, stupidly, without thought of the future. Well, somehow she was going to have to get all those silly, naive dreams out of her head and go on living as before. Boy, had she been dumb—no, desperate was a better description, she decided. Her whole life she'd longed to belong to a close-knit family like his. And had she ever fallen for his heritage, the Indian stuff! How dumb could she get?

CHAPTER SIXTEEN

ROBIN HAD NEVER REALIZED how many times a day she and Shelly took a break from work and chatted. And if they weren't poking their heads into each other's shops, then it was a quick telephone call or a lunch date at the burrito house around the corner from the Sena Plaza.

The day began with doughnuts. "Hi," said Shelly, brandishing her white bakery bag, "how about some calories, Skinny?" And for the first time in years, since she'd had the Taiwan flu, Robin had no appetite. For her friend's sake, she forced one down anyway.

"Thanks," she managed to say.

"Still down?"

"I guess I am," replied Robin, hating the deceit.

"I swear, that man may be a hunk, but he's definitely a killer, Robin. It's just as well you're through trying to find those counterfeiters."

Robin knew that all the blood drained from her face. "Why?" she asked in a whisper.

"Oh, you know," said Shelly, "that way Adam won't be drifting in and out of your life. You'll be done with the cad."

"Oh."

"Do you realize that I'll be a mother without children this Friday? Ericka's driving back to school," said Shelly.

"I know. I don't know how I'm going to manage without her," replied Robin, but she was glad she didn't have to see Ericka every day and treat her as if nothing had happened and wonder...

"And she's in Albuquerque today spending that bonus you gave her. A new mall or something just opened."

"I hope she enjoys it."

"She will." Shelly rolled her big eyes.

It wasn't even noon when Shelly called again. "How about a game of tennis after work?"

"I, ah..."

"Oh, that's right, there's the business association meeting tonight. Darn."

"Maybe another time," Robin was able to say.

She spent most of the afternoon studying proofs and getting together with clients, but by four, she was sulking again, alone, resting her chin on her hands, staring, unfocused, into nowhere. She had no idea how she was going to get through the meeting tonight, or the trite chores of the next day, or the next. Life suddenly didn't seem too grand without Adam around.

Maybe she should see a shrink. Maybe a doctor could tell her where she'd gone wrong and how to cope with the loneliness. Or maybe there wasn't an answer at all.

"Hey," came a voice at her door, "it's five after six." It was Chuck. "You're going to the meeting, aren't you?"

She couldn't even look her best friends in the eyes anymore. How *was* she going to cope?

The three-month-old Santa Fe Business Association seemed, that night, to be falling apart. Robin was amazed. And it had all started because Adam Farwalker had strolled by her shop one day and seen that photograph.

Niles Warner, a local restaurateur, had started the fracas. "So I'm supposed to chip in my money for a pamphlet that this so-called special committee has dreamed up? The hell I will!"

"Now, Niles," Julien said placatingly.

"I'm going to have my say here," Niles went on. "I don't even sell pottery or art of any form! And let me tell you all another thing, they can't forge a steak or a head of lettuce. Maybe you good folks ought to think about switching lines of business."

"I agree completely," piped up a lodge owner. "There's no reason why some of us here should be penalized because a few collectors buy fakes by mistake."

Good old Thad Mencimer was on his feet like a shot. "Who said that?" he shouted, red-faced.

"I did."

Thad faced the lodge owner. The purple veins on his neck stood out. "And I suppose if you need help with your lodge, like parking or whatever, you won't bring your problem in here?"

"I can take care of myself."

Lorraine Mencimer tugged on her husband's sleeve. "Thad, sit down, please."

"Can we come to order?" asked Julien from the podium.

It didn't work. "This association is never going to make it," said a Western gallery owner. "What we need is three or four associations."

"Brilliant." Thad snickered.

"Please," said Julien. "We are getting nowhere. We must come to order."

Madeline rose to her feet and turned to face the group. "Julien's right. The way to do things is to vote on them. Let's vote on the pamphlet and maybe we can work out payment on a sliding scale."

"Now you're talking," came a voice from the rear. "Let's hear more about this pamphlet, though. Let's find out what we'll be getting for our money."

"*Your* money, you mean," Niles jeered, and his wife shot him a scathing glance.

Robin sat and listened, feeling as tense as the rest of them. The town seemed polarized between various factions, each grinding its own ax in the room that evening. Maybe it was good to air things out, she thought; then again, maybe it wasn't. She couldn't seem to get things straight in her head anymore.

It took forty-five minutes, but the pamphlet passed by a narrow margin, and only because the gallery owners were at the top of the sliding-scale payment plan, and the others, the restaurateurs and hotel managers, at the bottom.

"Yeah, well," said Niles under his breath, "it might take me months to pay, if I can even find the bill."

"I'll help you find it," said Thad boldly.

"All right," said Julien, "now let's get on to something less controversial, if we can. I'd like Robin Hayle to step up here for a minute or two and address the members on an idea she brought up at one of our special committee meetings. Robin?"

It actually took Robin a moment to even remember what her idea had been. Then she wished Julien had saved it for another night—any night.

Dutifully she rose to her feet and slid out through the row of men and women. A friendly catcall sounded from somewhere, and she pointedly ignored it as she stepped up onto the platform and Julien yielded the podium to her.

"Good evening," she began. "As Julien mentioned, I have another thought on how we might thwart these counterfeiters." Robin cleared her throat, trying to formulate in her mind what she was going to say. It was terribly difficult, not just because she detested public speaking, but also because her heart was no longer in it.

"I hope this isn't going to cost us anything," someone said.

"Oh, don't worry," Robin replied to the unseen voice, "it won't cost a thing. What I have in mind is an Indian artisans' association, patterned after ours. I've been told that the Indian community has never before been organized and that the artists work very independently of one another. An association," she said, glancing around the room, "would mean communication, and eventually, the honest artisans would police the not-so-honest ones."

"How do you know it will work?" asked a woman in the front row. "The Indians don't exactly have a good track record in organizing. They're real clannish. The Pueblo tribes still hate the Navahos, the Zunis distrust the Rio Grande tribes. And anything the white community suggests they're going to suspect."

"I realize that," said Robin. "But it's something we could work toward. And, as I said already, it won't cost anything to try."

Thad Mencimer stood. "I'm afraid I agree with that lady over there. I'm not sure the Indians *can* be organized. Won't they just think it's more interference from the whites?"

"I hope not," Robin put in. "I'm planning on speaking to Mrs. Farwalker—I think we all know how influential she can be—and soliciting her help. There's another person involved, too, an Indian lady," she said, not wanting to use Josefina's name. "The person I mentioned will be of invaluable help. I believe it can be done." Robin smiled at the group. "Well? Any questions, comments?"

There were some. Several members were dubious, many reiterating doubts about the Indians' ability to organize. But Ben Chavez and Chuck Dalton were very supportive—as was Julien.

Julien finally climbed back onto the platform and stood next to Robin. "I don't think we need a vote, do we?" Heads shook. "Okay, then. Thank you, Robin."

She received applause as she stepped down and took her seat. Julien then pulled up a tripod that was covered. When he unveiled the object beneath, it was the mock-up for the *Travel and Leisure* ad. Naturally there were comments.

"Santa Fe doesn't look like that," said someone. "That's just a bunch of mesas in a sunset."

"Well, I like it."

"I don't; it's the wrong image."

"The caption is a cliché. Everyone's heard of the land of enchantment. We've gotta change that, it's been used."

"How about come visit the old world?"

"That's stupid." Thad, of course. "This isn't the old world."

"Pipe down there, Thad."

Nothing was resolved that evening and the man from the printer's who had done the mock-up at his own expense left, gritting his teeth, before the meeting was adjourned.

As Robin sat there growing weary and bored, she glanced around at the faces. Of course, Martinez had described the Daltons' van, but he could have been lying. Couldn't any knowledgeable gallery owner be involved? Counterfeiting provided easily obtained, tax-free money, and there were a number of fine artisans to do the work, especially if they were fed a cock-and-bull story. Sure, any one of the members here might be involved, thought Robin. A chill crawled up her spine. Any one of them could have been responsible for her accident, could have hired an Indian to do it, in fact. But right now the finger sure pointed to Chuck and Shelly.

She and Adam were going to find out when the next pickup of Martinez's pots was to be. They'd know then who it was. She hoped that day came soon.

Adam, Robin thought, as the voices still discussing the ad flowed in and out of her consciousness. Adam. A man she wanted desperately. A man who ran hot and cold, a man who spoke her language but had strange hidden corners to him. What had gone wrong? What had driven him back into that private world of his?

"Hey, Robin ... Robin?" It was Chuck, tapping her on the shoulder. "The meeting's over, kiddo. Where were you just then?"

She forced herself to smile. "Daydreaming."

"Hope it was nice. Say, are you all right staying here in town?" he asked.

"I'm perfectly fine, Chuck."

"Well, Shelly was sure disappointed. You know how fond she is of you."

In a minute, Robin was going to cry. "And I'm fond of her, too," she said genuinely. "I just needed some space."

"So Shelly said. Come on, I'll walk you out. You got your car here?"

Robin shook her head. "No. I'm staying in town... It's convenient, anyway."

"And you're okay?"

"Perfectly."

Members were still gathered in small groups outside the La Fonda Hotel. Robin saw the Daltons' van then, double parked, Shelly waving out the window at Chuck. "Come on," she called, "I've been waiting forever. Hi, Robin!"

Robin waved, but her eyes were fixed on the green van, on the desert scene artistically painted on its side. There couldn't be two vehicles like that within a thousand miles...

"Hey there, Robin." It was Thad Mencimer. "I don't think your idea's going to work out very well."

"Don't you think it's worth trying, though?" asked Robin irritably.

"If you need any help," offered Lorraine deliberately, "as soon as the baby comes, I'd be glad to pitch in."

"That's sweet of you," replied Robin as they all walked toward Chuck's van. "I'll call you."

"Do. I mean that."

"Well, how's business?" Thad was asking Chuck. "Say, I wanted to thank you..."

But Shelly was still waving, and Robin stopped for a minute to say hello. Later she would remember that she'd heard Thad say something significant, but everyone was talking at once, small talk, unimportant stuff, and she wasn't really listening. Only later would she remember that casual statement Thad made to Chuck, something very, very significant.

ROBIN TURNED the plastic clock hands to noon and locked up. She had no appointments that morning, and now was as good a time as any to start working on the Indian artisans' organization. Her first step, she had decided, was to see Christina Farwalker. If she could convince Christina to help her start organizing the Indians, she'd have the task half done.

Robin wondered, though, in her state of mind, if she'd make any sense at all to the woman. Maybe she ought to wait to pay this visit, wait until she had this forgery business behind her, and Adam along with it.

But she had to get out and do *something*. It was far better to act, to be productive, to solve a problem.

She drove up Canyon Road and turned onto the dirt road that led to the Farwalker ranch. Her car bounced and shook, and she felt as if her brain were rattling. She passed the time by thinking about last night's meeting and all the unsettling, petty arguments. And she thought about afterward when she'd been standing out in front of La Fonda, exchanging pleasantries with Chuck and Shelly while staring at their van.

There was something about the van, too, something she couldn't quite remember at the moment. Was it something Martinez had said? No, there was something else. Hadn't Thad been talking to Chuck about the van? He had, she recalled, but Robin had been busy speaking to Shelly and had only been half listening.

Thad. Yes, he'd been thanking Chuck, saying something about how, when his shop really got moving, he was going to buy his own van.

Robin's brow furrowed. Suddenly she had it. Thad had said, "Say, I wanted to thank you again for letting me use the van, Chuck."

Robin practically drove into the ditch. She stopped the car and gripped the steering wheel. Of course! Just because the van had been seen in San Lucas Pueblo didn't mean that the Daltons had been driving it!

Wow, it could be Thad behind the forgeries! And he had a motive, too; he was always complaining about money. He had a baby coming. And he was a terrible obstructionist at the association meetings. No wonder he'd put his two cents in about the Indians being difficult to organize!

A smile of relief curved Robin's lips. And what was more, she realized, maybe Chuck had loaned his van—innocently—to others. Almost *anyone* could have borrowed it; anyone who knew Chuck Dalton could be the guilty party. The suspect list was growing longer and longer, and now her plan to wait at Martinez's to see who showed up was even more vital. She'd have to tell Adam; then he'd believe the Daltons couldn't have done it.

Her smile faded. Tell Adam? How was she going to accomplish *that*? He'd said he'd be in touch, but would he?

Robin realized, as she parked in front of the hacienda, that she should have called ahead. When was she ever going to be able to think straight again?

But Christina was home, and welcomed her. "Oh, Robin, what a nice surprise. Do come in. I just made a fresh pot of coffee."

Christina had cleaning ladies at the hacienda, two short, almost identical Mexican women. But judging from the way Adam's mother couldn't pass a cushion on a couch without straightening it, it was difficult for Robin to tell who helped whom.

The two women were in the kitchen that morning. Three cups of coffee sat on the familiar pine table, and a pie plate of wonderful home-baked cinnamon rolls was just coming out of the oven.

"Maria and Pia, this is my son's friend, Robin," said Christina, and the two women giggled and exchanged meaningful glances.

"Hi," said Robin, "your rolls smell absolutely wonderful."

"Gracias, señorita," replied Pia. "You will have one?"

"And coffee, please."

They sat out in the courtyard, the morning sun on Robin's back. Beyond the walls a faint, cool breeze bent the tall grass, but inside the protection of the aged walls it was warm; not a breath of air stirred.

"I'm so glad you've come to visit," said Christina, offering the butter to Robin for her rolls, "although I wish you would have accepted our hospitality until this business is cleared up."

"To be honest," said Robin, "I would have, it's so lovely here, but being in town is really convenient for my work, and my car could only take so many trips on that dirt road."

"So," said Christina, folding her small hands on the table, "you look like a woman with a purpose."

Unconsciously Robin averted her glance. Adam's mother no doubt thought that she'd come with some problem concerning her son or, perhaps, something to do with the forgeries.

"I'd like to talk to you about something," she began. Then she told Christina all about her idea to organize the Indian artists. Christina watched her soberly, her dark brows drawn together. "And so I thought that if you could help me contact the artists that you know, or point out the leaders, the ones that would be listened to, you'd be a great help. You'd act as a sort of liaison."

"I see," said Christina, looking at her small, plump hands, and Robin was disheartened. Then the older woman glanced up. "Oh, it's a good idea, a really good idea. I was just considering the difficulties."

"But would you help me?"

"Did my son put you up to this?" asked Christina astutely.

"He only said I'd have to ask you myself."

"I'd like to help. Let me think about it. You know, Josefina would be invaluable to a group like this."

"I know. I even mentioned it to her, but she wouldn't commit herself to doing anything."

"Well, it's not exactly up Josefina's alley, but she might be convinced," said Christina. "It would be a lot of work, a lot of traveling and talking and explaining. It could be very disappointing, Robin. It might not come together in the end.''

"I've been told how private the Indians are. But wouldn't they see the benefits of an organization?''

"Maybe, if approached correctly.''

"But you see, *you* would know the right approach.''

"My dear, you flatter me," Christina said with a laugh.

"Well, you have influence with Josefina then,'' suggested Robin.

"To a point." Thoughtfully Christina sipped her coffee, then nodded her head. "It's a solid idea. All the artists: Navaho rug weavers, Hopi silversmiths, Pueblo potters, painters. Hm.''

Robin relaxed a little. She could see that Christina's brain was already at work.

"We'd have to choose one person in each pueblo to contact. The Navaho would be more difficult, they're so spread out. Maybe flyers in the native languages and in English.'' Christina spoke as if to herself. "I'm afraid there would be resistance. Some of the older artists will be afraid of getting involved. The younger ones will fear white influence. It won't be easy.''

"But I bet we can do it," replied Robin.

"Maybe I'll pull out my fund-raiser list and send off some notes to the Indians on it. Yes, that's a start.''

"And Josefina?''

"I'll talk to her.''

"Christina, you are a born organizer.''

"Well, an Apache woman is brought up to manage a whole clan. This is just practice.''

Things were definitely looking up, thought Robin.

Christina excused herself to get some more coffee, and Robin was left alone in the bright courtyard. She turned her face up into the sun and sighed. She'd been in this courtyard before, under quite different circumstances. Then, Adam had been the mysterious stranger who had only come into her life that day. She would regret that day, too, she guessed, for a very long time. Yet for one incredible moment, he'd brought hope to her existence. She'd been able to dream of being a part of something finally, of belonging. It was difficult and painful to imagine going through life so alone, but maybe that was her destiny.

Why couldn't she reach Adam, reach all the way into his soul, read his thoughts? Was it really just different backgrounds? Robin suspected that his mother could explain it to her. But she'd never have the nerve to ask. Never.

"More coffee?" asked Christina, holding the earthenware pot.

Robin opened her eyes. "Oh, sorry," she said, "I was off in space. It's so lovely here." She gave Christina a smile. "Sure, only a half cup, though. Thank you."

No, she'd never have the nerve to ask. It would be too embarrassing, too devious going behind his back like that. No, she couldn't possibly... "Christina," began Robin in a small voice, but then she stopped herself.

"Yes, Robin?"

She swallowed hard. "I was wondering... Oh, it's nothing. Really."

"Go on, dear, something's troubling you. What is it?" Christina seated herself and looked earnestly at Robin.

"You'll think I'm terrible."

"I could never think that."

"Look," said Robin suddenly, her face on fire, "I should be getting back into town." And she started to rise.

"This has something to do with my son," stated Christina solemnly. "Please...if I can help... We *are* friends."

Robin slumped back into her chair. "It is Adam," she admitted wearily, feeling as if her heart were in a vise.

"Go on."

"Well, he's very hard to reach sometimes, you know? Hard to get to." She tried to laugh, but it came out more like a hiccup. Christina said nothing, however; she only sat very still and looked pensive and sad. Robin knew she'd begun to squirm. Why had she said anything? It had been a hideous mistake...

"I can tell you one thing," said Christina slowly. "You understand, don't you, that I am loyal to my son?"

"Oh, of course I do," Robin murmured, her stare in her lap now.

"Adam is keeping something from you. That's all I can say. You yourself must hear it from him."

Robin managed to nod, unable to speak past the lump in her throat. A dozen things swarmed through her head, unbidden, tormenting thoughts, possibilities. What *was* he hiding, a family of his own somewhere? A woman that he was secretly engaged to? A problem because he was an Indian and she wasn't, something she couldn't foresee, something Apache, a rite he had to perform?

"Don't," came Christina's concerned voice, "don't torture yourself. Speak to Adam. Speak to him."

Finally Robin looked up. She knew that there were tears brimming in her eyes; she'd never felt so humiliated in her life.

"It's all right," said the woman softly. "We are friends, it's all right."

"I feel so foolish," Robin was able to say, and she wiped at her eyes and sniffed. "You know, I *never* cry..." she laughed then, at herself, at the whole crazy situation.

"Everyone should have a good cry once in a while, don't you think?" Christina returned her smile.

"Well," began Robin, taking a deep breath, "I really do have to get back to town." She looked at her watch. "And I suppose I better get started with this association thing."

"And I'll speak to Josefina," said Christina, but they were interrupted then by one of the Mexican women.

"There's a telephone call for you, *Señora* Farwalker," Pia said shyly.

Christina excused herself and disappeared into the house and Robin was left to sit alone again, only this time she was beginning to get anxious about leaving.

How could you have done that? Asking Adam's mother! Yet Christina had answered one question at least: Adam was keeping something from her. But what?

She was thinking, frowning deeply, when Christina came back to the courtyard. For a moment Robin didn't notice the grave look on the woman's face or the fact that she was wringing her hands.

"Robin," said Christina, her voice shaking, "that call. It was Josefina."

Robin was on her feet quickly, helping Christina into a chair. "What is it?" she asked carefully, holding the woman's hand.

"Her pots . . . her studio," whispered Christina, "someone wrecked everything!"

"Oh, no!"

"But it's worse." Christina's frightened eyes met Robin's. "John Martinez has been beaten up. My God," she whispered, "is no one safe?"

CHAPTER SEVENTEEN

ADAM LOOKED UP FROM HIS WORK for a moment as an odd sense of foreboding enveloped him, as if the raven were hovering over him, flapping its wings. The eerie sensation persisted, growing in intensity. Something, somewhere, had happened—something that affected him profoundly. But what?

"Oh, Mr. Farwalker!" came one of the student's voices, "lunch is ready!" He climbed up the ladder in the kiva and headed down the hill, but the feeling still held him with an unearthly will.

It probably had something to do with Robin and the fake pots, he told himself; neither subject was ever far from his mind. He knew Robin was all set and raring to play the detective. And if they *did* discover who was picking up Martinez's pots, everything would work out. *But*—and it was a big but—he kept remembering that case in Albuquerque, the counterfeiting ring, the investigating officer found dead, under mysterious circumstances. He remembered Robin's car lying in the ditch, and he knew he should have been more forceful and made her leave everything to Rod Cordova.

That afternoon Adam and his few remaining students worked on the collapsed kiva, excavating the fallen rock, trying to make it safe to leave for the winter. A chill was creeping into the air even during the day. Fall was on its way, the harvest season, the time to hunt, to butcher one's animals, to store supplies against the season of snows.

Adam, still held by that odd sensation, searched the immense grandeur of the sky. No clouds yet. But perhaps, one weekend when the clouds descended, he could go hunting with his father. They'd take a couple of pack-horses and ride up into the hills. He would feel totally in harmony with the world then, and remember the wonderful hunting stories his uncle had told him about the mountain spirits called *Gáhan* and about Coyote, the shrewd trickster of whom a whole series of tales existed. Was it Coyote who was disturbing his peace that day? Was it merely a trick?

Adam was brought back to reality when he heard a shout from below where he was working. "Mr. Far-walker! Josh from the visitors' center is looking for you," called one of the students.

Dusting his hands off on his jeans, Adam picked his way down the slope.

"Adam, I was going by anyway, so I thought I'd drop off the message," said Josh, the park ranger in charge of the center. "It sounds important."

"Thanks," said Adam, taking the pink slip. "I appreciate it."

"See you around. Say, you going to the goodbye party for Craig tonight?"

"Huh?" Adam looked up from the note. "Oh, I don't know yet."

"Sure am going to miss all the kids when they leave," said Josh in parting.

Adam read the message again. It was from Christina, and it was very disturbing. "Someone broke into Josefina's studio and Martinez is hurt. Call me."

He felt chilled; why hadn't he listened to his instincts earlier? Now he'd dragged more people into this mess. He wondered if Josefina had been injured, but it didn't sound like it, and he wondered how badly hurt Martinez was. It occurred to him instantly that if Martinez had indeed been beaten as a warning or punishment, then the man had not been lying to them.

Someone had been watching him or Robin, someone knew where they'd gone. Someone knew every move they made. My God—Robin.

He reread the note swiftly. There was no mention of her. Thank heavens she was staying in a hotel, but, still, "accidents" could happen anywhere. If someone were trying to warn Josefina and Martinez, they could do the same to Robin.

Ten minutes later he was dialing Robin's shop from the phone at the visitors' center, but there was no answer. He fought down panic. Hadn't Ericka Dalton been going back to college any day? Sure, she wasn't there, and Robin was out on a job.

On impulse he dialed her hotel. No answer. He even tried her apartment once, but there was no one there, either. He hung around until one-thirty, dialing her shop several times more, but it only rang and rang and rang.

Impatience ate at him—one of the white man's reactions he'd picked up over the years. Patience was nature's way, but this situation wasn't natural. Damn it, it was man-made and he felt irritable and worried. Finally he called his mother, wondering if Robin had decided to stay there after all. She could tell him more about what had happened to Josefina and Martinez.

"Adam? Well, you got *that* message fast. Isn't it awful?"

"How badly is Martinez hurt?" he asked.

"Josefina was hysterical. She didn't say. Just that someone beat him. She's half out of her mind. You know how timid she is, anyway. Adam, this is serious. I think you've got to go to the police."

"Rod already knows all the facts I have and neither Josefina nor Martinez will report these incidents. You know that," said Adam. "Mother, have you heard from Robin?"

"Oh, Robin. Yes, as a matter of fact, she was here this morning. She wants me to help set up an Indian artists' association."

Relief swept Adam.

"Well, I told her I would. Apparently she discussed it with Josefina . . ."

"When did she leave?"

"About three hours ago. I'm sure she's at her shop."

"She's not there."

"Oh," said Christina. "You don't think . . ."

"I don't know," replied Adam grimly.

By two he'd given directions to the kids, thrown a small bag in his Land Rover and was headed toward Santa Fe.

He should have checked in with Robin. In fact, he had been planning to call her that night, but what did that matter now?

He stepped on the accelerator, willing the lumbering Land Rover to go faster, but it went uphill only at a stubborn, sedate fifty. In the middle of the afternoon he stopped at San Ysidro and phoned her shop again. Still no answer.

Why hadn't he stayed with her?

The Daltons. Could they have realized that they were suspect? Were they really behind the counterfeiting ring? Could they have done something to Robin, lured her into a trap? Or Martinez. He could easily have called Robin and said he had some new information for her. She would have gone to San Lucas for that—and Martinez could also have lured her into a trap. She could be visiting Josefina, commiserating with her. Sure, she could be *anywhere*. But with Ericka gone, she damn well should have been in the shop.

The cottonwood trees still shadowed the facade of the Sena Plaza. The cute wooden sign still said Robin's Nest. The display in the window was just as attractive as ever. On the door a round plastic clock face hung, with its hands pointing to five o'clock. The words "will return at" were printed on the face.

But it was after six.

He felt as if a fist was crushing his heart, squeezing harder and harder. Something had happened to Robin. He could no longer fool himself into believing she was still out on a job. Not this late.

A small, calm voice told him to consider the possibilities, then his options. The possibilities he'd already been over—ever since he'd left Chaco Canyon. His options were to search for her himself, to ask her friends, to check every hotel in town in case she'd moved, to simply wait, or to call Rod Cordova. He went around to the back of the shop, in the alleyway, and looked through the blinds of her office window. The office was empty.

His next step was to check her apartment. He decided to walk, having spent too many hours in the car as it was. And, besides, it would kill time. She could show up any second, perfectly safe.

It was a lovely walk. The late afternoon sun warmed his face; a few trees were just touched with color, and the old city was smug and peaceful now that the craziness of the summer season was over.

He should have been enjoying the stroll, but his heart hammered too heavily, struggling to release the grip of that weighty hand. Her car was not in front of the building; no one answered his knock. The door was locked.

Swiftly he walked back to the Sena Plaza. Robin's Nest stood silent, staring back at him with empty eyes.

Okay, her friends were the next step. The Daltons' gallery was just two doors down. It occurred to him that the Daltons would lie about Robin's whereabouts if they were involved in the pottery scam, but he had to try.

Chuck Dalton was just closing up. "Hello, Adam. Silly to stay open this late in the off-season, isn't it?" He was the picture of innocence.

"Say, Chuck, do you know where Robin is? I just got in from Chaco and there's a notice on her door that she'll be back at five."

Chuck held his left wrist up. "And it's almost six-thirty. *Women.* Heck, I thought she was in her shop."

"Would Shelly know?"

"Hang on, she's at home. I'll give her a call." He went to the phone and started to dial. "I'd figure *you'd* know where Robin was, if anyone would." And Chuck winked knowingly.

Adam clenched his teeth to bite back a reply.

"Shel? Adam Farwalker's here looking for Robin. You know where she is?" Chuck said into the receiver. "No," he said to his wife over the line, "she's not in her shop. She was supposed to be back at five." He listened then turned to Adam. "Shel says she thinks Robin was going out to see your mother today."

Adam shook his head. "She left there this morning."

"She left there this morning, hon," Chuck repeated into the phone. He listened again then hung up. "Nope, Shelly doesn't know. Robin was at the association meeting last night, though." Chuck regarded him soberly. "You're worried about her. You think it has something to do with this counterfeiting thing?"

"I don't know," said Adam evasively.

"Did you try the hotel she's staying at? I think it was the Governor's Inn," suggested Chuck, looking at him oddly.

"I've tried."

"Hey, I'm sure she'll turn up. Tell you what, if Shel or I hear from her, where can we get hold of you?"

"Leave a message with my folks," said Adam, giving Chuck the number. "Would you mind if I used your phone for a minute to call her hotel again?"

"No, go ahead."

But no one answered in Room 223.

Chuck locked up and drove away in his bright green van. Adam stared after him, wondering, testing Chuck's reactions in his memory. His sixth sense told him Chuck was telling the truth, but this time he couldn't trust his senses. The Daltons would already be alert if they were involved with the forgeries.

He walked back to her shop. Would she bother coming here since it was so late? Was she staying with another friend somewhere? Damn, he should have kept in touch, insisted that she let him or Christina know where she was every minute of the day. He paced. He could try calling Julien or that Lassiter woman or...who else?

Or he could tell Rod Cordova that she was missing. Make it official. But *was* she missing?

The light faded to a dusty gold. Long stripes of brightness lay on the sidewalk, and the trees rustled in the evening breeze. He still paced in front of her shop, feeling helpless and anxious.

A car was coming down the quiet street. Automatically Adam looked up, as he had for every passing car. It was white, a little sporty white model, drifting toward him along the old brick street. A late ray of sun reflected off the windshield, making it difficult to see the driver. He stood with his fists clenched, keeping hope at bay. It seemed as though the car was driving toward him for a very long time, through a tunnel of trees, lit by the dying sun. And then it swerved, too fast, the sun flashed away as the car pulled up to the curb in front of him and he could see the driver.

"Adam! What are you doing here?" Robin asked, stepping out of her car and stopping short.

The fist released his heart at last, and his heart soared. A thousand questions flew around like a flock of birds in his brain. Ignoring them, he walked to where she stood by her car and pulled her into his arms in vast, unthinking relief.

Yes, she was there, unharmed, tall and graceful, smooth-skinned, glowing, sweet-smelling. He pressed her close then held her at arm's length, drinking her beauty in, a heady draught.

"Adam?" she said, cocking her head in that endearing way she had. "Is something wrong?"

He finally found his voice. "Where in hell have you been?"

"Working."

"This late?"

"I closed up this afternoon and went out to get some shots. Hey, do I have to tell you every time I . . . ?"

"You're late."

She glanced toward the clock on her door. "So I am."

He still held her shoulders in his hands. "Mother told me about Josefina and Martinez. I got worried."

She searched his face in the semidarkness, her pupils so large that her eyes looked like dark pools. "I appreciate that, but really..."

He finally dropped his hands, but they still burned with the feel of her. He turned away, raking his fingers through his hair, and swore softly in Apache.

"I'm sorry," Robin was saying, "I didn't know you'd be looking for me."

"Robin," he began, turning back, then he fell quiet. A long moment of silence stretched between them like a strand of the thinnest glass, perfect but fragile.

Her voice broke the strand. "Are you...are you staying in town tonight?"

"I haven't even thought about it."

She averted her face. "I was just wondering... Well, it's only an idea." She faced him again. "I would dearly love to spend an evening in my own place. I've been eating out and I hate it. As long as you're here..." She gave a funny little laugh. "Well, you could spend the evening with me..." Her voice trailed off.

He should have said no, but the trickster, Coyote, took his tongue and he heard himself saying, "I'd like that," and he could see Robin's face light up.

"Oh, good! Let me put my camera away, and then can we run by the grocery store. I'll cook..."

"I'll take you out."

"Oh, Lord, I've had enough restaurant food. I feel like cooking."

He gave in gracefully.

She fixed fat homemade hamburgers and a big salad, and they had coffee ice cream with hot fudge sauce for dessert. Robin was as happy as a lark to be back in her own apartment. She left the dishes in the sink and flung herself down on the couch next to him, put her stockinged feet up on the glass coffee table and spooned melted ice cream from the bottom of the carton.

"I was starved," she said. Then she sat up and got a serious look on her face. "I almost forgot."

"What?"

"Yesterday at the meeting I heard Thad Mencimer—you remember him?—thank Chuck Dalton for letting him use his van."

Adam sat up straighter. "You mean Thad borrowed Chuck's van?"

"Yes." She frowned. "So I figured that meant it could have been Thad who picked up the pots from John Martinez. I'd sure rather believe it was Thad than Chuck."

"There's no proof either way."

"So we still have to stick to our plan, I know," said Robin, rising and pacing back and forth, still holding the carton and licking the spoon. "It could be Thad or somebody else entirely."

"You realize, don't you, that if John Martinez really *did* get beaten up, he may be so scared he'll never let us know when the pickup will happen?"

She stopped short and her brows drew together.

"And Josefina, she's not going to stand up to harassment, either."

"*If* Martinez was beaten?" Robin said then. "You think—"

"I haven't seen him. I don't know if Josefina saw him. He could be making it up, a smoke screen," said Adam. "He could have been ordered to say that."

"But if he really did get beaten then he *is* innocent, isn't he?" she asked. "Can we find out somehow? Wow, this has really turned out to be a mess." She paced some more, her spoon stuck in the ice cream. Adam noticed that, for once, she wasn't eating. He would have been amused under different circumstances. "How are we ever going to convince Martinez to let us know when the pickup is now?" she said, half to herself.

"Okay," he said, "let's say Martinez *is* innocent, then he might be too frightened to pass word along to Josefina now."

"Oh, swell..."

"On the other hand, his pride must be on the line by now, so maybe he'll be willing to help us anyway."

"If," said Robin, "he's innocent. What if he isn't?"

"In that case, I'd say he has two choices. Either he can ignore us or he can get word to us through Josefina about a pickup but give us false information."

"You know," she said, "I wonder if we shouldn't—" She stopped short.

"Shouldn't what?"

"I was going to say, call Rod Cordova with all this. But why should we? I mean, what's he done but practically call us crazy?" Robin chopped away angrily at her dessert with the spoon. "The heck with him!"

Adam smiled at her. She was quite a woman. She deserved happiness and that big family she wanted, and all the love and security and belonging that went with it. She deserved someone special to love her and protect and cherish her.

But not him.

She'd fallen silent, staring at the spoon as if it were going to tell her something significant. "Adam?" she said after awhile. "Do you have to go soon? To the hacienda, I mean?"

He knew what she was getting at. A heat filled his body, a molten sweetness. He could stay with her. She was asking him to, and he desired her with a sudden force that shook him.

Adam stood and walked to a window, staring out over the lights of the city. How could he reject her beauty and her love? Yet how could he accept it?

"Adam?" she said, and he was aware of her behind him, moving across the floor.

He turned to face her and saw, deep in her eyes, the truth. There was nothing held back from him; her honesty stabbed at him with the force of a knife.

"What's wrong?" she asked. "Please, Adam...is there a problem?"

His heart dropped to his stomach like a stone, and the heat in him turned to ice, leaving a sheen of cold sweat on his skin.

"Tell me," she said in a passionate voice. "Whatever it is. I don't care. We can face it together. Please, let me help."

He swallowed. "It doesn't concern you, Robin. It isn't your problem."

"It is," she whispered, coming up close to him. "Whatever is bothering you is my problem, too. Don't you see? It's already hurt us both. Can't you tell me?" She laid her hand against his cheek.

He put his own hand over hers, feeling its softness, feeling the delicate bones under the silky skin. Feeling its strength. "Robin," he said hoarsely, "I don't want to hurt you."

A puzzled look crept into her eyes. "I don't understand."

Adam took a deep breath, lifting her hand from his face, holding it still, playing with her slender fingers. "Maybe it's because we're so different."

She stared at him for a moment. "I don't believe that."

"Maybe you should." His heart wouldn't stop hammering; it was pounding in his veins, in his head. She was so close. Her sweet scent wafted to his nostrils. He lifted her hand in his, turned it over and brushed it with his lips. He was filled with a vast sadness, a sweeping sense of loss, as if his clan had cast him out. For an instant he was going to tell her, no matter the consequences, but the moment stole off into the darkness beyond the window. She'd told him what it was in life she sought. He couldn't give her that, ever, and he knew in his heart that Robin would offer herself in spite of his failing.

She was terribly quiet, standing so close to him that her breath touched his neck. Then she was laying her head on his chest. "I'm sorry," he heard her murmur, "you don't have to say anything. Just stay here now, Adam, stay with me."

He knew he'd stay then. He'd stay and they would love each other and the sadness, for a short time, could be put aside.

Adam let the heat build inside him slowly, as if he were feeding kindling to a dying fire until small flames began to spark in his belly, his limbs. The warmth filled him, driving away the chill. She'd done that. Robin . . .

Her arms crept around his back and she raised her face to him and fire swept the blood in his veins. He lowered his head and kissed her, remembering abruptly the feel and taste of her. His arms tightened around her and the length of her body burned itself into his.

She leaned back in his arms then, her lips reddened from the kiss, her face shining. "Come on," she whispered, tugging at his hand.

Her bedroom was dark, with bars of light from the window lying on the bed. It was permeated with her scent and he breathed it in. She was unbuttoning his shirt, her fingers fumbling, tickling his chest, sending hot darts of pleasure shooting through him. Then her hands were ca-

ressing his bare skin and her lips covered his. He reached
under her blouse and touched her warm smoothness and
felt the ache in his body. "Robin," he groaned.

Then they were undressed and the faint light from the
window striped Robin's fair skin in broad bands, touching shoulder and breast and thigh. He cupped her face in
his hands and drank in her loveliness then softly brushed
her lips with his.

"You're the most beautiful man I've ever seen," Robin
murmured against his mouth.

He pulled her down onto the bed, caressing her, re-
learning the special, hidden places of her body. He kissed
the sensitive pulse on her neck, drew his mouth across her
taut nipples, flicked his tongue across her belly.

The fire rose in him, almost uncontrollable, but he
waited, wanting to give her pleasure. Her breath was ragged; small moans came from her throat. His hands
stroked, feeling her pleasure grow, learning to know her.

Then he was inside her, and she gasped, drawing him
close, rising to him, clasping him with her body. He was
gentle with her, holding himself back, loving her small,
incoherent cries, waiting until the time was right, until she
was ready. Then he plunged quickly, harder, and she rose
to his thrusts and cried out and they met on the pinnacle,
their bodies one body.

She moved under him later, then she traced a line on his
face with her finger. "Are you asleep?" she asked softly.

"No." He shifted his hips, rolling over, supporting
himself on an elbow. Silver light touched her face, washing it in radiance.

"Can you stay?"

"Yes, Robin, I can stay."

She snuggled into his side. "You feel so good."

He pushed her hair back and leaned over to kiss her forehead. "In Apache you'd be called *di-yin*."

"What's that?"

"A medicine woman. Powerful."

"I like that," she said seriously. "Would your clan need a new *di-yin*?"

"It takes years of study," he said mock solemnly.

"I've got years." She laid a hand on his stomach. "You see, I have no clan of my own. Everybody needs a clan, don't they?"

"Yes, they do. Otherwise they don't know where they belong."

"That's me in a nutshell." She sighed. "I don't belong to anybody."

A hint of morning paled the eastern sky as Adam stood by the window of Robin's bedroom. Pale gold touched the silent belfry of the time-worn chapel and filtered down to the plaza. He turned slowly and looked over to where Robin slept in the tousled bed. She lay curled on her side, her shoulders white as marble, her hair a great streaked mass half-covering her face. Yet even as she slept, a frown creased her forehead. He knew what was causing that frown. It was the wondering, the not knowing. It was the torment of not being able to trust, to commit, to depend on him.

The faint light outside took on a soft pearl glow, and with it, the room underwent a transformation as the deep shadows receded. She lay there so still, so perfect, so whole. He'd been unforgivably selfish to make love to her again.

For a moment he thought to awaken her and tell her that. He looked down at the shirt that dangled from his fingers. Somehow there had to be a solution, didn't there?

He pulled on his shirt and buttoned it up, recalling
Robin's fingers on those same buttons. He knelt by the bed
and placed a soft kiss on her cheek, padded silently out of
the bedroom, pulled on his boots, let himself out of her
door and closed it with a quiet snick behind him.

CHAPTER EIGHTEEN

By five o'clock on Monday afternoon Robin was thankful to see Mrs. Vermeil take her daughter firmly in hand and usher her out of the shop. The girl had been adorable in her Alice in Wonderland dress, but children's portraits were always difficult. And the fact that she'd had to include her white rabbit in the photographic session made things harder, but how could Alice in Wonderland be authentic without a rabbit?

"Whew," said Robin to herself, flipping the sign on the door to Closed. She stood for a few minutes, looking out onto the street. It was a gray day, promising rain later in the evening and, perhaps, snow in the high country. The sky had been low and grainy all day, autumn's first onslaught, and it matched Robin's mood exactly.

She wondered what the weather was like in Chaco Canyon. Was Adam still working, discovering buried pottery shards? Was he thinking about her?

It had been three whole days, she reflected, and no word from him. On Saturday night, it was true, the desk clerk at the Governor's Inn had told Robin that a man had called long distance and asked if she were still at the hotel, but he'd left no message. So he cared, at least enough to check on her.

Robin leaned her shoulder on the door and idly tapped a pencil against her teeth. But he hadn't cared enough to be there the morning after they'd made love. God, how she hated that, waking up alone with not even a note. They'd been so close, too, so loving, touching each other emotionally and physically. Why had he run from her? Why hadn't she been able to reach him?

The weekend had seemed endlessly long. She'd gone back to her room at the inn reluctantly, feeling lonely, inclined to forget his warnings and stay in her own apartment. She'd even tried to get Shelly for a game of tennis on Sunday in spite of everything, but Shelly and Chuck had driven to Denver with some of Ericka's things. It was just as well, she'd told herself, because she still crawled with discomfort every time she thought about her friends and the counterfeiting.

Wind rattled cottonwood branches outside the shop, making the leaves shiver. The street was practically deserted except for a couple of cars and an Indian lady, whose bright green skirt was being swirled around her legs by the breeze. An Indian lady who moved timidly, looking for something, her heavy silver earrings dangling as she turned her head apprehensively.

Quickly, her brain churning with questions, Robin unlatched her door and stepped outside. "Josefina!" she called, waving a hand.

Even when she was inside and out of the cold wind, the woman looked chilled and pale, anxious, standing near the door and glancing up and down the street.

"It's okay," Robin said, "we're safe here. I promise." She used the same quieting tactics as she had the first time Josefina had come to the shop; she made her a cup of steaming hot tea and sat her down in the privacy of the office. But Robin knew the woman was there for a purpose, and she was itching to know what it was.

"I heard about your studio being wrecked," Robin began softly. "I'm so terribly sorry. They did the same thing to me, but all your beautiful pots!"

"Yes, it was a terrible shock. But, after all, my pots are only small parts of Mother Earth and she has more to spare. I will make new ones," said Josefina as she held the teacup in both hands. "I was very frightened, but my two older sons are staying with me now and guarding the studio, so I do not worry so much anymore."

"Oh, good, that must be very comforting. I wish I had a few big strong sons to guard me," Robin said ruefully.

"You will, my child," replied Josefina.

"And John? Is he hurt badly?" asked Robin.

"John seems to be all right. He was very angry, very upset. He has no sons to help, only daughters. He sent his family to his brother at Isleta to protect them. This is a terrible thing, Robin," said Josefina, shaking her head sadly.

"I know," whispered Robin. "Have you thought about going to the police?"

Josefina shot her a glance. "No, they can do nothing."

"Then *we'll* do it. It's got to stop," said Robin, rising and starting to pace.

"Yes, we will do it. John has sent me to tell you . . ."

"Yes?" Robin stopped short.

"The men contacted him again. He acted frightened and told them he would do this one last order then no more. They are coming to pick up his work at his place."

"When?"

"Tomorrow," said Josefina, "at three in the afternoon."

"*Tomorrow?* So soon?"

"John thinks they are nervous. They know someone is looking for them—you, Adam. They know everything.

They know about me and they know we went to see John
that day. They threatened him and he lied to them. He lied
well and they believed that he told us nothing, but they
beat him anyway."

"Josefina," Robin said, thinking, "was John, um, well,
black and blue? Did he have cuts on him or marks anywhere? From the beating?"

Josefina shook her head. "He said they hit him here."
She indicated her own ribs. "It hurt him to breathe."

"No marks," Robin muttered to herself. What if he was
supplying false information through Josefina? What if...
But he was the only contact they had, and Robin would
have to go with it.

"Tomorrow at his place," repeated Robin.

"You will get word to Adam?" Josefina asked.

"Yes," said Robin, "I'll tell him, and we'll take care of
it from here on out. You've done a wonderful job. We'll
find out who's doing these awful things to all of us. They'll
be arrested, I promise. They'll go to jail."

"And if they do not?" asked the woman doubtfully.
"Then my sons stay forever at my house like soldiers?"

"No, no, we'll get them. All Adam has to do is write
down their license plate number and call Rod Cordova.
Rod will do the rest." Robin put her hand on Josefina's
arm. "You've been very brave. You'll see. Everything will
work out."

But when Josefina was gone, Robin was not nearly as
confident as she'd sounded in front of the woman. There
were so many ways the plan could go wrong. Adam could
have changed his mind about going through with it—because of the danger he imagined, or for any number of
reasons.

Then, of course, there was the scenario in which Martinez had made up the mysterious men who came for his

pots each month. Then no one would show tomorrow. But she couldn't think of that possibility, not now.

What if the men noticed her and Adam? They knew her car and they knew Adam's car. She'd borrow a vehicle, or rent one. What if Martinez gave them away? What if he'd set this up in order for the counterfeiters to try to trap them? Could John Martinez be that devious?

Robin paced back and forth in her shop, thinking. Maybe she just should forget the plan and notify Rod Cordova. But as soon as the notion solidified in her head she dismissed it. Both John Martinez and Josefina Ortega were only going through with this because they trusted her and Adam. To call in Rod now, to have him waiting at Martinez's place in their stead, might well spoil everything.

No, Robin decided, they'd stick to the original plan and alert the police when they had concrete evidence.

Rain was spattering her front window, and the thick, boiling clouds had moved lower, making the landscape seem very small, very limited in scope. Robin would have to go back to her lonely room at the inn; and she couldn't even call her best friend for a little gossip. Oh, God, she thought, let Shelly and Chuck be innocent. Let this awful mess be over tomorrow.

Adam. It was nearly six, and the visitors' center at Chaco Canyon was closed, but she could leave a recorded message for him. When would he get the message, though? Sometime tomorrow, maybe too late to drive into Santa Fe by three?

Would he come at all? And how would they act with each other? Robin couldn't bear another rejection; she'd have to stay very cool, very distant. It was hard for her to act like that, though. It wasn't *her*. Every time she tried to act cold and reserved she detested herself. Yet, somehow, despite the fact that Adam was at the root of her unhappiness, Robin couldn't hate him.

She sighed and, picking up the phone, dialed the number of the Chaco Canyon Visitors' Center. He'd come, her heart told her. He'd come because he couldn't stay away any more than she could.

BY ONE O'CLOCK THE NEXT DAY Robin was jumping nervously every time the bell over the door tinkled or the phone rang. Adam couldn't have gotten her message before nine, when the visitors' center opened, so he couldn't get to Santa Fe much before one. She'd phoned earlier and arranged to pick up an unobtrusive rental car at the Hertz agency, and it was parked outside Robin's Nest, a gray Ford station wagon. She kept looking at the clock on the wall, wanting Adam to come, afraid to see him, craving him, wanting to throw herself in his arms, hating herself for her weakness.

Where was he? Surely he would have called if he wasn't coming. Or maybe he never got the message. She took a deep breath. She'd leave by one-thirty whether Adam was there or not. She had a strong feeling she'd better be in place, hidden, watching Martinez's house, long before the three o'clock pickup. She'd just close up the shop and go, and if Adam showed up... She'd leave an envelope with his name on it taped to her door. Yes, that's what she'd do. A note, telling him to meet her at San Lucas, describing the gray station wagon. And if he got there in time, fine; if he didn't, she'd handle it herself.

At one-fifteen, she started fidgeting. A man came in to buy film, and she almost pushed him out the door. The minute he was gone she turned her Open sign to Closed, locked the door and leaned back against it, breathing hard, as if she'd just been running.

The phone rang and Robin's heart jerked wildly. She rushed to it, snatched it up. "Hello?" she said breathlessly.

"It's Shelly, home safe and sound from Denver. Hey, did you have lunch yet? Want to go to La Cocina?"

Shelly. "I . . . uh, gosh, I already ate, Shel."

"You want to just sit with me then? I have some great gossip to catch you up on."

"Look, Shel, I'm expecting a real important phone call . . ."

"Oh, sorry, I'll get off the line. Sure you don't want even a teensy little taco? You're always hungry."

"I just can't. How about tomorrow?" asked Robin, one eye on the clock: one twenty-five.

"Okay, call me," said Shelly.

My God, thought Robin. Could Shelly have been trying to keep Robin occupied while the pickup was pulled off? No, ridiculous. Her imagination was working overtime. Shelly had nothing to do with pottery counterfeiters and merely wanted to have lunch with her friend, Robin. Her *friend*.

She scribbled a note for Adam, taped the envelope to her door, grabbed a jacket and headed out the door. She looked up and down the street. No Land Rover, no Adam. Should she wait a few more minutes? She couldn't. She'd go without him. He was on his way, surely he was on his way right now.

She drove the big station wagon carefully, not used to such a vehicle. It was another gray day, but only overcast, not raining. The landscape was subdued, its colors subtle, its sweep more monotone. The mountains hovered on the horizon, dark masses with a faint dusting of snow on their peaks. She passed Tesuque, the halfway point. Glancing in the rearview mirror, she checked again to see if Adam was following her; maybe he'd gotten to the shop just after she'd left, and there was only the one main road up to San Lucas.

Her heart thudded; she'd feel immensely better if Adam were with her. She was a little scared. These men had used violence already. What if they were waiting for her? Where was Adam? Her foot seemed to have let up on the gas pedal, because when she glanced at the speedometer, she was only going forty-five. It took all her willpower to press harder, to inch the needle up to fifty, then fifty-five.

A car horn honked behind Robin, making her start as if she'd been burned. What? She looked around, slowing down. Behind her. A big grill, a dusty windshield, coming up fast. A truck. The sound came again, loud, insistent. She looked in the rearview mirror and, without hesitation, pulled off the road and stopped, bowing her head on the steering wheel, feeling her hands tremble under her forehead.

It was Adam.

In a second he was opening the car door. She sat there, drained, suddenly exhausted, and stared at him. "I...I couldn't wait," she finally managed.

"Sorry I was late. I didn't get your message right away," he said quietly, his dark eyes searching hers. "You okay?"

She gave a small hiccup of a laugh. "Yeah, sure. I was a little nervous about doing this alone."

He stood there for a minute, as if he wanted to say something.

"We better, ah, get up there," Robin said, looking away.

"Yes. I'll leave my car here. We can pick it up later," he said. "Do you want me to drive?"

"Yes," she replied gratefully, moving over to the passenger seat.

They were parked in an alleyway with a clear view of John Martinez's house by two o'clock.

"We may have to wait here a long time," Adam said, "so make yourself comfortable."

"Oh, I'm fine."

There was a period of silence, as if each was waiting for the other to speak.

"I'm glad you made it," Robin finally said.

Adam looked at her. "Would you really have come here without me?"

She nodded. "If I had to."

He turned to stare out the window at John Martinez's door. Robin tried not to keep looking at Adam, but he was so close. She would have liked to reach out and caress his copper-colored cheek. One of his hands lay on his thigh and she would have liked to grasp it, to be able to touch him when she wanted, the way a woman touched a man she loved. He'd given her incredible joy and caused her wrenching uncertainty in equal measure, but perhaps it was only the strange circumstances that had thrown them together after all. If they'd met casually and parted, none of this would have happened.

He was not going to talk about the other night, nor was he going to explain why he'd left. Was it the Indian in him, the Apache training that did not allow for intimate communication? Yet Apaches were gentle and affectionate in their personal relations, she'd seen that. He was keeping something from her.

"How's the dig going?" she asked.

"All right. The kids are leaving, except for a couple of graduates, but we've got that kiva mostly rebuilt."

"The kiva." She recalled the weight of his body on hers and the stifling dust. "That's good."

"Um."

"Did it rain at Chaco yesterday?" she ventured.

"It threatened."

"Gosh, it sure will be nice to get back to my own apartment when this is over."

"I hope it'll be today," he remarked.

"I'm sure it will, unless Martinez is putting something over on us," she replied. "You know, Josefina will be awful upset if John turns out to be one of the bad guys."

He nodded gravely.

"I asked her if Martinez was cut up or bruised, and she said he'd been hit in the ribs. So nobody would be able to tell if he'd really been beaten or not." She tried to keep her tone conversational. Was she chattering too much? "I don't suppose he saw a doctor about—"

"Wait." Adam put his hand out to silence her. He was watching Martinez's house intently.

Yes, someone was emerging. It was John, carrying a large cardboard carton. He took it to his old pickup truck and put it in the back. Returning to his door, he glanced around furtively.

"What's he doing?" she whispered.

"I don't know."

Martinez came out with another box.

"He's got pots in those boxes," said Adam with certainty.

"Is he trying to run away?" Robin breathed. "It's too early for them to come here."

"Josefina told you three at Martinez's house? You're sure?"

"Yes, I'm sure."

"Either Martinez is trying to avoid them or us by sneaking away early, or he's been notified to meet them somewhere else," said Adam.

"What do we do? Should we call Rod?"

Adam shook his head. "No time, I'm betting."

"Adam, we *have* to follow him."

"Yes, I'm afraid so." He pounded a palm on the steering wheel. "Damn, this is exactly what I didn't want to get into."

Martinez loaded yet another box onto the truck, then another. He moved quickly, stealthily, glancing around as if looking for someone. Then he climbed into his truck, started it up with a great blast of black exhaust and pulled away.

"Go on," urged Robin, "he'll get too far ahead."

"Look, Robin, you get out of the car right now. I'll do this alone. Call a cab and go back to Santa Fe. Tell Rod—"

"No! Go on, he'll get too far ahead!"

"Robin, who knows where he's going or who might be there?"

"You're not going to have all the fun, Adam!" she cried impatiently.

He muttered some Apache words under his breath and started the car. John's old truck didn't go very fast, so it was easy to catch up. Adam's main problem was trying to keep as far behind as possible—so as not to arouse Martinez's suspicion—without losing sight of him on the winding country road.

"Don't lose him," said Robin, leaning forward in her seat.

"I can't get too close. But he could turn off anywhere. There're dozens of dirt roads around here," replied Adam.

The road they were on dipped and curved, following an undulating ridge line. Stands of ponderosa pine, aspen and spruce dotted the brown hillside; there wasn't a house or a village for miles. It was a serene landscape, just touched with autumn's hand, tranquil under the gray sky, but Robin's heart raced and she only saw the hills as convenient obstacles to keep Martinez from spotting them.

The old pickup didn't go very fast, so there was no danger of him outdistancing them. It also left a trail of black exhaust floating behind it, so that even when the truck was out of sight they had no trouble following it.

"Where's he going?" muttered Robin, straining to see.

There was a long descending hill and a sharp curve ahead. When they reached the bottom the pickup was gone—and so was the black exhaust trail.

"Oh, no!" cried Robin.

"Maybe he turned off," said Adam grimly, wrenching the steering wheel around, turning the station wagon sharply on the narrow road. "Look for a dirt road."

Slowly he drove back around the curve and up the hill. "There," he said, pointing.

Yes, she could see it, a narrow track, merely two wheel ruts on the hillside. A faint blue of black vapor mixed with dust hung over its surface. "That's it!" she said excitedly.

Adam drove very cautiously on the dirt road, his tires catching the ruts occasionally, throwing the station wagon from side to side.

"Can't we go faster?" asked Robin, on the edge of her seat.

"We don't want to come around a bend and run right into him," replied Adam as he concentrated on the road. "In fact," he said, "we better stop and walk soon."

"Walk?"

"See the way the hills come together up there?" he said, pointing. "There's a canyon ahead. The road is going to end anyway."

"But Martinez—"

"Oh, he's up there somewhere," said Adam grimly, "but God knows what he's doing."

"Then we better stop, shouldn't we?" she said, starting to look for a spot. There was thick brush on either side of the road, a few trees, a rising bank on the left and a hillside sloping away directly on their right. "There's plenty of cover."

"I'll have to find someplace to park the car, a break in the bushes," said Adam. "I don't like this, Robin. It's too isolated."

"We'll be careful, and maybe we can see what Martinez is doing and then leave. Maybe he's just hiding out here. Maybe he's too scared to go through with the plan," she said. "We can't turn back now."

"You can," Adam said.

"And leave you here alone? Besides, we only have one car. I can't leave."

He steered around a fallen branch, bumping along slowly. The exhaust pipe scraped on the road, and the shock absorbers thumped alarmingly.

Robin noticed an opening in the thick growth on her side of the road. "Can you fit in there?"

Adam nosed the car off the road, pushing aside branches with the grill. The brush crackled and rustled and closed in behind them. When Robin squeezed out of her door, she found Adam standing in the road, hands on hips. "I guess that'll have to do," he said. "I hope we'll be gone before Martinez drives back out anyway."

They walked about half a mile, poised to dash into the bushes if they heard anyone coming. But there was only

silence, broken by the occasional cheery call of a chicka-
dee, and the crunching sound of their own footsteps.

Robin saw the smoke just as Adam put a hand out to
hold her back. "A fire?" she asked.

"A house probably. Now we better get off the road."

Robin was thankful she'd worn pants and low shoes. She
had to push through the prickly branches, trying desperately to be quiet, her heart pounding, her mouth dry. She
followed Adam's broad back, thankful he was breaking
trail. He moved effortlessly, silently, through the undergrowth, in his element. Suddenly he put a hand up and
stopped.

Just beyond the scrub oak and gnarled mesquite was a
house, an old Spanish-style adobe house, stained and
crumbling at the corners. Its windows were broken and
boarded up, its roof tiles cracked. The only new thing
Robin could see was a shiny padlock on the door, which
hung open. John Martinez's pickup was parked in front of
the house, and off to the side was a brown van.

"He's meeting someone," Robin whispered.

They crouched down, watching the house. She tried not
to breathe hard, but she felt terribly short of breath, excited, keyed up.

John Martinez appeared in the door of the old house,
then went to his truck and reached into the back for a box.
Two men followed him. They were too far away to see
clearly, and they wore hats that were pulled low over their
faces. Robin swallowed nervously.

A third man came to the door and spoke. His voice carried faintly, but she couldn't make out the words. He was
very obviously directing them to take the boxes out of the
truck.

"It looks like John is working with them," Adam said
quietly.

"Yes."

"Look, Robin, someone's got to go right now and call Rod before these men disappear. It'd be best if they were caught in the act, but we don't know how long they're going to stick around. I'm guessing they only store the pottery here until they find buyers, so they may leave soon." He thought a minute. "I think I better stay and keep an eye on them. You go back and get the car. Chimayo isn't far along the main road. You'll find a phone there."

"I can't leave you here! You wouldn't even have a car to get away in," she protested.

"Don't worry, they won't know I'm here."

"What if they leave before I get back with the car?"

"I'll get the license number of that van. The police can trace it. Of course, it'd be a lot better to catch them here, like I said."

"And Martinez?"

"We know where to find him, that's no trouble."

"I hate to leave you ..."

"I'll be fine. You hurry. Be careful. Can you find your way?"

"Sure. Oh, Adam ..."

"Go on. Quietly," he said, handing her the car keys.

She pushed her way back through the branches and burdocks, trying to be quiet, feeling as if someone were behind her every step of the way. Once she hit the dirt road she ran until she was out of breath and had a stitch in her side. Had she passed the place where the car was hidden by mistake? No, there were no broken branches.

Oh, Lord, what if those men were driving along the road toward her right now? What if they caught her alone? She stopped and listened—no sound came to her ears but her own harsh breathing. Slipping into the station wagon, she gunned it backward out of its hiding place and took off down the dirt road like a madwoman.

Chimayo, she thought, racing along the main road. *Isn't there a gas station closer?* But there wasn't, only an isolated intersection, with a sign: Chimayo 2 miles.

The old pueblo was charming, but Robin didn't notice. She pulled up in front of the general store, slammed on the brakes and ran inside.

"A phone?" she gasped to the startled storekeeper. "It's important!"

He tilted his head toward the back. She hurried over to the phone, jammed some coins in and dialed the operator. "This is an emergency," she said breathlessly. "Please get me the Santa Fe Police Department."

It seemed forever before there was an answer. "Detective Cordova, please," she said. "It's an emergency."

"Detective Cordova is not in today," came the reply.

"Oh, God, no! Then anyone, someone important! Please, this is an emergency."

A man came on the line. "Lieutenant Wilson here."

"Please, listen. My name is Robin Hayle. Rod Cordova has been handling this case. I'm at Chimayo..." And she had to tell the story, praying he believed her. "There are men with...with contraband goods. They're dangerous. Can you send some police up here?"

He was reluctant, she could tell. Her story sounded crazy. "Please believe me! We'll lose them if you don't send someone!"

"All right, Miss Hayle," he finally said. "I'll send a couple of cars."

"Hurry, please. And they're dangerous. I'm going back there right now."

"You stay clear of those men," warned Lieutenant Wilson. "We'll take care of it."

"Oh, yes, I will! Thank you! Please hurry!"

Robin hardly remembered the return drive. She pulled the car off into the same clearing and left it there, rushing up the road toward the house. Were the men gone? Was Adam all right? Would Lieutenant Wilson send the cars quickly, or would he dawdle, disbelieving her story?

A column of smoke was drifting up from the broken chimney of the house. Martinez's pickup was gone, but the brown van was still out front.

Adam was nowhere to be found.

Robin felt like crying. Had they discovered him? Was he being held inside the house? Squirming through the brush, she crept toward the house, worming her way closer. She had no idea what she was going to do, but she had to get near, to find out if Adam was inside, held prisoner—or worse.

She stopped, crouching, a few yards from the clearing, breathing hard, terrified, her heart racing uncontrollably. How long would it be before the police got here? Twenty minutes, half an hour?

A branch rustled behind her. As she half-turned, a hand covered her mouth and a strong arm drew her back against a hard chest. A scream welled up in Robin's throat; she stiffened and went wide-eyed with terror. "Sh!" she heard in her ear. "It's me."

She slumped with relief, falling back against Adam, shaking in reaction. "Don't ever do that to me again!" she whispered fiercely.

"Sorry, I didn't want you to make any noise," he said, steadying her, grasping her arms.

"Rod wasn't there," she explained. "A Lieutenant Wilson was. He said he'd send two cars. Adam, he thought I was crazy. I don't know if they'll get here fast enough."

"We've got to try to keep the men here. Martinez already left."

"The van. If we do something to the van so it won't drive," Robin suggested. "The tires?"

Adam fished in his pocket, came up with a knife and held it up; they exchanged glances over its sharp blade. "I'll have to get close to the house," he said, "but if I keep the van between me and them I should be okay. I'll try to get at least two of the tires."

"What if they see you?"

He shrugged.

"Adam..."

He was starting to make his way toward the van, but he stopped and turned to her, his dark eyes questioning.

"You'll...ah—" she swallowed convulsively "—be careful?"

He gave her an enigmatic smile and slipped off through the bushes.

Adam was beside the van before she could believe it. She could see him digging at the tires with his knife, but it seemed to be taking forever. The men could come out of the house any minute. She crouched there in the bushes, staring through the tangled branches, quivering with anxiety. *Hurry, Adam,* she thought, *hurry!* One end of the van settled slowly; Adam was moving to the front wheel. *Oh, good, halfway done!*

It was then that the door of the house opened, and the three men came out. Robin's heart stopped in mid-beat. Slowly, unsuspectingly, the men walked toward the van; they were talking, and one of them was laughing about something.

She could see Adam freeze—he heard them! Then he jabbed at the tire once more and the front of the van slowly settled. But it was too late. The men were splitting up, one getting in the driver's door, the other two heading around to the far side.

They'd see him! There was no time for Adam to reach the undergrowth!

Robin had no choice at all. Her mind was working clearly, logically. She stood and walked out of the mesquite into plain sight of the three men. Calmly, seemingly unconcerned, she strode toward them. "Yoo, hoo," she cried, "boy, am I glad to see someone! My car broke down out on the road and I—"

The three men stood there, paralyzed with surprise for a moment, and Robin got a good look at them.

Shock jolted her as if she'd been punched, and she could only stare stupidly and openmouthed at one of the men.

CHAPTER NINETEEN

ROBIN GASPED AND WHIRLED and started running, sickeningly aware that two of the men were shouting and chasing after her like hounds after a doe.

She was afraid to look back; if she did she'd trip. So she ran, her long legs eating up the yards, her face and arms sliced by the brush that crowded the road.

"Get her!" she heard from behind. The voice sounded close, too close. "You go that way! Head her off!"

Which way? wondered Robin frantically. *Which way?*

She braved a look over her shoulder, but just that quick move was enough to send her sprawling into a mesquite bush. But Robin wasn't down for long. She scrambled up and was off, her only hope to stay ahead of them until Adam caught up.

Where *was* he? Oh, God, had the third man gotten him? Did they have guns?

Breaking through the undergrowth was a nightmare, branches springing up around her like living creatures, reaching for her, grasping at her. She put her hands out in front and pushed furiously at the tangles, but they snapped back, striking her arms and shoulders, slashing at her head. And still, no matter how quickly she made her way through the growth, the sounds of crackling branches from behind grew nearer.

The police! Surely the police would come racing along the road at any moment, sirens wailing, frightening off her pursuers. *Oh, hurry, hurry!*

Robin's lungs felt as if she'd swallowed a ball of fire and her legs were giving way; her feet were cast in cement. Blood trickled down her cheek from a cut and she could taste it at the corner of her mouth when she gasped for air.

"There she is! Cut her off!"

Oh, God! Adam, help!

She ran into a piñon tree then, one of its gnarled branches seeming to snatch at her, monstrous, huge, throwing her to the ground where she landed so hard that the breath was knocked from her lungs. She tried to roll over; she tried to get to her hands and knees, but there was no air, and her chest felt as if it were caving in.

"I see her! Get her!"

It was over. Even if she could have gotten up, Robin knew that she hadn't the strength to flee. Broken and terrified, she lay there watching the men approach like wolves surrounding a lamb. The question struck her only then: why, why him?

Robin wasn't sure how long she stayed on the hard ground, panting like a rabbit, immobile, staring at him. It seemed like many long minutes, but logic told her it was seconds. Somewhere she was aware of sirens but they were so far off, in a distant place, a place she was never going to see. If Adam were able to come after her, she thought, he would already be there. A horrible regret filled her, driving away the terror for a moment. Adam...

"You should have taken the warnings more seriously," he said as he stood above her. "I'm sorry. I liked you."

Robin ran her tongue across her dry lips. "Why?" she managed to say. "Why did you do it?"

But he didn't reply; he only nodded to the other man, his eyes unable to meet hers.

It struck Robin suddenly that she was going to die. This was it, this was all there was. Even the sirens had faded, as if in farewell. She felt, oddly, like laughing at herself—all those dreams, all the hope...

The horror was gone from her eyes then, replaced by a sad kind of irony, a self-mockery. At first she didn't hear it. She was aware only of her mad thoughts, but then it came to her: a voice, a voice as if from her past. A deep, smooth voice, utterly in command.

"I wouldn't do that if I were you," the voice said, and it was a long moment before Robin could clear the cobwebs from her head to comprehend that it was Adam's voice coming from behind the two men. Relief washed over her.

He moved into her line of sight then, catlike, silent and ready. His feet were spread slightly, his arms hanging loosely at his sides. There was something deadly in his stance. A shiver crawled up Robin's spine.

Then the tableau exploded. One of the men, head down like a bull, rushed Adam. Robin cried out, shocked by the sheer violence of it, but Adam sidestepped deftly, grabbed the man by the back of the neck and swung him around, then slammed him against a tree. And it was over, just like that; the other man, cowed, gave up without a struggle.

After all, Robin was to think later, Julien Cordova was not at all a physical man.

IT TOOK ADAM A LONG TIME to explain everything to the police. And Robin guessed that the only reason they were buying his story at all was because of the evidence, the cartons of forged pottery, not to mention the fact that she'd been pursued and her life threatened.

"Look," said Adam, standing in front of the old adobe house, "why don't you just haul these three men into town and I'll follow. We can clear everything up at the station."

"Well," said one of the four officers, "the district attorney's got a case here, I guess, but Detective Cordova's not going to like this at all."

"I'd be surprised," said Robin, "if he didn't know about it already. I'll bet he was in on the whole thing. No wonder he wasn't much help."

"Now, lady, that's assuming an awful lot," began Lieutenant Wilson.

"She's right, lieutenant," said Adam quietly, and the man shut his mouth with a snap.

It was another few minutes before the three Cordova brothers and the boxes of pottery were all loaded into the police vehicles. Robin and Adam followed in the rented station wagon.

"You know," Robin said as they bounced along in the wave of dust from the patrol cars, "I was sure you were dead back there."

A corner of Adam's mouth lifted slightly. "Now, how could I have been in any trouble with you out there saving me? That was quite a little stunt you pulled."

"I rather liked it myself," she replied, "that is, until I saw Julien." She shook her head. "Amazing. *Julien*. But anyway, what happened to you when they were chasing me?"

"Oh, I stood up and said hello to Martin Cordova. We hadn't seen each other in years."

"What did he do, faint?"

"Just about." Adam gave her a sidelong glance. "Then following after the rest of you was really very easy. You were making as much noise as a three-ring circus."

"And here I thought I was being so quiet..."

The sun had already dipped below the western ridge of mountains by the time they reached the highway. Robin switched on the heater in the car and hugged herself with her arms. Suddenly she felt drained, scratched and bruised and exhausted. It was hard for her to even think.

"So it's over finally," she said wearily. "I never thought..."

"Didn't you? But you seemed so positive all along that we'd get them."

"That's me—" she smiled ruefully "—always the optimist."

"Um," he replied then fell silent.

Robin gazed out the window and watched the scenery drift by as if it were on a film. The adobe cubes of the pueblos looked dark now in the autumn light, as if they were a part of the earth itself, merely shaped more geometrically. And above them the willowy cottonwoods were already turning golden—soon winter would come, and the land would become brown and white, waiting, waiting those long cold months for rebirth. When spring came, wondered Robin, would she still be seeing Adam or were these to be their last few minutes together? She longed to ask him, but somehow the words just wouldn't come to her lips. It was too much like begging.

It was late by the time they left the police station. Even the district attorney, who had been called away from his dinner table, had told Robin to go on home and clean up. "Don't worry," he'd said, "we've got enough evidence to keep these men behind bars for a long, long while."

One last time, Robin climbed into the car alongside Adam. Was this it, then? Was this goodbye? "What about your Land Rover?" she asked as she drove toward her apartment.

"My father can give me a ride out to it tomorrow."

She would have offered, but he didn't ask.

"And I'll get this rental car back to the agency for you first thing in the morning."

Robin glanced up at the full moon, which hung huge and bright over the Sangre de Cristo Mountains. She sighed and looked over at Adam—strong, beautiful Adam. "You certainly are tying up all the loose ends, aren't you?" she asked, the hurt in her voice undisguised.

"I don't know what you mean," he said then fell silent. She could feel the tension, however, emanating from him like a terrible living thing. In the passing car lights his profile looked hard as marble, as if a sculptor had carved bitterness into his features. Adam sat only inches away, but he was a total stranger to her.

She was thinking frantically, searching her mind for a way to reach him, when suddenly he did an alarming thing. He spun the steering wheel violently and pulled into a parking space along the road. Robin was confused; her apartment was still three blocks away. "You won't let it go, will you?" Adam's voice was harsh, frighteningly so. *You just keep pushing, Robin.*

"I—"

But he silenced her with a sharp gesture. "Don't say another damn thing. You've asked for this, you acted as if you really wanted to hear it, so here goes..."

Her heart began to beat furiously, and instinctively she knew that she didn't want to hear it at all—not now, not like this. He was so angry, so in pain. She wanted to run, to cover her ears, anything.

"Do you think I'm blind?" he said as if demanding an answer. "I know what you want, Robin, and I can't give it to you. You want a husband and a family. You want to be a part of some man's life, to belong—"

She pushed his hand away. "Not *any* man's life, Adam Farwalker," she said in an angry voice.

"Okay. But can you deny that you want to be a mother, raise a family?"

What was he getting at?

"Well, I can't give you that, Robin. I can't give you those children." He slammed his palm against the steering wheel, and the force of his sudden rage made her heart leap. "It's the stupidest thing in the world but there you are," he ground out. "I was thirty years old... I had the mumps."

Robin sat utterly motionless for what seemed like an eternity. The mumps. He was sterile. So *that* was Adam's secret. She had no idea what to say to him, and she was afraid that anything she said would be wrong. He was so hurt, so angry, so very, very alone with his pain. She prayed for words of comfort to form in her head. Nothing came.

The silence drew out between them, a hollow, bitter, empty silence. She felt more alone than she'd ever felt in her life, alone with the beating of her heart.

It was finally Adam who spoke as he started up the car. "I'll take you home."

She bit back her tears of frustration. He'd certainly hit the nail on the head, hadn't he? She *did* want a family—she'd be lying to him and herself if she said otherwise. Oh, God, what was she to do? She *loved* Adam!

"I'm sorry," he said as he pulled up in front of her place and turned to her. "You can't know how sorry I am. It could have been good between us."

"Adam," she began, a thousand useless words swarming in her head, beating at her, "can't we... isn't there something..."

He shook his head slowly. "Facts are facts, Robin. I wish to God it weren't true, but I can't give you what you want, what you deserve."

"Isn't that up to me?" she asked. "Shouldn't I have a say in this, too?"

"I'm afraid," said Adam gravely, "you've already expressed your feelings on the subject. Maybe you shouldn't have been so honest, Robin Hayle." And even as he kissed her cheek softly she was thinking about that remark, hating it, trying to deny it, but there it was: she did want a family. No wonder at all, she thought darkly, he'd run from her. Good old honest Robin Hayle...

For long, miserable days those minutes in the car with Adam played through her mind over and over, endlessly, like a phonograph needle stuck in a groove. Robin went about her daily existence, opening and closing her shop, reading in the paper the breaking story about the counterfeit ring but hardly able to concentrate on its significance. She felt so empty, as if set adrift in a void where there were no stimuli whatsoever. There was no sight, no smell, no touch—just nothingness.

Thank God for Shelly. When the story of the van finally came out, Shelly was incredibly understanding and even laughed. "You should have told me," she said, "and saved yourself a big headache."

"I couldn't, I was afraid to. How can you ever forgive me?"

"Oh, how about you buy the doughnuts for the next week and then we'll call it even."

That was Shelly, the best friend a woman could ever have.

One other thing kept Robin going those days. She started planning for the new Indian artists' organization. If there was nothing left of her relationship with Adam,

something good had to come out of what Robin had
started thinking of as her "great adventure." She phoned
Christina, carefully avoiding the subject of Adam, and got
the names of some prominent Indian artists of the pueblos. She asked Christina to call a few then started on her
own list during the quiet hours in her shop.

It was discouraging. So many of the Indians were suspicious or doubtful. Some didn't speak English. But she
kept at it, gritting her teeth at the rebuffs, determined to
have something to show for her great adventure.

She called Josefina, too, begging the woman to lend her
support to the concept of the organization.

"I am not sure," said Josefina. "Why would anyone
listen to me?"

"You are one of the most famous, respected Indian artists in the Southwest," Robin said firmly. "Every Indian
in New Mexico will listen to you, Josefina."

"That would make me very nervous. Who am I to tell
others how they should act? Every Indian must search his
own heart to know what to do," said the woman.

"But you agree this organization is needed?" pressed
Robin.

"I think it is a good idea, but I do not know how you
can make it work."

"With your help I can. I know Christina thinks it's a
good idea, too."

"Yes, she was very persuasive. But, you see, Christina
does not always understand . . ."

"But, Josefina, if I can persuade some of the artists to
get together for a meeting, would you come? Would you
give it your support?"

Josefina sighed. "I must think about it. I will talk with
my sons."

"Oh, thank you. I know you'll do the right thing."

"The right thing for an Indian is not necessarily the right thing for a white person," replied Josefina quietly.

It was difficult, but it kept her occupied at least, the endless, frustrating phone calls, the attempts to penetrate an alien culture that was wary and guarded, having too often been betrayed by Anglos. But she kept at it tenaciously; Robin was, if nothing else, determined.

And she never heard from Adam.

It was finally Shelly who broke through her silence on the subject and got her mad. "Okay, kiddo," said her friend one morning as she popped in, "what gives?"

With much coaxing and hugging, Shelly finally got the whole story from Robin. "Go ahead and cry," Shelly advised, "you deserve it." Then, when Robin's sobbing finally subsided, she said, "So? What are you going to do? I don't see that this decision is entirely Adam's."

"Well, he *made* it his decision," replied Robin, sniffing into a Kleenex. "He thinks that all I want is kids."

"Do you?"

"Yes...and no." Robin felt an odd sort of anger begin to bubble up inside her. "I mean, they don't have to be *my* kids, do they? Shouldn't I have a say?"

"You bet."

"After all, hundreds of people get married every day and then find out they can't have children, don't they? And that doesn't stop them from loving each other."

Shelly shook her head emphatically.

"And I bet if they had known before they got married, they still would have."

"They adopt," offered Shelly as she took a doughnut from Robin's white bakery bag.

"Oh, sure," said Robin, feeling alive again for the first time in days, "I'd like to have my own kids... But Shelly—" she looked at her friend intently "—we can't have it all, can we? It might hurt at times, but I've got so much love stored up inside me, enough for Adam *and* a bunch of children.''

"Even if they aren't yours?" asked Shelly.

"They'd need me even more, wouldn't they?" replied Robin pensively. "There're so many kids without homes..."

"Thousands and thousands," agreed Shelly.

Robin stared at her friend. "Indian children, too. Can you imagine the wealth of knowledge a man like Adam could give them?"

Indian summer touched the land with a generous hand, flashing in the rivers, gilding the mountainsides, kissing the desert with a last, frantic bloom of colorful wildflowers. Day after day the sky was clear, the air cool and crisp. Robin felt peaceful and vibrant; for the first time in her life she truly knew what she wanted. And she came to a decision: even if she never again saw Adam, even if there was never to be *any* man in her life, she was going to stop waiting for love to come to her; she was going to go out and grab it and hold it to her. She was going to adopt a child.

Her decision made, Robin knew that there was one thing she had to do first: she had to see Adam one last time; she had to try to make him believe how much she loved him, how much she *would* love him even if he were missing an arm or a leg or an eye. But if she failed she was not going to bury herself behind her superficial, fun-loving exterior. Not ever again. But just how was she going to see him?

The opportunity finally presented itself, however, when Robin got an encouraging call from Christina late in the month.

CHAPTER TWENTY

THE GATHERING AT CHRISTINA'S was to be a preliminary organizational meeting for the New Mexico Native American Artists' Association. It was off the ground, at last, Christina had told her on the phone, and Robin had to be there. It had been all her hard work that had finally persuaded at least some of the Indians to consider the idea.

Robin drove out to Las Jaritas in an unsettled frame of mind. She was thrilled that some of the Indians were organizing, and she was gratified to be involved. So many benefits could come from the fledgling association, and Robin was to be a part of it all. She knew, also, that John Martinez was going to be there today, and she was looking forward to seeing him again, to thank him in person for all his help.

Everything had turned out for the best, just as Robin's eternal optimism had always led her to believe. Everything but her and Adam.

Would he be there today? It was a Saturday; perhaps he'd taken the weekend off.

Why should he be there? If he'd wanted to see her he would have called—he'd had days and days to contact her.

The familiar hills lay under the brilliant yellow sun, the horizon standing out as sharply as a cactus thorn. Indian summer. The summer of Robin's Indian. Was her great adventure over? Was it the end of their love?

But his mud-caked Land Rover was parked in the driveway, behind the dozen or so other vehicles. Robin's heart gave a frightened thump, then a glad one.

She pushed her hair off her shoulders, straightened her long, slim navy-blue skirt and belted blouse and closed her eyes for a second, then walked to the front door and knocked.

Adam opened it. Had he been waiting?

"Oh, hello," she said.

He stood in the doorway, gazing down on her. "Hello, Robin."

"Ah...I'm, ah, here for the meeting," she said inanely.

"Yes, I know. Please come in." His face was expressionless, his voice carefully neutral.

Rigid, Robin walked past him then stopped. Was this all there was going to be between them now, strained politeness?

"They're all in the living room," he was saying, then he moved past her, leading the way.

She couldn't help staring at him as she followed. He had no right to look so handsome, so tall and dark and beautifully put together. And yet, she knew, there was that imperfection that scarred him. Suddenly she wanted to reach out and touch his back, to tell him that it was okay, that she would love him no matter what.

"Oh, hello, Robin!" Christina rose from her seat and came to greet her. Then Robin was whisked away from him and introduced to the assembled group, representatives of the pueblos and of the Navaho and Apache tribes. Robin had trouble concentrating, her whole being focused on Adam, who took a seat in the corner of the room. But she smiled and replied correctly to questions, she guessed, because no one seemed to notice her preoccupation.

Josefina Ortega was there with her son Manuel. John Martinez was there, as expected, and many other Indians whom Robin did not know, but whom she'd spoken to on the phone.

"We've been working all morning," Christina said, "organizing. They've elected me president." Then she smiled. "But only temporarily, until things get going. Now, we have a few small problems, Robin. We have to decide on dues and we really need to see a copy of that pamphlet your association is going to put out."

The discussion went on for another half hour. Robin answered questions about her own business association, trying to help. She could see there were going to be a couple of factions, as there were in all such organizations. Some of the Indians were distrustful still, but, with Christina and Josefina's influence, she was convinced that they'd learn to compromise for the good of everyone.

And all the while she was aware of Adam's attention on her. Her skin felt oversensitive, as if she had a fever, as if his big hands were on her flesh, setting her on fire.

"Well," she was saying to an artisan from San Claro, "when we have a disagreement at our meetings in Santa Fe, we always take a vote." Why was Adam doing this to her? Didn't he know what torment it was for her to be so near without having the freedom to touch him?

"Will everyone pay the same in dues?" asked another artist.

Eventually Robin was handed a plate of Christina's *chiles rellenos*, cheese-stuffed green peppers, and found herself seated on the couch next to Adam's mother. During the lunch break, the conversation turned from the new organization to the recently exposed counterfeiting ring. John Martinez, of course, had to explain to the group his role in the scam.

"I was told," he said in English, "that the pots were for a museum. I was paid so little..." And then he spoke in Tewa to a few of the Indians.

Robin half listened to his words, but she was more aware of Adam than anything else. He'd pulled a chair up close to the couch and, with a plate of food in his hand, seemed to be engrossed in Martinez's explanation while he ate. Robin's appetite, however, was entirely gone for once; she couldn't seem to get the food past the lump in her throat.

Christina said something in Apache to a woman seated on her right then turned to Adam. "Many here today," she said to her son, "are still confused about the forgeries. Perhaps you can explain better than I can."

Adam put his plate down. As usual, when he began to speak, everyone paid attention. How did he do that? wondered Robin once again.

"As I'm sure you all know, it was Julien Cordova," he was saying, "who was the head of the ring."

"But why would a fine man like that do such a terrible thing?" Josefina shook her head, and a man sitting next to her patted her clasped hands.

"Essentially," replied Adam, "it was an act of revenge. The Cordovas were an old Spanish land-grant family. They lost their land, of course, years ago, but apparently they still harbor bitter feelings."

"They did it for the money," put in Martinez angrily.

"Yes," agreed Adam, "that, too. When they lost their land, they lost their livelihood. There was a lot of money to be made from the forged pots, more, as it turned out, than most of us realized."

"Julien and his brothers were very clever," said Josefina.

"And," said Robin slowly, "they were in the right position to pull it all off smoothly." She fell silent, uncomfortable, too aware that Adam's gaze had shifted to her again.

"Go on," he said, "you know as much about it as anyone, Robin."

"She was very brave," put in Christina, laying a hand on Robin's arm.

Robin laughed lightly. "I didn't *feel* brave, though. Not at the time." She took a sip of her water then looked around the room, avoiding Adam's eyes. "If you think about it," she went on, "Julien was placed perfectly to organize the ring. He knew everyone in Santa Fe and he's one of the foremost experts in the area of Indian art. Heck, he even had me telling him every move I was making. It was no wonder he was always one step ahead of us."

"Of course," said Adam, "he had his brother Rod in with him, too. It was just pure luck that Rod wasn't there when Robin called for help that day."

"I wonder why the Cordovas made the last pickup of John's work?" Christina asked. "It was their downfall..."

"They thought they had John completely cowed," said Robin. "Although they did get a message to him to make a delivery to that isolated house instead. They were still being cautious even then."

"The van," put in John Martinez, "I was very taken in by that."

"Anyone would have been," agreed Adam. "Julien, of course, had borrowed it from Chuck Dalton for just that purpose. In fact, Julien used a different vehicle every time he sent his brothers out to make the pickups."

"A very careful man," said Christina.

"It was lucky," said Robin, "that Adam threw him off the track, though, when he told Julien at the Daltons' dinner party that we were washing our hands of the forgery business."

"And my poor pots," said Josefina, "all ruined."

"Your pots," Adam said, "and John's injuries, not to mention Julien having one of his brothers follow Robin to Chaco Canyon and try to kill her."

"He dressed like an Indian," Christina explained to the group, "and made a roof collapse on my son and Robin. Then he ran her car off the road. A horrible man."

"No worse than Rod, though." Robin frowned. "As a policeman, it was so easy for him to follow us to John's house in San Lucas. He even had John watched by a stakeout team with the excuse that John was involved with black marketeers. And," she said, her tone growing angry, "it was Rod himself who broke into my shop and my apartment! The creep."

"And," interrupted Adam, "the police in Albuquerque did pick Rod up at the airport there. He had a ticket to Mexico in his pocket."

"What will happen to these men?" asked Tina Sanchez, a weaver from San Claro.

"There'll be a trial. The district attorney is working on the charges right now," said Adam.

"I will tell my story at the trial," said John Martinez. "I believe now that it is the right thing to do."

"Oh, good," said Robin. "Your testimony will help so much."

"I do not like these ways of your law," said John, "but I trust you that it is right to do. My family is back at San Lucas and safe. My wife tells me I should do it and that she will come and watch me in the court."

After lunch Christina asked Robin to explain to the group what the Santa Fe Business Association was doing to see that this kind of thing didn't happen again.

"Well, we're doing several things. We're going to print and distribute a quarterly pamphlet containing information of counterfeit artwork, ways of spotting forgeries, lists of reputable dealers and so on. We're also going to lobby the state legislature for stricter laws governing the sale and documentation of Indian art.

"And it's the first time the association voted for something without arguing," she reported with a smile. "People finally realized we have to cooperate to stop this kind of thing. And, oh, yes, we had to elect another president. It's Chuck Dalton—of the Dalton Gallery. Some of you may know him."

There was a murmur of assent. Robin sat back, feeling relieved that the forgery matter was closed and that she had been able to help. She was glad to see, too, that the Indian artisans were willing to organize. There was going to be a new trust between the whites and the Indians after this, a breakthrough. It was no small thing, either, that John Martinez had agreed to testify in a white man's courtroom.

"Thank you so much, Robin," Christina was saying, "for coming here today," and then the meeting was breaking up. Many people shook Robin's hand and spoke to her. John Martinez said goodbye gravely, but it was Josefina who came up to Robin with a smile on her seamed face and a box, which she held out.

"This is for your help," said Josefina shyly, "and for all the danger I put you in."

It was one of her black-on-black pieces, a large shallow bowl decorated with stylized feathered serpents and jagged lightning. Reverently Robin took it out of the box and held it. "Oh, it's *so* lovely. But Josefina..."

"It is the least I can do for you," said the older woman. "You will remember what happened whenever you look at it—and that is as it should be."

"I'll never forget *you*," said Robin. "And I can never thank you enough."

Carefully Robin put the pot back in the box. She hugged Josefina and smiled some more and thanked people and shook hands, but all the time she was still conscious of Adam, standing quietly in the back of the room, and she knew there was one more matter that was not quite closed.

It was terribly awkward. Robin didn't know whether to leave with everyone else or to say something to him, to wait around in case he wanted to talk to her, or to keep the last shred of her dignity intact and say goodbye firmly, once and for all.

Suddenly the house that had been overflowing with people minutes before was absolutely quiet. Even Christina had vanished. There was only Robin, who stood in the living room fingering her purse straps, and Adam, his stare resting on her, impenetrable and calm.

"Well," said Robin, "guess I better get back to the shop."

Adam came to life then, finally, seeming to cross the distance between them without actually moving. He stood so close to her that she was afraid to breathe. "Can you try to understand?" he said in a deep voice. "I wanted to give you time."

Maybe she said something, or maybe she only nodded. But she would always remember that sense of nearness, and the fact that she was gazing at him in bewilderment as his strong fingers found hers and entwined them warmly.

"Come outside," he said, "I think better there."

The four-hundred-year-old stones of the patio were sun-warmed; the air smelled of ripe apples from Christina's trees and the sharp, dry odor of mesquite and creosote bush and piñon from beyond the thick aged walls. They sat across from each other, Adam still toying with her fingers. Robin was afraid to speak, in an agony of apprehension.

"I've been taught to avoid excesses all my life," he finally said. "It's the way of the Diné. I've been taught to be careful of other people, especially outsiders, and to walk hand in hand with the natural world." He paused and studied her. "We're a selfish people, the Diné, very self-centered."

She listened, feeling that Adam was trying to tell her something vitally important.

"My uncle gave me my war name when I was three. It is Changing Man. Do you understand, Robin?"

"Changing Man," she repeated, "but you shouldn't tell me. I'm not..."

"You need to know."

What was he saying? She couldn't quite grasp the significance of his words. He couldn't mean...

"You know everything about me now. It's your choice, Robin. You, alone, have the right to choose."

She lowered her head over their joined hands and felt tears dim her eyes. "I only need to know one thing, Adam."

He raised her chin. "What is it? Anything..."

"Do you love me?"

"I love you," he replied solemnly.

"Well, then, there's no choice. I love you. I want you for my husband, forever. I want Changing Man, just as he is," she said, "for my clan."

"Robin..."

"Don't try to change my mind, Adam. I love *you*, not what you can give me." She smiled shyly. "I know I've got a lot of insecurities, and I'll probably drive you nuts from time to time. But, Adam, I love hard."

He pushed her hair back. "And you'll be happy without children?"

"We can have children. We'll adopt them. Lots of them. Indian children." She took his hand. "They need us so badly. It's as if someone planned this. Don't you see? And you can teach them to walk hand in hand with the world."

"And you can teach them to love," he said softly.

"They'll have the best of both worlds. It will work, Adam, we can make it work."

"I live in Albuquerque usually, you know," he said then.

Robin's face fell. "Oh," she said, "I guess I can..."

Adam smiled. "You'd move from your precious Santa Fe? You'd even do that for me?"

She straightened her back. "Yes, of course," she said staunchly. "I'd just forgotten."

"Something's come up, though," he went on, "just recently. The Governor's Palace museum is currently without a curator."

"Julien."

"Yes, Julien was the curator there."

"And?"

"I've been approached to fill the position."

Robin's eyes lit up. "Oh, Adam, wouldn't that be wonderful? We could live here, and we'd spend summers on the ranch, wouldn't we? I can see your father teaching his grandchildren to ride and hunt and speak Apache."

Adam laughed. "You have things all planned, don't you?"

"Oh, yes, we're going to be very busy," she said, her face shining, her joy swelling like a bubble in her breast, "and very happy."

Adam drew her close. "As your bride price," he whispered, "I demand a kiss," and the warm golden sun illuminated the embrace sealing their contract, the difficult but enduring bond between the trinity of Anglo, Indian and Spanish that was New Mexico, the land of enchantment.

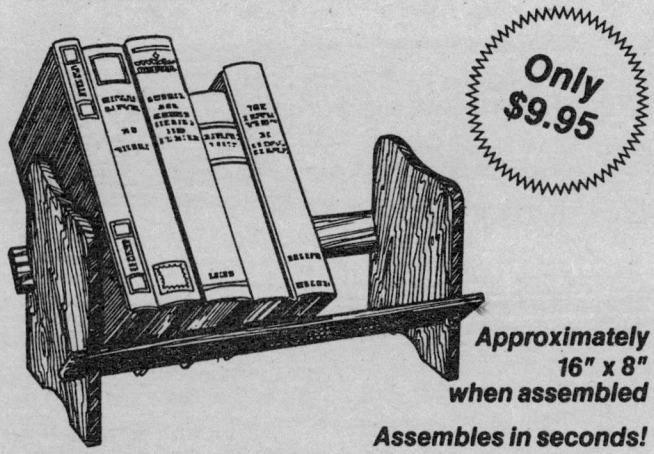

HARLEQUIN SIGNATURE EDITION

VIOLET WINSPEAR

HOUSE OF STORMS

Editorial secretary Debra Hartway travels to the Salvador family's rugged Cornish island home to work on Jack Salvador's latest book. Disturbing questions hang in the troubled air over Lovelis Island. What or who had caused the tragic death of Jack's young wife? Why did Jack stay away from the home and, more especially, the baby son he loved so well? And—why should Rodare, Jack's brother, who had proved himself a man of the highest integrity, constantly invade Debra's thoughts with such passionate, dark desires...?

Violet Winspear, who has written more than 65 romance novels translated worldwide into 18 languages, is one of Harlequin's best-loved and bestselling authors. HOUSE OF STORMS, her second title in the Harlequin Signature Edition program, is a full-length novel rich in romantic tradition and intriguingly spiced with an atmosphere of danger and mystery.

Watch for HOUSE OF STORMS—coming in October!

HOFS-1